WITHDRAWN

WANING MOON

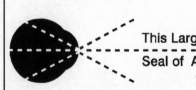

This Large Print Book carries the
Seal of Approval of N.A.V.H.

WANING MOON

JIM JONES

WHEELER PUBLISHING
A part of Gale, Cengage Learning

GALE
CENGAGE Learning·

Farmington Hills, Mich • San Francisco • New York • Waterville, Maine
Meriden, Conn • Mason, Ohio • Chicago

GALE
CENGAGE Learning

LIBRARY OF CONGRESS CATALOGING-IN-PUBLICATION DATA

Names: Jones, Jim, 1950– author.
Title: Waning Moon : a Jared Delaney western / Jim Jones.
Description: Large print edition. | Waterville, Maine : Wheeler Publishing Large Print, 2016. | © 2013 | Series: A Jared Delaney western | Series: Wheeler Publishing large print western
Identifiers: LCCN 2015041373| ISBN 9781410481696 (paperback) | ISBN 1410481697 (softcover)
Subjects: LCSH: Outlaws—Fiction. | Large type books. | BISAC: FICTION / Action & Adventure. | GSAFD: Western stories.
Classification: LCC PS3610.O62572 W36 2016 | DDC 813/.6—dc23
LC record available at http://lccn.loc.gov/2015041373

Published in 2016 by arrangement with Cherry Weiner Literary Agency

Printed in the United States of America
1 2 3 4 5 6 7 20 19 18 17 16

ACKNOWLEDGEMENTS

I'd like to express my heartfelt appreciation to my editor, Ruthie Francis, for her valuable feedback, suggestions and her ability to recognize my blind spots (she calls them "author tics"). I know I still have a great deal of room for growth in my writing. With her able assistance, however, I made significant strides with this work. She not only identified problems, she helped me see solutions. As a result, this book is better than it would have been otherwise.

Many thanks to my cowboy pard, Randy Huston, for his invaluable input, both in the "cowboy-specific" areas and in the overall feel of the book. Any errors in the "cowboy-ology" of this book are mine alone, as Randy sure nuff knows his stuff. He is all about keeping it real.

I would also like to thank friend, author and historian extraordinaire, Don Bullis for his contributions of numerous historical details from this period in New Mexico history. In particular, his assistance in identifying insults which were common to the period was especially helpful. Don can insult you in the vernacular of three different centuries . . . pretty impressive!

AUTHOR'S NOTE

wane (wān)
intr. v. **waned, wan•ing, wanes**
1. To decrease gradually in size, amount, intensity, or degree; decline.
2. To exhibit a decreasing illuminated area from full moon to new moon.
3. To approach an end.

It is purely by coincidence that this historical novel is being published in the year that marks the end of the Mayan calendar. If the alarmists are right, it signifies the end of the world. In that case, you probably won't be reading this. If, on the other hand, the Mayan calendar is a reflection of the cycle of life in which living things grow and expand (*wax*) to a zenith, only to diminish (*wane*) and ultimately die, leaving room for the next cycle to take place, then this book is a microcosm of that process. The waning phase of a cycle can involve sadness, conflict and uncertainty. At the same time, there is room for hope, excitement and the promise of something new. Endings are followed by new beginnings.

Although the characters in this novel are fictitious, the events that take place are based on historical fact. There was a group known as the Santa Fe Ring in the New Mexico Territory during the time period from just after the Civil War until the late-1880s. The members of that informal group used their connections in Washington, D.C. as well as the legal framework of the Maxwell Land Grant to engage in what many consider the largest land speculation conspiracy in U.S. history. At one point during this period, Thomas Catron owned more land than any other individual in the United States. During what was known as the Colfax County War, individuals who stood up to oppose the Ring were murdered . . . attorneys, law-enforcement officers and a Methodist Minister among others. In this fictional account, I attempt to honor the heroic efforts of those very real men and women who lived in this time and who courageously made a stand against corruption and injustice. I also tried to tell a good story along the way.

CHAPTER 1

October 18, 1884

Sunlight streaked through the trees in Cimarrón Canyon, creating shafts of light and shadow on the trail, obscuring his vision. He rode out of the light and into a shadow. Ahead, he could see the outline of two riders coming around the bend in the canyon approaching from the west. His eyes, dimmed by age, adjusted slowly to the change in light. He squinted to see if he could make them out as they approached. His pupils began to dilate. In disbelief, he saw the man on his left whip his rifle out of its scabbard, raising it to fire. His heart began to hammer furiously. He felt that familiar surge of energy that's partner to fear and anger. He reached to draw his own weapon. *Too slow.* He felt a bullet slam into the upper right side of his chest. The force spun him back around to the right as his horse reared. Luckily, he caught a firm grip on the horn with his left hand, otherwise he would have fallen. Blindly, he spurred his horse up into the rocks on the north side of the canyon.

The sound of gunfire thundered in his ears. He frantically urged his horse up the side of the canyon on the treacherous path between the huge boulders. He heard the whine of a bullet. He felt the sting as it punched through his vest and creased his skin. *Too close.* Maybe sixty yards up in to the rocks, he grabbed his Winchester out of the scabbard with his left hand, nearly dropping it in the process. He dismounted in a quick stumble. His right side was on fire. A bullet hit the rock beside him. Shattered fragments buried themselves in his cheek. *Damn near got my eyes.*

Desperate now, he sought cover behind the biggest rock he could find, his legs trembling as he squatted down. He clumsily jacked the lever with his left hand . . . one in the chamber, fourteen in the magazine. He didn't think he could hit a barn shooting one-handed. Lord, he hoped that if he fired enough shots their way, maybe these anonymous assailants would decide it wasn't worth it to follow him up the hill. He blazed away ferociously, counting his shots as he went. *Eat lead, you sorry bushwhackers!* He stopped after thirteen. *I'm savin' these last two bullets,* he thought, *on the off chance these sidewinders ain't givin' up easy.*

The echoes of his shots died away. He strained to hear hooves striking rocks indicating they were storming his precarious fortress. All he had left was his pistol. If they chose to attack, he knew it would only be a matter of time before he was overwhelmed. Instead, he heard the sound of horses galloping away to the east, their hoof beats muffled by the pine straw on the trail. Peering out through a crack between two rocks, he saw a welcome sight . . . nothing.

He was leaking blood from his chest wound. He had just two bullets left in his Winchester. His horse had taken off towards home. He knew the stream ran along the north side of the trail. Whether he'd have the strength to drag himself over to it was another matter entirely. No one expected him back in Cimarrón from this trip to Taos for a couple of days. They likely wouldn't start searching for him until at least the third day. He'd been in some tough spots during his long career as a lawman. This might be the worst.

This is bad, he thought. His head felt like it was floating off his shoulders. The world grew dark around the edges of his eyesight.

This is real bad.
He was right.

CHAPTER 2

October 19, 1884

Jared Delaney was as nervous as a long-tailed cat in a room full of rocking chairs. The preliminary hearing for William Chapman and his hired gunman, Daughtry, was scheduled to start on Wednesday the 20th, just one day hence and Nathan Averill had left for Taos on Monday. He was to meet with a man to get some letters that provided clear evidence that Chapman had not only conspired to illegally take land from citizens of Colfax County but also had directed Daughtry to rustle cattle from the Kilpatrick Ranch. This cattle rustling resulted in the death of Jared's partner and best friend, Juan Suazo. Everything depended on Nathan's returning in time with the letters, as the evidence against Chapman and Daughtry was pretty slim otherwise. Jared felt like he hadn't slept a wink the previous night although when he commented on this, Eleanor assured him that she had heard him snoring loud and clear. Still, he was bone weary and wound up tighter than a cheap watch.

"Relax, Jared," Eleanor scolded. "You're making me nervous, too. You know Nathan said he would make the trip over in one day and back the next. He's done it plenty of times and this time will be no different."

Jared tried to smile at his wife but the sides of his mouth just wouldn't go up very far. "I know, Eleanor my love, but the stakes are higher now than they've ever been before. I don't know if Judge Cardenas is a straight shooter or if he's in the Ring's pocket. Without those letters, I'm worried Chapman is gonna get away with killin' Juan." Jared clinched his jaw. It took a moment before he could speak. When he began again, his voice was husky with emotion. "Too many good people have died, Eleanor. We can't let that happen. We just can't."

"I know, Jared." She sighed as her own tears brimmed over and spilled down her cheeks. "I know."

"I know, papa, I know." Young Jared Delaney made a loop and did his dead level best to rope the saw horse steer his papa had set up for him but he kept overshooting his mark. His

14

father had patiently instructed him to take his time and relax as he let the loop fly but he could feel himself tense up as he released. This time he came up short. He turned around and waited sheepishly to accept his father's gentle rebuke but he didn't see him anywhere.

"Papa, where are you?" Terrified, he panicked. He felt his heart race like a stallion galloping across the prairie. Louder this time, he called out, "Papa, I can't see you. Where are you?" He started to run, racing in rhythm with his heart although he had no idea where he was running to or for that matter, what he was running from. As he came over the rise, he saw a figure in the distance and ran toward him. "Papa, is that you?" He was within ten feet of the man he hoped was his father when the man looked up. Jared skidded to a halt as he gazed into ice blue eyes that did not . . . could not . . . belong to his father. In a trembling voice, he asked, "Who are you?" The man said nothing. His cruel smile spoke volumes.

Jared woke up in a cold sweat. The nightmares were back.

CHAPTER 3

June 3, 1884

After the success of his first cattle drive up through Raton Pass and on to Pueblo, Colorado in '81, Jared Delaney had established a solid financial base for the Kilpatrick Ranch. Even though Lizbeth Kilpatrick was dead, murdered by the killer known as Gentleman Curt Barwick, Jared had kept the name for the ranch to honor Lizbeth and her late husband, Ned. He and Eleanor had even named their first child after Ned. Edward Nathan Delaney, he was, but everyone called him Ned.

With his compadre, Juan Suazo, as his new partner, Jared became a regular provider of beef to the Colorado Coal and Steelworks Company in Pueblo. They fattened up the cattle on the ranch and had a plentiful supply of beeves available so they could act quickly when there was a demand for their product. Juan took his outfit up the trail several times a year with a herd of several hundred steers. Business was so good that they sometimes had to buy a few head from other ranchers just to keep up with the demand. The money was coming in regularly and Jared was looking to expand the operation to include some other coal mining outfits in Trinidad. He had talked to the company stores at the Starkville and Morley coal mines and they seemed interested in having him provide their beef.

Jared was plum tickled at how his life was playing out. He had a beautiful and intelligent wife, a rambunctious three year old boy and a thriving ranching business. A cowboy couldn't ask for a lot more. Well, maybe a little more rain but you take what you can get and forget the rest. He just wished that two of the people in his life whom he held most dear could work out the kinks in their friendship, or whatever the heck kind of "ship" they wanted to call it. He and Eleanor spoke of it often.

"I don't know what Nathan is thinking, Jared." Eleanor frowned and brushed a wisp of hair from her forehead. "Christy has turned in to a fine woman. She's made it clear to him that she's there for him if he wants her. He's been alone for so long, I just wish he could see how much better his life would be if he'd just go ahead and marry her."

Jared chuckled. "You just think everybody'll be as happy as us if they tie the knot. I know you got your eye on Tommy and Mollie, too. You're turnin' into a regular matchmaker."

Eleanor smiled. "You're right, they're my next project." Her smiled faded. "Seriously, I'm worried about Nathan. Ever since the troubles with Barwick a few years ago, he just hasn't been the same. It's like he's lost all his confidence."

"I know," Jared replied. "He just doesn't have that spring in his step that he used to have. Bein' laid up and not able to help when the shootin' came down was somethin' new for him. I think he felt like he let us all down."

"Christy's getting hurt was what hit him the hardest, though." Eleanor grimaced as she recalled the confrontation with the sadistic gunman, Dick Cravens. "He knows she could have lost her arm or even died if that cut had gotten infected."

"There wasn't anything Nathan could have done about that, though," Jared protested. "If anyone was to blame, it was me, for goin' off on that cattle drive to Pueblo. I should have been there to deal with Barwick and the others."

Eleanor put her hand on Jared's arm. "You know you had no idea of what Catron and Chapman were planning. None of us did." Eleanor's eyes flashed. "I think if anyone deserves blame, it's those scoundrels in Santa Fe. All they're interested in is lining their pockets and they don't care who gets hurt in the meantime."

"Well, maybe we're done with them," Jared said hopefully. "I don't know how many times it'll take for those no-good Santa Fe Ring thieves to see that we ain't gonna just lie down and let'em have their way here in Colfax County. We handled O'Bannon and we handled Gentleman Curt Barwick. I don't know who else they think they can throw at us that'll have any more luck."

"I don't know." Eleanor shook her head. "I don't want to spend all my time looking over my shoulder and wondering what those rapscallions are up to. I'd rather look ahead."

As she finished speaking, a little pint-sized tornado rushed into the room, followed by two dogs. They were a whirligig of arms, legs, paws and tails, making noise and tumbling around. When their gyrations threatened to knock over the hat rack Jared

19

had made out of a large cottonwood limb, Eleanor raised her voice as her almost three year old son rolled on the floor with the dogs.

"Ned!" she yelled. "You stop right now." Eleanor loved her son more than life itself but there were times she felt totally clueless about how to rein in his seemingly bound- less energy. She turned to Jared, who was doubled over laughing. "Would you quit laughing and get those flea-bitten dogs out of here before something gets broken!"

Jared continued to laugh but scooped his young son up in his arms and shooed the dogs out the front door. "Easy there, little guy," he said, "you don't want to get your mama mad at you."

Eleanor frowned, tried to look stern, but could only hold the pose for a moment before she broke in to laughter. She held out her arms and Ned eagerly came to her. "You're getting almost too big for me to carry, young man." Ned squirmed with pleasure and hugged his mother's neck.

"Yep," Jared said. "If he gets much bigger, we're gonna have to put him to work with Juan on the drives." Jared scratched his head. "Speakin' of Juan, I wonder how he and Tommy and the boys are doin'. They should be past Raton by now on their way home."

CHAPTER 4

June 3, 1884
The man is huge, Juan thought. *He's as big as a grizzly. I bet he could crush me like a bug. I wonder does he remember the last time I was here? That could be trouble.*

The giant slowly approached Juan Suazo with his right hand slightly raised. A chill ran up Juan's spine as he prepared himself. The man's hand came down and clapped him on the back. With his other hand, he pulled Juan into a bear hug.

"Juan Suazo, you rascal," Big Jim Rogers squeaked in his strangely high-pitched voice. "Don't think I've forgotten about the last time you were here. You won ten dollars from me at poker, you sly dog. I know you were cheating, I just don't know how. You must've been, though. Otherwise a terrible card player like you would've never beat a card sharp like me."

Juan tried to catch a breath as he struggled

to get free from Big Jim's friendly if somewhat smothering embrace. Once he'd extracted himself, he looked up at the big man.

"Don't blame me because you can't play cards. I hit a lucky streak, that's all." Juan looked around the crowded Wild Mustang bar and eating establishment. "Looks like you still serve the best beefsteak in Raton, though. I got to hand it to you. Your daughter can sure cook."

Big Jim laughed, then he turned his gaze down on Juan's two companions. "Tommy Stallings, how are you? I haven't seen you boys in a while. Who's your friend?"

Tom Stallings grimaced as he reached out to shake Big Jim's hand. He knew there was always a risk of getting your hand crushed accidentally when you shook hands with Big Jim Rogers. Not that he meant to hurt you, he just didn't seem to understand how strong he was.

"I'm doin' mighty fine," he responded with his Texas drawl. "My pard here is Joe Hargrove. Joe's been workin' for Mr. Jared now for about three years on and off." He turned to grin at Hargrove. "There's been a couple of times he's stayed up in Pueblo after we've run a herd up there. I think he's even been up to Denver a time or two." Stallings laughed. "Sometimes we don't see

23

him for a few months at a time when he's enjoyin' that city life. You probably missed him when we've come back through after the drives."

Hargrove nodded politely to Big Jim as he wisely kept his hands at his side. It seemed the big man had forgotten they'd met once before. "Good to see you, Mr. Rogers. The boys all speak highly of you."

"Mr. Rogers is my father. You can call me Big Jim." Big Jim laughed. "So you take your hard-earned pay up to the big city and spend it all on the nightlife, do you? I guess we're too tame for you here at the Mustang."

Joe recalled his experience at another tavern in Raton a few years ago when he thought he and Stallings both were about to meet their maker. A trio of double-dealing gunslingers had them backed into a corner. If it hadn't have been for Jared Delaney and Big Jim, they would surely have wound up six feet underground at the Raton boot hill just outside of town. Things had gotten pretty busy for a time and apparently, Big Jim didn't recall meeting him. It was understandable under the circumstances.

"The Mustang is pretty tame, Big Jim. I'll tell you what, though, I'm surely afraid to go in to the other joints you boys have here.

I feel a lot safer in those big city spots." He grinned. "I got some ladyfriends up in Denver that take pretty good care of me."

"They take all your money, too, I bet." Big Jim turned back to Juan, his smile fading. "How did this drive go for you? Any trouble?"

"Mostly, it was pretty quiet," Juan responded. He frowned and shook his head. "We lost some steers after we got through the pass, though. We had them spread out pretty far one night grazing in a big meadow. I think one of my new hands was sleeping on the job. When I counted in the morning, we were down ten head."

"Indians, do you reckon?" Big Jim looked sharply at Juan.

"Whoever did it was sure sneaky enough to be an Indian." Juan looked pensive. "I don't think that's who did it. We'd already run into our friends, the Utes. We'd given them a couple of steers. We got a pretty good understanding with them, you know. I can't see them breaking their word." Juan shrugged. "Next time, I'll see if I can get me enough cowboys who'll stay awake when they night herd."

Big Jim recalled Juan and Jared's first hair-raising drive through Raton Pass three years before. They'd gotten caught in a brutal blizzard that had claimed the life of one of their best hands. Even before they'd made it into the pass, however, the gunslingers who tried to cheat Stallings out of his pay also attempted to steal their cattle. Two of them wound up dead for their trouble and the third one vanished.

"Well, at least there wasn't any gunplay," Big Jim said. "I've heard some tales lately from other drovers coming through that they've had more and more trouble with rustlers. I don't know who's behind it but it makes it even riskier to make the drive up north."

"You're right about that, Jim." Juan took a deep breath, then exhaled sharply. "I have an idea about who is behind it . . . the same no-good, thievin' Santa Fe lawyers that have plagued us for years." Juan looked like he wanted to hit someone. "Me and Jared, we got a good thing going, selling beeves to these coal miners up here. We'd be in the high sweet grass if we didn't have to worry about those rotten thieves."

Big Jim nodded in understanding and gave Juan a consoling pat on the shoulder. Juan staggered. "Well, you boys need to be careful. You're some of my best customers. I don't want anything bad to happen to you." He grinned. "At least, not until I've won my ten dollars back from you." Big Jim cut loose with his high, squeaky laugh. "Now, let's get some of those beefsteaks in front of you boys."

CHAPTER 5

October 19, 1884

Robert Elkins was nervous. Well, no, that wasn't really the truth, not that lawyers often dealt in the truth. The truth was, he was scared out of his wits. He just hated meeting with his clients, Bill Chapman and the one they called Daughtry. Chapman treated him like he was just a pawn in this corrupt chess game, not a human being with feelings and opinions of his own. Chapman seemed to view him as just another one of his flunkies. The truth? That was indeed what he was.

Daughtry was something else entirely. Elkins had read stories about the crocodiles over in Africa. He'd even seen drawings of them in books. That's what he thought of when he thought of Daughtry. Like some big old lazy dinosaur lizard that was just waiting to make you his dinner. When that time came, Elkins knew that there would be no reasoning with the man . . . no pleading, no mercy. If he wanted you dead, you were dead.

After Judge Cardenas granted his request for bail, he'd been able to get Chapman and Daughtry out of jail after only two nights. Their release was on the condition that they return for a preliminary hearing in two weeks. The fact that they'd had to spend two nights in jail, however, was a bit of a sticky issue. Truth, again? They were very unhappy about that. When he showed up to spring them, he had tried to explain that he'd moved as quickly as he possibly could but they were unhappy nonetheless. Perhaps livid was a more accurate description of their mood when he arrived at the sheriff's office to have them released. The subsequent meeting had been extremely disagreeable and set the stage for his current anxiety.

"Gentlemen," Elkins said as he closed the door to the room the mayor had loaned them for meetings like this. "We need to go over our case and decide how we're going to plea." With a handkerchief, Elkins wiped his brow. Beads of sweat reappeared almost immediately.

"How're we going to plea?" Bill Chapman's voice carried equal notes of incredulity and scorn. "Elkins, you idiot. We're pleading not guilty, of course." He rolled his eyes in disgust. "They don't have a case against either of us, how the hell else would we plead?"

Elkins avoided looking at Daughtry. "Of course, Mr. Chapman, I know that. I was just trying to conduct the meeting in an orderly fashion and that seemed like the first order of business."

"Well, I guess we got the first order of business out of the way." Chapman smiled. "What else do we need to talk about?" Daughtry didn't say a word, he just stared at the attorney.

Elkins was sweating profusely now. His collar had wilted and his cravat lay limp on his rather concave chest. He exhaled deeply and continued. "There's the matter of the evidence that Sheriff Averill is supposed to be collecting. I'm rather concerned about that."

Chapman guffawed. The right corner of Daughtry's mouth turned up just the slightest bit. "Counselor, that's nothing to worry about," Chapman said in his booming voice. "Trust me, the sheriff won't be bringing any evidence to this trial."

Elkins was puzzled. "But I thought he was riding over to Taos to collect something that just might incriminate . . ." Elkins stopped in mid-sentence. Choosing his words more carefully, he continued. "I mean, I'd heard that he might bring some letters back that could be twisted by the prosecution to cast aspersions on your conduct." Elkins held up his hands in a protective gesture. "Not that there was anything about your conduct that could be construed as . . ." Elkins stopped, again searching for the right words so that he wouldn't become a lightning rod for Chapman's anger.

Chapman lit a cigar, taking the time to let his lawyer dangle in the wind. Daughtry looked out the window, a bored expression on his cruel face. Finally, Chapman turned back to Elkins. "Relax, Bobby, they have nothing." Chapman managed to smirk and puff on his cigar at the same time. "They can't prove that Daughtry was involved in the cattle rustling or the . . ." Chapman flashed his own reptilian grin . . . "unfortunate death of that poor Mexican cowboy. What do they call them? Vaqueros? Quaint word."

"Well, sir," Elkins stammered, "they do have just the slightest amount of physical evidence that Mr. Daughtry might have been . . ." Elkins began to tremble as he glanced at Daughtry out of the corner of his eye. Daughtry was watching him like a roadrunner eyes a baby bird.

"Elkins, lots of men wear derby hats. Hell, Bat Masterson wears one. Why isn't he on trial?" Chapman began to pace and puff furiously on his cigar. "Just because they found a hat where this fracas took place doesn't mean it belongs to Daughtry. If you can't make that little bit of 'evidence' disappear, maybe we need to make you disappear."

Elkins felt as if he might faint. He took a seat in the chair next to the small desk the mayor had provided. "No, Mr. Chapman, that's certainly not necessary. I believe there is sufficient question about whether that evidence points to Mr. Daughtry that I can sway the judge in our favor." Elkins smiled weakly. "Maybe I'll mention that Bat Masterson wears similar head attire."

"You do that," Chapman said. Clearly, his patience for the meeting was wearing thin. "The other thing you need to convince the judge of is that I had no connection to any of this." He turned and stabbed the terrified lawyer in the chest with his finger. "No connection," he roared, "you understand me?"

"Yes, sir, Mr. Chapman, yes, sir!" Elkins could tolerate not a second more of the tension and threat that hung in the air of the room like an evil mist. "I'll take care of all of it, don't you worry." He rose quickly and gathered his papers from the desk. As he began to back out of the room, he repeated his reassurances. "You have nothing to worry about, I promise."

Chapman smiled as he had the final word. "That's good, Elkins. If I've got nothing to worry about, then you've got nothing to worry about."

Elkins turned and fled from the room. Chapman turned to Daughtry and grinned. "Lawyers! I'd rather pester one than set a cat's tail on fire. It sure is fun watching that weasel squirm and dance."

Daughtry smiled.

Eleanor frowned as she cleaned up the dishes. Jared was playing with Ned for a few minutes before they put the boy to bed. She was doing her best to support her husband. In truth, she was expressing an optimism she didn't really feel. Achieving justice for everything that had happened . . . Juan, the reverend . . . it all hinged on Nathan retrieving that vital evidence against Chapman. There was a time when she would have been confident that he would succeed no matter what obstacles were in his way. Now, as she and Jared had discussed earlier, she wasn't so sure. Bad things had been happening in Cimarrón Canyon. A person would need to be alert. No, that's not right. They would need to be as watchful as a hawk. She hated to think that Nathan might be getting too old to do the job. *I hate to think it . . . but that's what I think.*

CHAPTER 6

June 13, 1884

"And how long are you expectin' to be gone this time, Mr. Tommy Stallings?" Mollie's tone was melancholy as she walked hand in hand with Tom Stallings down the main street of Cimarrón.

"Why do you want to bring somethin' sad up when we're havin' a nice time, Mollie?" Tommy squeezed Mollie's hand. He smiled at her as they sauntered along, oblivious to the other citizens of the town. It's fair to say that they were in a world of their own.

"Because I need to plan for how long I'm going to be sad, silly." Mollie's brogue came through clear and strong although she had been in the New Mexico territory for a number of years now. "We Irish like to plan ahead for sadness and tragedies, you know. We know they'll be comin'. It helps us if we prepare."

Stallings looked at the girl with a perplexed expression. "I can never tell for sure when you're joshin' me and when you're bein' serious. How in tarnation do you plan for bein' sad?"

"It's not difficult, sweetheart," she said. "You try to figure out how long you'll be sad, then you think about something good that will be happenin' on the other side of it." With her free hand, Mollie reached around and lightly punched Tommy on the arm. "That's why I'd be after askin' you how long you'll be gone and when you'll be comin' back. Do you see now?"

Tommy chuckled and said, "That's silly, Mollie, but if it helps you feel better, it's okay with me." With a feigned look of pain on his face, he said, "And there's no need to be assaultin' me. You pack a pretty powerful punch there, young lady."

Mollie giggled. "Oh, don't be such a baby. And answer me question, cowboy. I need to know when you're leavin' and when in thunder you'll be back. I've got to prepare for me grievin'."

Tommy Stallings was secretly thrilled that this lovely young lady would be saddened by his departure and heartened by the prospect of his return. He'd met her three years ago in the Colfax Tavern just before he was critically wounded in a gunfight with

Gentleman Curt Barwick. Fortunately, he was able to squeeze off a shot and wound Barwick in the leg. Who could have known that Barwick's bum leg would've given Jared and the others just enough of an edge to prevail in their furious gun battle? Thanks to Mollie's quick action in getting the doctor to his aid, Stallings was able to survive his wounds. After he recovered, he went to work as a ranch hand for Jared Delaney and Juan Suazo at the Kilpatrick Ranch. Mollie's care and attention during his recovery also kindled the spark that led to their courting.

Mollie grew impatient with Tommy's silence as he reminisced about the beginning of their relationship. "Don't make me punch you again," she said with mock fury. "Answer the question."

Stallings sighed. "We leave day after tomorrow. We're gettin' pretty handy at makin' this drive so we ought to be able to get up there and back in about two weeks . . . that is, if nothin' goes wrong." Tommy made a face at her. "There. Are you satisfied now?"

Mollie's face fell as she contemplated Tommy's departure. "I'm not satisfied, I'm sad. I didn't think you were leavin' until next week."

Father Antonio Baca approached from the other direction and tipped his hat to them as he came. Tommy said, "Padre, you got to save me from this wild woman. She's taken to punchin' me."

Father Antonio smiled mischievously and said, "It is not likely she will hurt you badly, my son. If she is hitting you, I suspect that you deserve it."

Mollie laughed with delight at the padre's taking her side. Tommy blushed and said, "Reckon I can't argue with a man of God, now can I, Father?"

"You most certainly can not." The priest's demeanor changed from mischievous to concern. "You have not by any chance seen Reverend Richardson today, have you?"

"No, Father, we haven't," Mollie said. "Is he missing?"

"Well, no, I would not say that." Father Antonio's expression clearly conveyed his concern. "It is just that he was supposed to meet me at the Marés Café at noon for our daily spiritual debate. He never showed up." A hint of his mischievous smile returned. "You do not suppose he has conceded, do you?"

Mollie and Tommy laughed. "From the brief time I've spent around the Reverend," Tommy said, "I'd say it wasn't likely."

"I suppose you are right." The priest tipped his hat and said, "One can always hope though. If you see him, please tell him I am looking for him."

As the padre walked away, Tommy turned back to Mollie. "You were tellin' me how much you were gonna miss me before we got interrupted. I wouldn't mind hearin' some more about that."

When Mollie encountered Stallings at the Colfax Tavern three years earlier, her life was in the process of changing as well. An immigrant who had followed her older brother from Ireland out to the West, she found her prospects for advancement, and even for survival, rather bleak. She took a job serving food at the Colfax Tavern. Soon, however, she found herself sliding down the slippery slope into the other primary occupation of the girls at the tavern, serving the baser needs of the cowboys who frequented the place. Although this went against her nature, there were times when she was so desperate for money, she saw no other way. She was only a step or two away from losing herself completely to the degradation of the alcohol and laudanum-laced fog of prostitution when she found herself in the middle of a crisis not of her making.

When Barwick and his murderous companions bushwhacked the sheriff, she found that she couldn't just stand aside and let it happen. Instead, she sought help from Christy Johnson, the former "soiled dove" and now a reformed school teacher. Christy, Eleanor Delaney, Maria Suazo and Lizbeth Kilpatrick made a stand against Barwick's gang. With the timely arrival of Jared, Juan and Tommy, they were able to take them down in a violent encounter that claimed the life of Lizbeth as well. Christy recognized Mollie's fighting spirit and took her under her wing, encouraged her to attend school, and helped her find a way out of the dead end life she had been living. She had turned her life around. Most of the time, she was hopeful and optimistic about her future. Right now, however, she was sad.

"Don't be sad yet, Mollie," Tommy pleaded. "I don't leave until day after tomorrow. We still have this time to be together." He released her hand and put his arm around her shoulder, comforting her as best he knew how. "I've got it. We could go on a picnic tomorrow. I need to gather a few head of steers in the mornin' and then I've got to get my gear together. Shucks, that won't take long. I could come get you in the buggy just before noon. We could go out to that meadow just north of town.

What do you think about that?"

Mollie looked uncertain. "I'm not sure, Tommy. I don't finish lessons at school until the middle of the afternoon. Then I need to help Miss Christy get ready for the next day's lessons."

"Come on, Mollie, just this once. I know Miss Christy would understand." Tommy turned to face her and took both of her hands. "I want us to have a happy day to remember while I'm gone. Don't you see? This will help us both not be so sad."

Mollie's face brightened like the sunrise over the mountains. "You're right. It will be part of the plan to help with the sadness." She looked sideways at Tommy. "Are you sure you're not Irish?"

Tommy laughed. "Not that I know of . . . maybe I'm learnin' from you." He let go of Mollie's hands and clapped his together. "I know just the thing," he said. "I'll ask Miss Eleanor to kill one of her chickens and fry it up for us. I bet she'd do that for you. She thinks a lot of you, you know."

Mollie's face reddened. "Oh, go on with you. A fine lady like Miss Eleanor has little use for the likes of a workin' class Irish lass like meself. Why would you say such a thing?"

"Because she said so just the other day,

miss smarty-pants." Tommy's face shone with pride. "She told me she was proud of the way you were workin' so hard at your lessons and tryin' to better yourself. She said you had class . . . and I don't think she meant 'workin' class.' She thinks you're special."

"Special? I don't know about that." It was clear that Mollie was pleased with the compliment, even if she had trouble accepting it. "Did she really say that?"

"She sure did," Stallings replied. "You are special, you know." Tommy's face took on some color as well. "What do you think I've been tryin' to tell you all this time?"

"Ah, you with your smooth-talkin' cowboy ways," Mollie replied in a sassy tone. She took Tommy's hand and they resumed their walk. To any casual observer, it was clear that they were in love.

CHAPTER 7

June 11, 1884

"This is going to make Maria loco. Every time I make a drive, she's convinced I'll get caught in another freak storm and die." Juan had a worried frown on his usually sunny face. "We just got back from Pueblo last week and now we've got to take off again." He rolled his eyes and said, "I might wind up sleeping in the stables tonight after I tell her."

"I know," Jared said. "This ain't the way I would have planned it but Pedro Flores over at Morley just sent me the telegram yesterday. Somebody raided their pens in the middle of the night. They made off with over a hundred head." Jared shook his head in disbelief. "They roped the posts and just pulled a whole section of fence down. They weren't expectin' anything like this so they didn't even have any guards posted."

"Whoever's doing this is getting bolder

every time," Juan said. "They come at night like they did with us on this last drive. We may need an extra hand for this one so we can double the watch."

"I wish we could do that, amigo, but I don't know who we could spare to go with you," Jared said reluctantly. "If you, Tommy and Joe take this herd up the trail and Estévan handles the wagon, that just leaves me to keep an eye on things around here." He shook his head in exasperation. "I wish Sean and Patrick hadn't decided to stay up in Pueblo and paint the town red with Sullivan." Jared had to smile in spite of his frustration. "Three Irishmen together in one place is at least two too many, if you ask me. I don't know if Pueblo is ready for 'em."

Juan grinned. "No telling when they'll come dragging back in. Those boys sure do like their drink, don't they?"

"That they do," Jared said. "Doesn't do us any good though. Still, we got to jump on this if we want to keep things goin' with the Morley outfit. If we don't come through with some steers in a hurry, there's other lined up that'd jump at the chance to do it."

"I know you're right," Juan sighed. "I just hate to have to tell Maria about it."

Since becoming Jared's partner in the Kilpatrick Ranch, Juan had learned a lot about the responsibilities over and above the day to day work with the cattle. He knew that in order to keep the ranch profitable, they had to be in the right place at the right time, every time. That meant being able to respond quickly to the needs of the mining companies for beef to feed their employees.

Jared couldn't pass up the opportunity to rib his compadre. With a twinkle in his eye, he said, "If she kicks you out of the house tonight, come on over to our place. You can sleep in our stable. It's not all that comfortable but at least no one is gonna throw any pots or pans at you."

"Thanks, pard," Juan said, shaking his head. "It's good to know I have friends I can count on."

CHAPTER 8

June 12, 1884

Clinking glasses and loud voices collaborated to create a happy bedlam in the Colfax Tavern. Tom Lacey surveyed the scene from his position behind the bar, taking in all those small details that make up a successful business. He smiled. Drinks were being served at a furious pace, the faro tables were full and his girls were doing a lively business as well. It was late afternoon and the working folks were drifting in to join the regulars who had been there since much earlier in the day. Tom did the mathematical calculations in his head . . . he was quite good with figures . . . and his smile got bigger as he thought about the profits he was accruing as a result of all this merriment. He lifted his glass of whiskey and toasted himself. *Here's to hard living and wicked ways. May they continue to flourish.*

His smile slowly faded as he glanced surreptitiously at the table over in the corner that was being studiously avoided by the patrons and working girls alike. Since he'd taken over the tavern a few years back, he'd seen his share of hard cases. Barwick and his homicidal friends, Dick Cravens and Pancho Vega, had been both frightening and bad for business. Once the dust had settled after the gunfight that resulted in their deaths, he was on the receiving end of a blistering lecture from Sheriff Nathan Averill. Apparently, the sheriff felt like he needed to be alerted of the activities of such unsavory characters so that he might inter-vene earlier before things got out of hand as they had that day.

Bill Chapman and his gun slinging friend, Daughtry, were deep in conversation at the table in the corner and seemed totally unaware of the revelry and happy business transactions taking place around them. Daughtry had just come in the tavern a few minutes before, covered with dust from the trail. Lacey couldn't quite put his finger on it. Somehow, even without adequate words to describe it, it was abundantly clear to him, and apparently everyone else in the tavern, that peril lurked at that table. Prudent folks would do well to stay away. He wondered if it might be in his best interests to let Sheriff Averill know of their presence here at the tavern. He weighed the odds carefully . . . after all, he *was* good with figures . . . and decided that he would indeed alert the sheriff. This would have to be done in a most discrete manner in order to avoid any negative and perhaps violent repercussions from the pair in the corner.

"Jim," Lacey yelled at his bartender at the other end of the fine mahogany bar he had imported from Chicago. "I'm going to the bank. You watch over things. Make sure the girls don't linger too long upstairs."

Receiving a surly nod of affirmation from his assistant, Lacey headed for the door. He made a great show of greeting various patrons, bantering with several about their unfortunate financial reverses at the faro table the previous evening. Once he left the tavern, he greeted a few citizens as he walked straight to the bank and entered. He actually did conduct some business, making a deposit of last night's earnings. He visited briefly with the bank president, who appreciated having his money in the bank, even if he didn't appreciate the source of the money. It amused Lacey that the self-righteous hypocrite was so effortlessly able to set aside his disapproval as long as the money kept rolling in.

He announced loudly that he was headed back to the tavern and walked out the front door. However, instead of turning right to return to the tavern, he turned left and quickly walked the half block to the sheriff's office. Looking around carefully to make sure no one was observing him, he knocked and waited anxiously for the sheriff to invite him in.

"Come on in, the door ain't locked."

Lacey entered quickly and saw the sheriff standing over by his gun rack, replacing a rifle that he'd been cleaning. As Lacey shut the door behind himself, he thought, *he looks old.*

"Good afternoon, sheriff. How are you doing this fine summer evening?"

Averill turned and looked hard at the tavern owner. "Lacey, I know you didn't come here to inquire about my health. State your business. Let's get it taken care of, whatever it is."

Lacey nodded. "All right, sheriff, if that's the way you want to do this." He took off his hat and set it on the chair by the door. "I know we've gotten crosswise a few times in the past. I'm here to show you that I've been paying attention to the things you've told me. I want to be your ally. It's impera-tive, though, to know that you'll be discrete." Lacey looked around the office nervously. "There's not anyone in the jail cells, is there?"

"Nope," Averill said brusquely. "It's just you and me."

"All right, then," Lacey said. "I want to tell you about a situation that may be developing. I need your assurance that this information is a warning that's being passed along in strictest confidence. Can you guarantee this to me?"

"I'm not sure I can guarantee you that, Tom," Nathan said carefully. "I can only tell you I'll do my best not to let word get out that you've talked with me." Nathan looked at the tavern owner quizzically. "Somethin's got you spooked, Tom. What is it?"

Lacey hesitated for a moment, then continued. "Sheriff, I don't know for sure what's going on. That Santa Fe politician, Bill Chapman and his rather frightening companion, Daughtry, have been in deep conversation at the tavern on several occasions of late. As I said, I haven't overheard anything that would be of use to you. I suspect, however, that they're up to no good." He looked over his shoulder at the door. "Sheriff, I hope you appreciate that I'm trying to turn over a new leaf here. I did learn my lesson with that nasty business with Barwick and his compatriots."

At the mention of Barwick's name, Averill's eyes narrowed. "Well, Tom, I do appreciate that you got the message from that 'nasty business,' as you call it. Good people died that day. You might have done something to prevent it from happenin'."

Lacey glanced down, then back over his shoulder at the door, avoiding the sheriff's eyes. Finally, he spoke. "I know, sheriff, you're right. That's why I'm here today, in hopes that we don't have a repeat performance of that unfortunate episode." Finally, he looked the sheriff in the eye. "You must understand that I'm in a precarious position here, though. If word gets back to Chapman and Daughtry that I gave them up, things will go very badly for me."

Averill took a deep breath and then shrugged. "I see your point, Tom. I do appreciate you fillin' me in. You're probably right that they're up to no good and I'm in a better position to do somethin' about it thanks to you. I'll do everything I can to keep this little talk between you and me under my hat."

Lacey nodded. "Thank you, sheriff, I appreciate your circumspection." He glanced out the window. "I hope you don't mind if I take the back exit. I believe the alley leads

51

right behind the bank, which is where everyone thinks I am." He looked away, shame briefly reflected in his expression. "I don't want you to think I'm gutless," he said softly. "It's just that I don't need the kind of trouble those two gentlemen might cause."

"I understand, Tom," Averill replied evenly. "Those are two bad hombres. You don't need that kind of grief." He motioned to the door leading to the jail cells. "The back door is at the end of the hall. Feel free to use it . . . and make sure you let me know if you hear anything that might be important. *Anything,* you understand?"

Lacey nodded as he walked through the door and down the hall.

After Tom Lacey left by the back door, Nathan sat at his desk and pondered his next move. Although he appreciated Lacey's belated and somewhat feeble attempt at being a solid citizen, he did, in fact, already know about the presence of Chapman and Daughtry in his town. Chapman was a charter member of the notorious Santa Fe Ring, that group of crooked politicians which had been a blight on northern New Mexico landowners and Colfax County in particular for at least ten years. Just three weeks before, someone had killed five cowboys and stolen the entire herd. *They just won't give it up,* Nathan thought.

Nathan opened the drawer and pulled out a letter he had received several days previously. He read it again for at least the fifth time and contemplated his course of action. His friend, Taos deputy Ronald Markstrom, had written to inform him that he had documents in his possession that very clearly linked William Chapman to the cattle rustling epidemic that had been occurring throughout Colfax County for the past six months. Specifically, he had letters from Chapman to Thomas Catron, the acknowledged leader of the Santa Fe Ring, stating that Chapman had a plan to destroy the cattle trade of the ranchers in Colfax County. He intended to make it impossible for them to deliver on their contracts to the coal mining operations in southern Colorado and put them in a position where they were forced to sell their ranches to him. Accomplishing that would then put Chapman in the saddle to take over those contracts.

If I could get ahold of those letters, I'd have all those boys right where I've wanted'em. Nathan's friend had stated in his letter that he felt it imperative that Nathan come to Taos personally to pick up the letters. He didn't trust the mail delivery. He also was worried that members of the Ring might have gotten wind of the fact that he had documents that could cause trouble for them. In fact, he had been more specific. He had instructed Nathan to send him a telegram first before he headed out for Taos. His words had been "if you don't hear back from me in two days, it means I had to fade away for a time." Markstrom was not a man to run from trouble but he was no fool either. If he thought he might have to head for the hills, Nathan was sure he had good reason to be afraid.

Nathan thought Markstrom was probably right that it would be the safest thing for him to make the trip over to Taos to get the letters; he just hadn't had time to do it. The spate of rustling had kept him riding from one end of Colfax County to the other trying to get a handle on who these rustlers were. *You'd think I could find more than one deputy,* he fumed. *Course it ain't legal for me to have more than three anyhow and that's not nearly enough to cover Colfax County.* That particular Territorial law made no sense at all . . . that is, unless you happened to be engaged in shady endeavors and didn't want the eye of the law focused on you. Although he was dead sure that Chapman was behind these illegal acts, he was just as certain that he wouldn't be directly involved. It was the style of the Santa Fe Ring to have others do their dirty deeds. Once he got those incriminating letters, though, he just might be able to cut the head off of the snake.

I think maybe I'll head down to the Tavern tomorrow to see if those boys are sittin' there plottin' their next caper. Maybe I can stir up the hornets nest a bit.

CHAPTER 9

June 13, 1884

Jared was finishing up his coffee when he heard a horse approaching. Reflexively, his eyes immediately tracked down the twelve gauge shotgun hanging on the wall by the door. He walked cautiously out onto the portal and saw Juan riding in his direction. With that welcome sight, he expelled the lung-full of air he'd been holding without realizing it. It was a mighty relief to discover that the rider was a friend rather than a stranger and potential foe. He shook his head wistfully and sighed. *It'll be nice when the day comes that we don't have to look over our shoulders all the time for the next batch of mankillers those dang political hacks in Santa Fe keep comin' up with.*

Juan grinned and waved as he approached the house. He instinctively knew what his friend had been thinking as he rode up. "Thanks for not shooting me." He dismounted and tied his horse to the hitching post. "I think we'll be ready to go in two days, amigo," he said. "Tommy has been bringing steers down from the high country. Joe will help him finish the job tomorrow morning. We should have one hundred head gathered and ready to go by the day after."

Jared nodded approvingly. "Good job, pard. Sounds like you 'bout got everything together. Sorry we can't spare one more hand to go with you. I think you, Tommy and Joe ought to be able to handle a herd that size, though." He looked out over the foothills, avoiding his friend's eyes. "How did Maria take the news that you'd be headin' up the trail again so soon?"

"Not good." Juan shook his head wearily. "Not good at all. She just about went through the roof when I told her, is what she did. Then she got quiet. She hasn't spoken to me since then. I tried to tell her that it was business. When these coal miners need steers, we got to jump." He smiled ruefully. "She wasn't listening."

"I'm sorry, Juan. It's hard enough to leave home and head up the trail. It's sure enough harder when your wife is mad at you," Jared said. "Maybe I'll ask Eleanor if she'll go over to check on Maria after you been gone a day or two."

"That might help," Juan said. "Sometimes she'll listen to somebody else when she's mad at me. Yeah," he said, after a moment's reflection. "That would be good."

"At least Eleanor could help her out with some chores," Jared said. "Maybe talk to her about that little ruckus the two of you had, maybe not, dependin' on how the wind is blowin'." Jared grinned. "Eleanor's got a feel for that sort of thing. She knows when to take on somethin' head on and when to kind of work her way around it."

"You got that right, pard. She's a lot better at it than you and me, that's for sure." Juan grinned mischievously. "Might have been smart to just have Eleanor tell her in the first place. Least she wouldn't have thrown pots at her and made her sleep in the stable."

Jared was concerned enough that he ignored his friend's joshing and changed the subject. "I'm a little worried about all the rustlin' that's been goin' on up north. You boys need to be cautious."

"We'll try to keep an eye out," Juan said. "With just the three of us, we're gonna have to take turns doin' nighthawk solo. I don't see any other way around it. Estévan has got to handle the wagon chores. We can't have him do it."

"That's what I figured, too," Jared said with a frown. "That's part of what's got me worried. One cowboy can't be all around a herd, even a small one like you got. It'd be pretty danged easy for a few thievin' curs to sneak twenty or thirty head out and get'em movin' before you realize what's happenin'."

"I don't know about that," Juan said. "We're all pretty fair hands. I don't think anyone will be snoozing on the job this time. We'd spot rustlers before they did too much damage."

Jared thought, *I'm afraid this gang that's pullin' these raids wouldn't be afraid to shoot if it came down to it.* He decided to keep that thought to himself, however, as Juan was already stirred up enough about Maria's being mad at him. *He's a top hand, he'll know how to handle whatever comes along.*

CHAPTER 10

June 13, 1884

Nathan checked his Colt and made sure he had bullets in all six chambers. Then he got his Remington .10 gauge and stuck a few extra shells in his vest pocket. Even though he wasn't planning on gun play, he figured he'd best be prepared just in case. He'd heard rumors that this Daughtry was a pretty deadly customer. Since he didn't know him, he wasn't sure what to expect. He hefted the shotgun and thought, *better to have it and not need it than need it and not have it.*

Although he didn't plan on starting a war, Nathan fully intended to put a bee under Bill Chapman's bonnet. Before their little parley was through, Chapman would know for durn sure that he didn't have a free pass to come into Cimarrón and start trouble. There was no doubt in Nathan's mind that Chapman was up to no good. If he'd been the least bit uncertain, the presence of a killer like Daughtry confirmed that fact. Chapman was a charter member of the Santa Fe Ring. While their thieving ways seemed to ebb and flow depending on who the territorial governor was and how willing he was to look the other way, they'd never completely stopped their efforts to grab land all over northern New Mexico.

Nathan took a deep breath and walked to the door of his office. *I don't know how much longer I'll be able to do this,* he thought. *But I don't know who'll do it if I don't.*

Chapman and Daughtry were deep in conversation when the saloon doors swung open. Chapman hadn't noticed the intrusion until he looked up and saw that Daughtry's eyes had narrowed. He looked down at the whiskey glass Daughtry was holding. He noticed the index finger on his right hand was twitching. The saloon, which had been filled with the boisterous chatter of happy customers and employees yelling out orders to the bartender, suddenly grew silent as the prairie at midnight. Carefully, Chapman scooted his chair around. He saw Sheriff Nathan Averill walking deliberately in his direction. He was carrying a shotgun. He was holding it carefully with his right hand just behind the trigger guard while the business end was cradled in the crook of his left elbow. It appeared to be aimed at a spot just above the derby hat on Daughtry's head. From where he sat, Chapman could swear that both hammers were cocked.

"Good afternoon, sheriff," Chapman called out with false cordiality. "Did you stop by to buy us a drink?"

Nathan's eyes never left Daughtry. "Nope." The silence hung in the air like a soap bubble about to burst.

Finally, Chapman broke the silence. "Well, if you don't have any business with us, then please excuse Mr. Daughtry and myself. We were engaged in a conversation about some important matters."

Daughtry's right hand moved almost imperceptibly back toward his body. "You make one more move, I'll blow you out of that chair," Nathan said in a quiet, matter-of-fact voice. As he spoke, he lowered his shotgun just enough to where it was pointed square in the middle of Daughtry's chest. Daughtry stopped where he was. His right eye began to twitch. "Put your hands flat on the table and leave 'em there."

"Why, sheriff, I believe you're threatening my friend." Chapman spoke in a cheerful voice. The cheer did not extend to his eyes.

"If you shoot him down, it would be cold-blooded murder here in front of a room full of witnesses. You don't really think you could get away with that, do you?"

"I don't know, Chapman," Nathan said in the same steady voice. "It wouldn't make much difference to your friend here either way, though. He'd be dead."

"Sheriff, my friend Daughtry has done nothing to warrant this treatment by you." Chapman drew himself up a little bit straighter in his chair when he spoke, attempting to sound indignant without moving enough to appear threatening.

With a look of disgust, Nathan responded. "Your 'friend' there is an outlaw and a murderer. The world would be a better place if I pulled both triggers right now."

Daughtry cut his eyes toward Chapman for a signal on how to proceed. The threat of violence hung so thick in the air you could easily imagine that you smelled it. Slowly, Chapman shook his head. Just as slowly, he raised his right hand in Daughtry's direction to indicate he should stand down. With obvious reluctance, Daughtry placed both hands flat on the table and sat back in his chair. It appeared to dawn on him that no matter how fast he was, he didn't have a prayer of getting his gun drawn and aimed before the sheriff cut him in two. He also seemed to have gotten the clear message that Nathan wouldn't mind doing so . . . in fact, might relish the deed. He knew what it meant to have the drop on someone, it's just that he wasn't used to being on the wrong end of the transaction.

"Mr. Daughtry is a law-abiding citizen, sheriff," Chapman said with a tad more indignation in his tone. "I repeat. He's done nothing to deserve this treatment from you."

"Mr. Daughtry is low-life rat," Nathan said with a sneer on his lips. "He kills people for money. He's a lily-livered coward who's just as likely to back shoot'em as to face'em fair and square." Daughtry's eyes narrowed to slits again. His trigger finger began to twitch again, this time more rapidly. Once again, Chapman raised his hand slowly to indicate that he wanted Daughtry to calm down.

"Can you prove this, sheriff?" Chapman asked. "If you can, produce a warrant and arrest the man. If not, state your business and then leave us be."

Nathan shook his head. "What rock do you find these varmints under, Chapman?" Chapman began to reply but Nathan talked over him. "First, you and your gang of yellow-belly thieves sic the O'Bannons on us. Then it's Curt Barwick and his cronies. Is there some special place where you find these worthless, lowdown bushwhackers? When are you gonna learn that we'll handle all comers here in Cimarrón?"

"As I heard the tale, Sheriff," Chapman said with a smirk, "you didn't handle much of anything with Mr. Barwick. In fact, I heard you were holed up in some line shack without the nerve to join the party."

Nathan smiled in return but his gray eyes were flint-hard. "Don't believe everything you hear, Chapman."

Chapman continued to smirk. "Well, I understand, sheriff, that as you get older, your reflexes slow down. Maybe it's better to let others do your dirty work."

"If you're lookin' to start a fight," Nathan said very softly, "you're just about there. I'm not too worried about the legalities. Neither should Daughtry be, 'cause he'll be dead." Nathan smiled. "For that matter, I don't think you'd have to worry much either. I got a barrel for each of you."

Chapman's smirk vanished. "Sheriff, I'll try to overlook your threats and ask you your business again. Daughtry and I really do have pressing matters to discuss."

"I don't doubt that you do," Nathan said carefully. "In fact, that's the very business

65

I've got in mind to discuss with you. I know you're up to plottin' some more foul deeds. I want you to know that I won't let it happen here in Colfax County." Nathan shifted his shotgun so that it was aimed at a point halfway between Daughtry and Chapman. He favored them with a smile as cold as the winter snow. "As I've already made clear to you, I'd be happy to let the law sort it out after the fact. Do yourself a favor. Believe every word I'm sayin'."

Chapman tried to meet the sheriff's gaze with a cold stare of his own. He couldn't sustain it. He was the first to look away. "Your message has been delivered, sheriff. Thanks for your time." With that, he turned his chair back to the table.

Nathan returned his gaze to Daughtry. "Whatever else happens, compadre," he said almost in a whisper, "I've got a bullet for you."

The right side of Daughtry's mouth turned up ever so slightly. Nathan gave him a look of disdain. He turned and walked to the door, showing him his back in an invitation to fly his true colors. Daughtry's hand started to move down to his side. "No," Chapman hissed forcefully. "Not here, not now." Daughtry looked at him. He raised his eyebrows inquiringly. "There'll be a time later."

Sweat ran down Nathan's back as he walked towards his office. He remembered a few years back when he'd told Eleanor Delaney to never let them see you sweat. *Looks like I'm sweatin' more now than I ever used to,* he thought. *Just hope they didn't see it.* This trouble just never seemed to end. Like he'd told Chapman, so far they'd handled everything the Santa Fe Ring had thrown at them, but he knew that a high price had been paid. Ned and Lizbeth Kilpatrick, two of the finest people he'd ever known, were both dead. There were others among the living who were carrying scars, too. Some, like Christy Johnson, carried theirs on the outside. Others, like Maria Suazo, had to bear the pain of wounds that no one could see. In his agitated frame of mind, he didn't notice that the door to his office was slightly ajar until he was already halfway in the door.

"Hello, Nathan."

Nathan almost jumped out of his skin. He had the hammers cocked and his shotgun swinging up to fire before the voice, mercifully, registered. "Good Lord almighty, Christy, you just about scared me to death!" He lowered his shotgun shakily. "You coulda got yourself killed, young lady. What were you thinkin'?"

Christy Johnson cocked her head and frowned at Nathan. "Well, excuse me, but I was thinking that you might want to join me for a cup of coffee at Miguel's place. I didn't know you might shoot me just for asking."

Nathan was flustered and embarrassed. He walked over and sat down in his desk chair. "I'm sorry, Christy, I shouldn't have barked at you. I'm just on edge because of that damned Bill Chapman. Him and that snake they call Daughtry." Nathan scowled. "What the hell kind of name is Daughtry anyway? Decent folks got two names, a first and a last. Daughtry, be damned!"

Christy's jaw dropped in amazement. That was three times as much profanity as she'd heard from Nathan Averill's lips in the more than six years she had known him. Unsure of how to proceed, she meekly tried her invitation again for coffee. "I'd still be pleased to have you join me down at Miguel's. I'll bet Anita still has some of that apple cobbler she makes left over from the noon meal."

Nathan began shaking his head vigorously before Christy had even finished speaking. "I can't let you be around me right now, Christy, it's way too dangerous. If those gutless wonders come gunnin' for me, they won't think twice about shootin' you as well."

The frustration Christy had experienced for three years boiled over. She stamped her foot and practically yelled at Nathan. "Then when exactly in this lifetime do you expect that we can be together? Will it ever be safe?"

Nathan sighed. "I wish I knew, Christy." He looked out the window for a moment, then back at her. In a voice raw with emotion, he said, "I hope you know I got feelin's for you. I care about you, I care a great deal. That's the reason I have to think about your safety, even if it means we can't spend time together."

Christy was not mollified. "I'd like to know what makes you think you're the one who gets to decide how to keep me safe. This is *my* life, Nathan Averill, not yours. Being sheriff means you arrest folks who are breaking the law. If it's against the law for me to want to be with you, then go ahead and arrest me. Otherwise, I wish you'd just shut up about it."

"I wish I could, Christy." A look of deep sadness came over Nathan's face. "You're wrong, you know. It ain't just my job to arrest folks. It's my job to protect good people from bad people." He shook his head in frustration. "You know better than most that I haven't done a very good job of that the past few years."

"Are we back to that?" Christy asked in exasperation. "You're not perfect. You can't be everywhere at once. You've done a far better job than most any other lawman I've ever heard of. Most people would be satisfied with that."

"Good people are dead," he said bitterly. "I should have prevented it. I didn't. Other people have been hurt, you included. How do you expect me to be satisfied with that?"

"We've gone round and round about this, Nathan. I know you have a dangerous job. I understand that if I want to be with you . . . which I do, by the way . . . I have to accept that part of you with all the rest." Christy threw up her hands. "Have you forgotten how I made my living when I first met you? Don't you think I might've run into some dicey situations back then? I'm not some prissy little school girl who faints at the sound of gunfire."

"I know you're not, Christy," Nathan grudgingly acknowledged. "Right now, I just don't think it's safe for you to be around me. I hate it, but that's the way I see it. That's the way I've got to play it."

A tear rolled down Christy's cheek. "You're a stubborn and sanctimonious man, Nathan Averill." She saw his eyes widen and snapped. "Yes, I used a big word . . . sanctimonious. I'm the school teacher now, I know big words."

Nathan shook his head in resignation. "I know you do, Christy. You're a smart, beautiful lady who deserves to be safe. I wish I could give you that. Right now, I can't."

Christy looked at Nathan for a moment, then she shook her head. "I can see this discussion is going nowhere, just like it has in the past. I'll stop for now. I'll even stay away from you." She took a step closer to where he sat. "I'm not giving up, though. You'd better know that. You're not the only one around here who knows when something is worth fighting for."

Christy turned without a word and walked out of the sheriff's office. As she walked away, she felt her heart sink. What a cruel joke the fates were playing on her. Just when she thought she might have a chance to be happy with Nathan, that worthless bunch from Santa Fe showed up again to cause trouble. Her mind wandered back through her checkered past, searching for any vestige of pleasant memories.

Chapter 11

June 13, 1884

Christy would swear she'd been born under a bad sign. In fact, she had sworn about it often. She had distant memories of moving west from her home in East Texas a few years after the Civil War. In her hazy recollections, it was an exciting time for her family. Her father had saved up his money and had dreams of starting a mercantile in the town of Mesilla in the southeastern corner of the New Mexico Territory. The Butterfield Stage ran through Mesilla and Fort Selden was close by, offering protection from the dangerous Mescalero Apaches. They were going to be rich . . . her daddy said so.

After a few prosperous years, however, things went bad. The fort became run-down due to a lack of funds and was eventually abandoned. When the troops left, the citizens of Mesilla were essentially abandoned as well. Attacks by the Apaches increased. No one was safe beyond the village limits. Christy had a vivid memory of her mother coming to get her at the school house on her eleventh birthday to tell her that her father had been murdered while delivering his weekly wagon load of supplies to Fort Selden.

Christy was devastated. Her daddy had always been strong. It had never crossed her mind that something awful like this could happen to him. She had always felt safe before. This tragedy led to a fundamental shift in her view of the world. She had the painful realization that terrible events could strike like lightning and there was nothing you could do to stop it or protect yourself.

Her mother was immobilized with grief. She'd relied on her husband to keep the books and make all the purchases for the store. Although she tried her best to take up where he'd left off, she was soon overwhelmed by the multitude of details involved in running the business. Money flowed like blood from an open wound. Within two years, the bank began foreclosure proceedings.

With no income and little in the way of savings, Christy and her mother were cast adrift right at the time Christy entered young womanhood. Her mother increasingly relied on laudanum and elderberry wine to cushion herself from the pain. She was immobilized by a drug-induced fog and there were times when they did not eat for several days. Christy increasingly relied on her wits. If not for the generosity of the man who owned the café in town, they might have starved.

She was way too young, Christy recalled, when she began her career as a working girl. It happened quite by accident. As her mother became more and more helpless, Christy tried desperately to think of a way to make money. Somehow, she took it in her head that the president of the bank that foreclosed on the store owed it to them to help with their dire financial straits. As it turned out, she was right, just not in the manner she had imagined.

When she went to the bank to see the president, she was initially met with resistance from the secretary who made his appointments. This officious little man told her that the president was much too busy to see her, both that day and all days to come. It was only after she very quietly threatened to make a scene in front of the bank customers that the man relented and grudgingly showed her in to the president's lavish private office.

The bank president looked her up and down. He instructed his secretary to leave and shut the door behind him. When he was gone, the man turned and asked her to be seated on the plush velvet love seat in his office. He pulled a chair up uncomfortably close to her. For the first time in her life . . . but certainly not the last . . . Christy had the experience of being undressed by a man's eyes. After an uncomfortable few moments of leering, the bank president asked what he could do for her.

Christy had prepared a speech about why the bank president should help her family. She launched into it with great enthusiasm. She hadn't gotten very far into the speech when the man raised his hand to stop her. He then placed that same hand on her knee and told her not to worry because he was willing to help her. Christy's sense of relief and gratitude vanished quickly when his grip on her knee tightened and he explained what she would need to do in order for him to help her. Her initial outrage was met with indifference. He let her go on for a minute, then he told her that if she wasn't interested in his offer of help, she could starve as far as he was concerned. Her desperation outweighed her disgust. Before she knew it, she was the concubine of the Mesilla bank's president.

For the next few years, the man kept his promise. As long as she provided him favors, he provided food and shelter for her and her mother. Christy still felt a twinge of resentment that her mother never asked her how their fortunes had managed to turn around so dramatically. Her drinking and laudanum habits continued. The time soon came when her lucid moments were few and far between.

Several months after she turned sixteen, Christy's mother died. Christy came home one afternoon after yet another degrading tryst with her banker to find her mother slumped over in the chair in the sitting room. Christy's efforts to wake her turned into frantic attempts to revive her. It was to no avail. The banker paid for the funeral and a rather plain-looking plot in the town cemetery. A week later, Christy went to the bank. She asked the same officious secretary if she might speak with the bank president in his office. He sullenly led her back to the office. When he was leaving, she quietly asked that he not close the door. Although puzzled, he did as she requested. She then told her benefactor she was leaving and that after one last transaction, their financial arrangement was finished. This transaction would involve his giving her one hundred dollars in cash to help her with moving expenses. The man had actually become quite fond of her and was heartbroken by the news. He created quite a scene, first begging her to stay, then threatening her with violence if she left him. At the end of his rant, she pointed out that the door to his office was open and if he tried to assault her, she would scream at the top of her lungs. She told him if he made any effort to stop her from leaving town, she would make a beeline to his home and have a heart to heart talk with his wife. He relented.

With her paltry stake of one hundred dollars, Christy headed north to Santa Fe where she found ample opportunities to ply her new trade. It's not that she didn't try to find other jobs, it's just that the choices for women were slim. She might have found some financial security if she married a rancher or shop owner but the "proposals" she received rarely included marriage. On the rare occasions when they did, that part of the offer was always retracted once the other party had taken what they really wanted from the encounter.

The cowboys who were her best customers were not the worst part of the job.

Certainly their odor would never be confused with the fresh smell of pine trees in the mountains. Occasionally, one of them might become too rough while under the influence of alcohol. For the most part, however, they were hardly more than boys trying to do a man's job on the trail. Spending time with the ladies of the evening was one of the ways they tried to convince others . . . and themselves . . . that they were really grown men. The worst problem most of them gave her was that they tended to fall in love with her, or at least with the image in their head of who she was. When the sun came up and their heads cleared, they usually got over that.

Far more difficult to deal with were the men who ran the establishments where she was employed. If the cowboys had a distorted image of who she was, at least they considered her a human being. To the businessmen for whom she worked, she was just a piece of meat to be bought and sold as rapidly and for as high a price as she could draw. As long as she followed their directives, they treated her with complete indifference. If she displeased one of them, however, retribution was swift, merciless and painful. She was much more afraid of her employers than of the occasional rowdy cowboy with too much liquor in his system. Her bosses tended to be cruel. A number of them appeared to relish inflicting pain on the ladies who worked for them.

The brightest spot in her dim existence was her relationship with her fellow working girls. When they weren't working, they spent time telling stories about clumsy or humorous things their customers did or sharing fantasies about what they would do when they "got out of the trade." These fantasies were always tinged with sadness, as if at some level they all knew there was no way out. Most of the girls indulged heavily in alcohol, laudanum or opium when they could get it. If these medicinal helpers dulled the pain of their hopeless existence, they took a terrible toll on the bodies and spirits of the girls. Christy had known more than one girl who finally sought lasting relief by taking the long laudanum sleep.

With her own mother as a tarnished example of the folly of bad habits, Christy tried her best to stay away from the dangerous temptations surrounding her. At her most optimistic moments, she still held out some hope that she would find a way out of the downward spiral she was caught up in. She knew if she succumbed to the temptation of spending most of her time in drugged oblivion, there would be no way out. While she sometimes drank alcohol, she tried hard not to make it part of her routine to get drunk. She refused to use the other drugs common to her trade. Still, as the years went by, it became harder and harder for her not to give in to the tug of sweet narcotic haze.

However jaded she was before she arrived in Cimarrón and went to work at the Colfax Tavern, it could not compare to the cynicism and bitterness she acquired once she took up residence there. The bartender Heck Roberts, a sadistic Yankee, took perverse pleasure in inflicting pain on her. He was quite adept at not leaving any bruises that would show, if in fact anyone had cared to look. His boss, Morgan O'Bannon, was, in her opinion, the physical embodiment of evil. He came close to destroying her very soul. If the fates hadn't intervened to bring Jared Delaney, Nathan Averill and Eleanor Coulter in to her life, she knew beyond the shadow of a doubt that she would be in Hell by now. They had thrown her a lifeline, showing her a way out and giving her the opportunity and encouragement to take it. Not only that, they had each treated her as a human being with dignity and the potential for self-respect that comes from pulling yourself up out of the gutter. They reminded her of things she had long-forgotten . . . that she was intelligent and had the capacity to take back control of her destiny. They had saved her life.

After the range war with the O'Bannons had ended, Eleanor Coulter, who not long thereafter became Eleanor Delaney, had taken her under her wing at the school. Building on the rudimentary skills she had acquired in the one-room school in Mesilla, she'd given her the tools to take over as the teacher. Much more than that, she had given her the treasure of her friendship. Most of what Christy knew about being a lady came from her association with Eleanor. She somehow found the confidence to let Nathan Averill know that she had a romantic interest in him and the stubbornness to stick with it when he exhibited feet of day. She thought they had turned the corner and were headed for the kind of partnership she had barely let herself dream about when the fates showed their ugly side once again and brought Gentleman Curt Barwick and his murderous associates to town. As her recent maddening conversation with the sheriff indicated, they were still dealing with the aftermath.

CHAPTER 12

October 20, 1884

"This 1st Judicial District Court is now in session, the honorable Judge Roberto Cardenas presiding. All rise." The bailiff opened the door to the judge's chambers, not much more than a closet, actually. Judge Cardenas strode out. As he walked to the table that served as the bench, he looked down his nose and surveyed the crowd. His eyes stopped briefly at the table for the defense. A ghost of a smile flickered across his lips.

"Did you see that?" Jared whispered indignantly in the ear of John Budagher, the prosecuting attorney. "He smiled at Chapman."

"Easy, Mr. Delaney," Budagher whispered back to Jared. "That could mean anything . . . or nothing."

Hearing the small commotion, the judge shot a disapproving glance their way. Jared sat back and resolved to remain quiet through this initial phase of the proceedings. Inside, he was fuming. All they needed was a judge who was in the pocket of the Santa Fe Ring.

The judge banged his gavel rather unnecessarily and said in a stentorian voice, "Mr. Budagher, would you please tell the court what your business is here today."

Budagher was a young man who was already losing his hair. He was not tall, he was not handsome and he was developing a paunch that marked him as a man who spent his time indoors. Had there been a jury, they would not have been impressed with his appearance. He wore a suit that was most likely the only one he owned, judging from its threadbare appearance. He exuded under-confidence as he arose anxiously to address the court.

"If it please your honor," he said in a quiet voice that could barely be heard, "this is the preliminary hearing to determine if the state has sufficient evidence to proceed in the prosecution of a Mr. Daughtry, first name unknown, for murder and grand theft, specifically cattle rustling. In addition, the state is bringing charges of conspiracy to commit murder and grand theft against Mr. William Chapman."

"It would please the court," Judge Cardenas said in a supercilious tone, "if you would speak up so I could hear you clearly, prosecutor. If I have to strain to hear your words, this will not favorably dispose me toward your case, I promise you."

Looking sheepish, Budagher cleared his throat. When he spoke again, his voice was only slightly louder. He sounded like his cravat was tied too tight. "Yes, your honor. I'll do my best."

"Thank you, Mr. Budagher. Now, would you care to tell me about the state's allegations?"

"Yes, sir, your honor," Budagher mumbled as he reached for his notes. The judge banged his gavel down with a noise like a gunshot, startling Budagher so that he dropped his papers.

"Mr. Budagher, if I have to tell you again to speak up, I will find you in contempt of court. Is that understood?"

Struggling to gather his notes from the floor, the young prosecutor responded with a muffled "Yes, sir." Standing up quickly, he said in a louder voice, "I mean, yes sir, your honor. I'll do my best."

Jared's heart sank as he watched the drama unfold. Clearly the judge was hostile towards the prosecution for some reason. It looked like the case against his friend's murderers might unravel before it ever got started. He supposed it was possible that Judge Cardenas held a grudge against young Budagher that had nothing to do with this particular case. Somehow, Jared doubted that. The influence of the Santa Fe Ring ran wide and deep. If the judge really was a pawn of Catron's and the Santa Fe crowd, Daughtry and Chapman might just get away with murder.

"See that you do, prosecutor. Now, please continue."

Budagher cleared his throat again and Jared could hear that he was straining to raise his voice. "Your honor, in June of this year, a herd from the Kilpatrick Ranch was being driven up the trail to supply steers to the Morley coal mine north of Raton pass. Sometime during the night of June 19th, the herd was attacked by rustlers who drove off twenty head of cattle. In the process, they fired multiple shots at the cowboys driving the herd, wounding one young man and killing a second."

"Tragic, Mr. Budagher," Judge Cardenas interjected. "But incidents such as this happen from time to time. Do you have reason to believe that Mr. Chapman and Mr. Daughtry were involved in this foray or are you just looking for someone to pin it on?"

Budagher looked stunned. He glanced back at Jared, then looked back at Judge Cardenas. "Well, Judge, I was in the process of sharing with you why the state believes those gentlemen were invoked. If you could be patient, I will do my best to present sufficient evidence that we might proceed with a trial."

The judge froze the young prosecutor with an icy glare. "Do not ever presume to question my patience again, Mr. Budagher. I'm not inclined to sit here all day long while you meander around making some convoluted argument linking men who are well-respected in the community to your random crime just because they happen to have been in the general vicinity when it happened." The judge had both hands on the table now. It almost appeared as if he was about to come out of his chair and launch himself at the attorney. In an angry voice, he exclaimed, "We will need some hard evidence and we'll need it soon, Mr. Budagher. If it is not forthcoming, I will declare this proceeding finished. Do you understand me?

"Yes, your honor," the prosecutor said meekly but most definitely loud enough to be heard.

Jared squirmed in his seat. He looked over at the defense table and saw that Chapman was grinning broadly while Daughtry had a barely perceptible smirk on his lips. In an odd contrast, their attorney, Robert Elkins, looked anxious and uneasy. Jared wasn't sure what to make of that. He filed the information away in his memory.

"Now, Mr. Budagher," Judge Cardenas said with exaggerated patience as if he were speaking to a child, "would you please lay out in general terms the basis for your allegations against these gentlemen so I can begin to make a determination on how to proceed."

"Yes, your honor." Budagher took one more look at his notes and then set them on the table. He approached a spot about halfway between the judge's bench and the gallery of curious and excited onlookers crowding the benches in the courtroom. Although this was only a preliminary hearing to determine if there would be a trial, he hoped to plant in the minds of potential jurors some seeds that would flourish in to a guilty verdict at a future date.

"As I stated earlier, on the night of June 19th of this year, a number of men attacked the Kilpatrick herd in the middle of the night, driving off twenty head of cattle, killing one man and wounding another. We have reason to believe that one of the men leading the attack was Mr. Daughtry, who is sitting to my right at the table for the defense. Furthermore, we have reason to believe that Mr. William Chapman, also seated at the table for the defense, was the organizer of this incident and therefore a co-conspirator in the action."

At the defense table, Bill Chapman reached over and grabbed Elkins' arm in a vice-like grip, pulling him over so that he could whisper in his ear. "Are you not going to object, you bumbling nincompoop?"

Elkins wriggled in his grasp, trying to get his arm free. He leaned over to Chapman and said in a voice strained by the pain he was experiencing, "Now is not the time, Mr. Chapman, he's just making his opening statement. I'll make my opening statement after he gets done and I've had a chance to hear all he has to say." He wriggled more vigorously. "Please, you're hurting my arm. This won't look good to the judge."

Chapman smiled a cruel smile. He held on a moment longer just to show Elkins who was in charge, then loosened his grip. "Don't concern yourself with the judge, counselor. I don't think you're going to have to worry too much about him."

In fact, Jared noticed that while almost everyone else in the court was watching this interchange between Chapman and his attorney, the judge was entirely focused on the prosecutor and seemed totally oblivious to the disruption. *I don't like this,* Jared thought.

"Well, Mr. Prosecutor," the judge said in a voice that fairly dripped with sarcasm, "you've made your accusations against these gentlemen. Can you enlighten me as to whether you have any type of evidence to back these claims?"

"Yes, your honor, we do. We have a hat that I believe we can show belongs to Mr. Daughtry, thereby placing him at the scene of the crime. We have one of the cowboys who was present during the attack that can identify Mr. Daughtry as one of the attackers. We also will have letters to present in evidence that were penned by Mr. Chapman's own hand and which clearly indicate that not only did he know about this incident, he was directly involved in the planning of it."

The judge cocked his head. "Did my ears deceive me, Mr. Budagher? Did I just hear you say that you 'will have' letters to present in evidence?" He shook his head in disbelief. "Can I take this to mean that you don't currently have these letters in your possession?"

To his credit, Budagher didn't wilt under the judge's withering gaze. "No, your honor, we don't currently have the letters in our possession. However, we have an officer of the court who is riding to Taos as we speak to obtain these letters and bring them back for you to inspect. He should be here no later than tomorrow."

Jared felt a cold chill of apprehension rise up his spine. In fact, he had expected Nathan to return today. He had no idea what might have delayed his travels and there had been no communication via telegram to indicate that he was detained for some reason. This was totally out of character for Nathan. Jared had a bad feeling about it.

"Well," the judge said sharply, "you had better hope he gets here quickly. If I don't see this evidence by the end of court tomorrow, I will be inclined to drop all charges against Mr. Chapman and his associate. Do you understand me, Mr. Budagher?"

"Yes, your honor," the prosecutor responded in a quiet voice that sounded as if he had a mouth full of oatmeal. Too late, he realized his mistake.

Judge Cardenas' gavel slammed down

with authority. "I'm fining you for contempt of court, Mr. Budagher. I have warned you repeatedly to show this court the respect of speaking in an audible tone. You are hereby fined five dollars. Pay the bailiff at the end of the session."

About an hour before sundown, Eleanor heard a horse approaching. She looked out the window to make sure it was Jared. There hadn't been any trouble at the ranch in a while; still old habits die hard. She shivered in spite of herself as she recalled the outlaw, Curt Barwick, who had threatened her while she was pregnant with Ned. A blood curdling shriek from her three year old son reassured her that he was very much alive. Ned saw that his father had returned and ran out the door before she could stop him. He raced over to where Jared had dismounted and gleefully launched himself at his father.

"Papa, papa," he squealed. Although he had learned a number of other words by now, papa was the first one that he had spoken and the one that tumbled from his lips most frequently. Eleanor smiled as Jared scooped up his son and swung him around several times. She knew how much Jared missed having a father in his life when he was growing up. It warmed her heart to see that he was determined to give his son all the best a father has to offer.

"I'm gonna put you down now, cowboy," Jared said. "We've got to get this saddle off old Red and get him fed and watered. You step back over there. I'll let you carry his saddle blanket when I'm done."

Ned calmed down immediately and did as his father had said. Eleanor felt a twinge of envy at how obedient Ned was with his father. She spent half her time during the day at the ranch keeping an eye on her wild child. She spent the other half telling him repeatedly to get out of things. She smiled ruefully at the irony of her being a former school teacher who had dealt successfully with many rowdy children over the years. With Ned, it often took the threat of her getting a switch to get him to pay attention to her, whereas the sound of his father's voice seemed to calm him down almost immediately. Fortunately, Ned had a good-natured streak to go along with his exuberance. *He's all boy, that's for certain,* she thought.

As Jared unsaddled his horse, he explained each step of what he was doing to his son. Ned listened with rapt attention. Jared was very patient with Ned and let him carry the saddle blanket to the barn. In spite of his calm demeanor, however, Eleanor could sense that something was bothering her husband. With the trial starting today, they both had high hopes that they would see the wheels of justice begin to turn and call those who were responsible for the murder of their clear friend to account. Judging from the sound of his voice, she suspected that the wheels weren't turning as smoothly as they would like. She decided to wait until they had gotten the horse put away before she asked him about it, though.

Eleanor got the table set and fed her two cowboys when they came in from the barn. Ned babbled happily throughout the meal. He made a big mess, getting as much food *on* himself as he did *in* himself. Although Jared was patient with him, Eleanor could see that he was distracted. When they were done, she gathered up Ned and carried him over to the water basin where she did her best to scrape away the remains of dinner that he was wearing. He became fussy as she did this. It became abundantly clear that he was ready to go to bed. He had run around most of the day and had only taken a short nap early in the afternoon.

"I'll put this young man to bed and get these dishes cleared away. After that, you can tell me about the trial," she said.

Jared nodded absently to her and walked out to sit in the rocking chair on the portal. He gazed over the land that stretched out in front of him . . . land of which he was the steward. To the east, as far as he could see, there were rolling hills covered with enough good grass to feed more cattle than he could ever sell. As the sun sank beneath the foothills behind him, it bathed the landscape with a light the color of a pink rose. Off to the north in the hazy distance, he could just make out the silhouette of the mountains rising majestically out of the prairie, providing the gateway up through Raton Pass into Colorado. Owning this glorious land was, to him, both the culmination of a dream and the acceptance of a tremendous responsibility . . . to his family and to the generations that followed. The land was the foundation that sustained the way of life he loved. It allowed him to provide for his family and to offer work for wages to his friends so that they also could provide for their families. Most of all, it allowed him to be who he was . . . a cowboy. The notion that greedy men with no love for this land were trying to steal it away from him made his blood boil.

After a few minutes and several lullabies,

Ned finally nodded off. Eleanor took care of cleaning up, then joined her husband. They sat in silence for several minutes, staring at the purple afterglow from the sunset. Eleanor knew her husband well. She waited patiently until he was ready to speak.

"It makes me so mad I could just spit," Jared said vehemently. "The judge was falling all over himself to kowtow to Chapman. That prosecutor was a gutless wonder. He was pretty much worthless." Jared shook his head with disgust. "It was about all he could do to speak above a whisper. If the judge had said 'boo!' I believe he'd have died of fright."

"It was just the first day, Jared. When the judge hears Tommy's testimony and sees the letters that Nathan is bringing back, he can't help but find enough evidence to go ahead with a trial."

"I don't know what he's gonna make of Tommy's testimony, Eleanor my love. He didn't get that good of a look at the man who shot him. He was lying on the ground bleeding at the time. It could go either way."

"Maybe so," Eleanor said, "but the documents Nathan has will be crystal clear. They are written in Chapman's own hand, as I understand it."

"Well, the problem is that Nathan isn't

back from Taos yet." Jared exhaled deeply. "That's got me worried, darlin'. It's just not like Nathan to not show up when he says he will. I got a bad feelin' that somethin' may have gone wrong."

"I know the waiting is hard. Couldn't there be any number of explanations for why he's not back yet, though?" Eleanor was trying to reassure her husband. She could see from the worried look in his eye that it wasn't working. As they talked, she, too, began to have a sense that something was amiss. *If something has happened to Nathan, I don't know what I would do,* she thought.

With a deep breath, Jared pulled himself out of the rocker. "I don't reckon it's doin' any good to stew about all this. Let's turn in, try to get some rest for tomorrow."

Eleanor took the hand that her husband offered to help her out of the chair. As she rose, she pulled it close to her heart and squeezed. "We'll get through this, Jared. You know that, don't you? We've been through hard times before and the sun generally comes on up the next day." She smiled at him. "I suppose it will come up again tomorrow morning." He led her to their feather bed where they sought comfort in

each others' arms. There were no nightmares this night.

CHAPTER 13

May 22, 1884

Two cowboys were riding nighthawk under the dim light of the waning moon. The other three were deep in their bedrolls back at the wagon. The two night hands were on opposite sides of the herd, one east and one west. The wagon was just a short distance to the east of the herd. The cowboy . . . he really was a boy, not more than sixteen . . . thought he heard a noise in the brush back off to his left. He was afraid it might be a wolf or even worse, maybe a mountain lion, but his horse didn't act skittish. *Must be my imagination,* he thought. *That sure enough can happen out here in the dark.*

Setting aside his fears, he turned his head back towards the herd to check for any signs of unusual activity. Too late, he heard the sound of footsteps running in his direction. He turned and only managed to squawk, "what the . . . !" before he was jerked from the saddle. He hit the ground hard and lost his breath. The last sound he heard was the whisper of metal sliding against leather, right before his throat was slit from ear to ear. Although there was little light, his assailant could see the boy's eyes growing wide with disbelief as his life's blood ran out onto the prairie. He tried to speak but could only gurgle helplessly. The attacker wiped the blade of his bone-handled knife on the young man's chaps, stood up and waved to his unseen companions.

Four men rode out of the underbrush. A man wearing a derby hat was leading the horse of the stealthy attacker who trotted over and mounted up. Once in the saddle, he leaned over to the man in the derby, who appeared to be the leader. He whispered, "Bob'll take care of that boy on the other side. Once he's down, we can start movin' these steers out of here."

The man just nodded. They sat still on their horses until they heard the sound of homes approaching. Their guns were drawn and ready. Once they recognized their partner by his top hat, they holstered their pistols. The man with the derby waved his hand in the direction of the herd and the rustlers spread out to begin moving the cattle. They got in position and waited for the signal they knew would be coming.

Several minutes passed. Suddenly, the silence of the night was shattered by the sound of gunfire . . . three shots. The rustlers began whooping and waving their hats to get the sleepy bovines moving. They planned to head off in a northwesterly direction but they had been instructed to first run some cattle through the camp. It seemed like overkill, even to these hard case outlaws. They'd learned through bitter experience though that if the man in the derby hat gave you an order, or even deigned to speak to you at all, you did what he said.

Over by the wagon, the man in the derby hat looked down at the three cowboys he had just shot in cold blood as they lay sleeping. The first two had been close together and hadn't even waked up. The third one, who had been a little further from the fire, pulled himself to a sitting position in his bedroll before a shot to the chest laid him back down almost gently. If anyone had been near enough to see in the dim light, they would have found the expression on the face of the man in the derby hat to be bloodcurdling. As he rode away, he appeared to be smiling.

CHAPTER 14

June 17, 1884

He smiled. It warmed his heart to watch Eleanor as she sat in the old rocker on the porch, crocheting a blanket for little Ned that would keep him warm and snug when the north winds began to swirl on the prairie. *Well, maybe not so warm,* he thought wryly. She squinted as she worked and Jared could hear her muttering with apparent frustration as the yarn failed to cooperate with her. Eleanor was about as handy with a crocheting needle as she was with a frying pan. Jared, not having been born yesterday, was certainly not about to complain, at least not to her. He might make sport of her shortcomings when he was joking around with Juan but he loved, respected and to a certain degree, feared his wife too much to say anything about it to her directly. While she was not particularly adept in the traditional uses of crocheting needles and frying pans, he was concerned that she might prove rather nimble at using them as weapons. *At least,* he thought, *she knows I don't stay with her just because of her cookin'.*

Jared looked out in the yard at his son trying his best to rope the steer Jared had fashioned for him out of a stump with branches for horns. He smiled again. Sweat was running down the side of his face. He had his tongue stuck out the side of his mouth as he carefully shook out his loop. By Jared's count, he roped the stump about one out of every ten throws. When he did, you could tell it from a mile away . . . he'd whoop with pure glee. Although he was only three, Ned was determined to be a cowboy just like his father. Jared had to admit he was mighty pleased with that turn of events, as he believed there was no higher calling than being a cowboy. Now that he had a spread of his own, he wanted to keep it in the family for generations to come.

"I believe that boy's gonna make a hand one of these days," Jared said to Eleanor.

She looked up from her work. "I think he has his father's knack for cowboy skills." She frowned. "I'm glad he's not a girl. No one would want to inherit my skills . . ." Eleanor grimaced, "well, my *lack* of skills at cooking and sewing."

Jared decided to tread very carefully. He knew he should say something complimentary to his wife at this point. However, she was sharp as a tack and could see through any false bouquets he might toss in her direction. "Any child of yours is sure gonna have a good head for figures. A gift for dealin' with people, too." He sat back in his rocker, quite pleased with himself.

Eleanor looked sideways at him. She smiled an impish grin. "Jared, honey, I was fishing for a compliment on my cooking. Isn't there something nice you could say about that?"

Jared could feel himself turning red. "Well, sure, I reckon there's plenty I could say," he said with all the self-righteous indignation he could muster. "I just didn't think you liked it when I go on and on about how you cook."

With the grin still on her face and now a twinkle of mischief in her eye, Eleanor said, "I'm trying to recall the last complimentary thing you said about my cooking. I'm having a little trouble remembering. Would you mind repeating it?"

Dang, he thought. *She's got me.* Looking around for some means of escape, he could see no way out. He was trapped. That didn't stop him from making one last feeble attempt. "Why just last week, I was sayin' to Juan what a fine job you did cookin' up beefsteak. If he was here, I know he'd tell you the same thing."

"Well, I'll make sure to ask him when he gets back from this drive." Eleanor looked thoughtful. "It really is a shame he had to turn around and leave so soon after just getting back from the other drive. I'm sure Maria wasn't happy about that."

"No, she sure wasn't," Jared said quickly. He sensed in this change of subject a chance to escape from his predicament. "You know how she gets when she's upset. Juan's gotten pretty fast on his feet from dodgin' pots and pans."

"I know she acts mad," Eleanor said sympathetically, "but underneath it all, I think she's frightened. We know every time you men go on a drive, something bad could happen. That first trip to Pueblo three years ago was terrifying. Rustlers, snow storms, Indians . . . just about everything that could possibly go wrong. You've been awfully lucky since then. I'm sure Maria believes it's just a matter of time before another disaster strikes."

"I know you're right. It ain't somethin' we like to think about much." Jared sighed. "Tell you the truth, I'm a little worried myself. There's been more problems with rustlers lately and I had to send Juan short-handed. He knows his job, though. I expect he'll pull'em through." Jared sat forward in his rocker. "I sorta mentioned to Juan before he left that you might go over and speak with Maria. Maybe help her out a bit, say some words of encouragement."

To Jared's relief, his wife didn't miss a beat. "I can do that," Eleanor said. "I'm sure she could use the company and a willing ear. Believe it or not, we miss you fellows when you're gone."

Jared felt a twinge of guilt for his unkind thoughts earlier about his wife's cooking skills. She really was one of the most honest, caring individuals he'd ever met in his life. He hadn't been fabricating when he had mentioned her gift for dealing with people. He knew he would be lost without her. "Thanks, Eleanor my love, I knew I could count on you."

"It's really nothing," Eleanor said. "I enjoy visiting with Maria. We both get so busy that we don't take the time to do it enough."

"It's *not* nothin', though," Jared said earnestly. "It's real important. When a cowboy says another cowboy is always in the right place at the right time, it's one of the highest compliments he can pay. It means he can count on the other fella." Jared searched for the words to tell his wife what he was thinking. "I know you ain't a cowboy . . ." Jared grinned. "Thank goodness for that! What I'm sayin' is I know deep down in my bones I can always count on you. I don't think there's a better feelin' in the world than that. I just want you to know what it means to me."

Eleanor turned in her rocker and looked at her husband for a long moment. "Why Jared, I think that's one of the nicest things anyone has ever said to me. Thank you very much." She paused, then she broke out into a grin of her own. "But don't think for a minute it makes up for you not complimenting my cooking."

"Do it."

Daughtry's eyes were cold and dead like those of a rattlesnake. There was a faint trace of a smile at the corners of his mouth. He nodded.

"I only wish Delaney was on the drive with them," Chapman said. "That would be perfect. I'd like to wipe them all out . . . that smart-mouthed wife of his, that shotgun-wielding woman that belongs to Suazo. All of them!"

Chapman's voice had gone up a notch.

He suddenly realized he was standing and waving his arms around wildly. He sat back down in the chair, aware of the uncomfortable hush that had come over the barroom. No one looked in their direction however. In fact, the patrons of the Colfax Tavern were intently studying just about anything else there was to look at other than Bill Chapman and Daughtry.

Behind the bar, Tom Lacey appeared to be busily wiping out whiskey glasses with a dirty rag. In fact, he was thinking furiously while trying to keep all expression off his face. He could have sworn he'd just heard Bill Chapman say something about "wiping them all out." He couldn't quite make out what he had said before and after that but he was pretty darned sure he'd heard "wipe them all out." He knew that was bad news for someone.

"Jim," Lacey shouted out above the din. "Come on down here."

Lacey's bartender strolled slowly and insolently from the other end of the bar. Ordinarily, this would have enraged Lacey, who found his assistant to be impertinent and rather sullen. He had a passing thought that he probably needed to get rid of the boy before his attitude infected other members of his staff. However, at this particular time, he figured that his moving slowly would call less attention to them, which was a good thing.

"No need to rush down here," Lacey said, his voice dripping with sarcasm. Jim looked away, cleared his throat and may have made a derogatory remark under his breath. "I've got to run some errands. I need you to take over. Do you think you can manage that?"

Jim looked at him for a long moment, then he said, "Sure, boss. I think I can handle that."

"Good." Lacey returned the insolent young man's gaze for a moment. "I just counted the till. I have a pretty fair idea of how many people are in here and how much they drink. I expect the tally at the end of the day to match up pretty close with what I expect."

The bartender stared at Lacey for a moment longer, then averted his gaze. "Sure, boss," he mumbled.

Lacey decided to take the time to make him sweat a little. "I'm sorry, Jim. I couldn't quite make out what you said over all the noise."

The young man cleared his throat. "I said, yes sir, Mr. Lacey, you can count on me."

"That's what I thought you said. And I won't just count on you; I'll also count every penny in the till. Are we clear?"

"Yes sir." Jim appeared to be studying the shine on his brogans and couldn't seem to meet Lacey's eye.

Yes, I think it's time I address this problem before it gets further out of hand, he thought. *First things first, though.* Tom Lacey walked out through the back exit to the Colfax Tavern and headed down the street towards the sheriff's office.

CHAPTER 15

June 17, 1884

Nathan was leaning back in his chair with his boots up on his desk. He had a frown on his weathered face and appeared lost in thought. Father Antonio had been in to see him two days before to express his apprehension that Reverend Richardson hadn't returned to Cimarrón. Apparently, the Reverend had taken a notion that he was going to tackle the Santa Fe Ring head on. He had made an announcement in church that he was going to make a pilgrimage to Santa Fe and demand that the Territorial Governor do something about this crooked bunch of robber barons. He set out eight days previously on his mule and was long overdue to return. He'd even missed the church service that week, something he'd never done before. The thought crossed Nathan's mind that he had never seen Father Antonio look so worried.

In fact, he had a number of thoughts running around loose in his head like steers milling after a stampede. He was doing his dead-level best to get them circled, calmed down and sorted out. Now, Tom Lacey had just brought him information that sounded ominous. It was so vague, however, that it wasn't much help. Lacey thought he'd overheard Bill Chapman threaten to wipe someone out. Unfortunately, he had no idea who that someone might be.

Although most of the recent rustling had taken place on the trail up through Raton Pass and on to Trinidad and Pueblo in Colorado, there had been a few incidents down towards Santa Fe as well. Nathan's official problem was that, as sheriff of Colfax County, neither area was in his jurisdiction. Even if they had been, he didn't have the manpower to cover all that ground and try to prevent crimes from being committed. He supposed he could send Tomás Marés, his deputy, south to see if any herds were being trailed to Santa Fe. Even if there were, though, the best he could do would be to warn them of potential danger and tell them to stay alert. Since word had already spread about the rash of rustling, any trail boss worth his salt would already be posting double guards at night if he had the cowboys to do it. *Maybe I should send Tomás out through the canyon to see if he can find out what happened to the Reverend. Lord, if it's not one thing, it's another.*

Nathan had a gut feeling that if any cattle rustling was going to get done, it would be to the north. He felt a rush of relief knowing that Jared Delaney's crew had just returned from taking a herd up to Pueblo. *Least I know his boys aren't in any danger,* Nathan thought. He doubted if Bill Merritt would be trailing any steers north. His cowboys had been ambushed a few weeks ago. He didn't figure he had enough hands to mount another drive this soon. Even if he did, he would have ample reason to be cautious after what he'd just been through.

Shaking his head in aggravation, Nathan contemplated his options. He came up blank. Although it was not his nature to be indecisive, right now that's exactly how he felt. He thought back to the many times in his career as a lawman where he'd been faced with a life and death situation. He'd always just seemed to know instinctively what to do. It would make sense that the older you get, the more certain you would be. Why was it that just the opposite had occurred? *Damn, this gettin' old is a chore,* he thought. *That badge I wear seems to just get heavier and more tarnished as time wears on.*

June 18, 1884
Nathan heard an uproar in the street and sprang to his feet. He started to draw his pistol as he ran for the door. An instinct honed by years of responding to uproars told him it was unnecessary. Still, he kept his hand close. When he cleared the door, he looked north first and saw nothing unusual. Turning his head quickly to the south, he saw a crowd of folks milling around in the street. Beyond the crowd, he saw Tomás Marés riding slowly his way leading a mule. There appeared to be a body draped over the old saddle on the mule. Squinting, Nathan had trouble recognizing who it was because of the people running this way and that. As Tomás got closer, Nathan was able to begin making out some details. The realization slowly dawned on him. He was looking at the body of Reverend Richardson. The sight made him catch his breath. For a moment, he felt a wave of nausea. *This can't be.*

Nathan stopped where he was and waited for Tomás to ride up even with him in front of his office. Some rational part of his mind was thinking that they would need to unload the body and take it . . . funny how, in death, the Reverend had become an "it" . . . inside where Doc Adams could examine it in private to determine the official cause of death. At the same time, another part of his mind was wondering just how low those polecats could go.

Apparently, someone had sent for Father Antonio who came running up the street from the church. Nathan heard a sobbing, keening noise. It took him a moment to realize that it was coming from the padre. Before he could stop him, Father Antonio ran up to where Tomás had stopped. He threw himself up against the body of the reverend, causing the mule to shy and almost throwing the body onto the ground. Nathan quickly stepped over. He took the priest firmly by the shoulder, whispering in his ear that it was important they get the reverend into the office with some shred of dignity. Somehow, this reasoning resonated with the padre. He stepped back, although he continued with his keening.

Tomás was already in the process of dismounting when Nathan said, "Tie your horse and that mule to the post here so we can get the body down and inside before there's even more of a commotion." He stepped forward to assist Tomás in getting

114

the mounts secured. "Let's get him inside, then you can tell me what you know."

Accomplishing the task was more difficult than he'd anticipated. Reverend Richardson was a big man. He was quite a load for the two of them to manage. *I always forget what they mean by "dead weight" until I'm in a situation like this. I don't know how Tomas got him on the mule by himself,* Nathan thought. Father Antonio hovered close-by, moaning and getting in the way. Finally, they were able to get the body inside and on the cot up against the wall.

"Father, I'm afraid I'm going to have to ask you to wait outside," Nathan said.

Wringing his hands, the priest said, "I cannot. I must . . ." he broke down into a fit of sobbing. Nathan waited patiently for it to subside. When he had regained a modicum of composure, he said, "I need to know what happened, Sheriff. I can't wait outside."

Nathan was unsure of how to proceed. Fortunately, Tomás stepped forward and spoke in a calm and authoritative voice. "Perhaps we might allow Father Antonio to stay if he agrees to remain quiet while I give my report. After that, he may have some information that could help us as we investigate this crime."

115

Nathan shrugged. As he sized up the situation, he agreed with Tomás that they would probably have more difficulty with the padre if they excluded him than if they let him stay. "All right, Father, you can stay, but please try not to interfere with my deputy." Turning to Tomás, he said, "Let's hear about it."

"I found him in the canyon, sheriff," Tomás said grimly. "There was blood everywhere." He walked over to where Reverend Richardson's body was sprawled on the cot. Nathan followed him. "I'd say the likely cause of death was these two bullet holes in his chest."

Nathan looked down at the body. He observed where the bullets had entered. He also noticed that there were powder burns. Someone had shot the reverend at very close range and Nathan wondered how they had managed to get so close. Although the reverend was a peaceable man, Nathan wouldn't have expected him to just allow himself to be shot without putting up some sort of a struggle. Then he looked at the blood and lacerations all over the man's face. Some teeth had been knocked out as well.

"Looks like someone gave him a helluva beating before they shot him."

"Sí, sheriff, that's what I thought as well," Tomás said. "It looks like they tortured him before finally shooting him."

"Wonder why they would do that?" Nathan asked.

From behind them, Father Antonio rose from his chair and approached. "Por favór, señors, I apologize for not remaining quiet. I think I can answer your question."

"All right, father," Nathan said patiently, "why do you think they would beat the . . ." Nathan hesitated self-consciously.

"Sí, Sheriff," Father Antonio said, glancing down at the lifeless form of his friend, "they did beat the hell out of him."

Nathan allowed himself a tentative smile. "All right, padre, why do you think they beat the hell out of him?"

Father Antonio stood up very straight. He looked Nathan in the eye. "I believe those worthless cabrónes wanted to send a message to anyone who planned to stand up to their so-called 'ring.' They are saying 'this is what happens when you show some backbone.' That is what I think."

"Is that what the reverend was doing, father?" Tomás gently inserted himself back into the conversation. "Was he standing up to the Santa Fe Ring?"

"That is exactly what he was doing, young

man. We had many conversations about the foul, evil deeds these men were committing. My friend was outraged . . ." Father Antonio stopped, overcome with his grief. Nathan and Tomás stood by helplessly, not really knowing how to comfort the man of God. After a moment, he continued. "My friend preached about right and wrong. He preached about good and evil. He preached about free will. He finally decided that he could not stand by silently and let these men continue their evil deeds." Father Antonio took a deep breath. "He told me that he was going to Santa Fe to seek an audience with the territorial governor. He believed that this man might do something to stop these . . ." The padre stopped again and closed his eyes. He crossed himself and continued, ". . . these evil men from stealing land from good people and murdering the citizens of the territory."

Nathan frowned and pursed his lips. "So you think Chapman and his crowd heard about the reverend's plans and decided to stop him and send a message to the rest of us at the same time?"

The priest nodded. Off to the side, Tomás nodded as well. *Torturing and killing a man of God,* Nathan thought as he shook his head in disgust. *Those lily-livered backshooters can't get any lower than that.* He was wrong.

CHAPTER 16

June 18, 1884

Daughtry and his men left Cimarrón two hours after Bill Chapman gave him his deadly instructions. They rode steadily the first day and made good time. The first night, they found a spot near a stream to camp. Off to one side, there was a rock fire pit with a six foot rattlesnake coiled up in it. Daughtry shot the snake. They cooked it for supper . . . so much for professional courtesy. If they didn't hit bad weather going through the pass and were able to take the side trail up through the woods to avoid Dick Wooten's toll station, they should get within shouting distance of the herd they were stalking by late afternoon of the next day with no one the wiser. That would give them plenty of time to get in position where they could wait for dark.

An hour or two after midnight would be the ideal time to attack. They had a waning moon on their side so the darkness would cover their approach. The cowboys would've changed nighthawk for the first time by then. The hand who'd been relieved would be deep in his bedroll. Daughtry knew for a fact they were short-handed and were having to make do with one cowboy on night watch. That man would have had an hour or two to get a little drowsy himself. He would be a prime target. *This will be as easy as shooting that rattler in the fire pit.* Apparently, Daughtry relished the thought. His mouth turned up in a cruel smile.

June 19, 1884
Eleanor had procrastinated in going over to visit with Maria Suazo. She meant to go over the next day after her conversation with Jared. As usual, there were chores to be done and, truth be told, she was having so much fun with her young son she just couldn't tear herself away. When he was in an obliging mood, he was the most agreeable child in the world. With nothing more than a wooden horse, his rope, a small wooden pistol his father had carved for him and their imaginations, they were able to entertain themselves for hours.

Maria had a mercurial temper, there was no doubt about that. As Eleanor had explained to Jared, though, her strong reactions were indicative of the powerful love she felt for her husband. Juan was a good man . . . in Eleanor's estimation, one of the best she had known in her life . . . and he was every bit as dedicated to his wife as she was to him.

That being said, the couple had their ups and downs. There were times when their fights would last for days. Pots and pans were indeed thrown on occasion although Eleanor could not remember a time when any had actually connected with Juan's body. Having seen Maria shoot, Eleanor was pretty sure that Maria hit exactly what she was aiming at when she went on her rampages. She made her point without inflicting any real physical damage.

As she approached the small adobe dwelling that Juan and Maria called home, she called out to alert Maria that she was coming, trying her best not to awaken the sleepy three year old she was toting. Given all the trouble they had encountered over the past few years, 'hello the house' was a habit they had all adopted. Startling your neighbor could be unsettling at best, lethal at worst. Waking up your slumbering little boy might lead to a bout of grumpiness but it was worth it to Eleanor not to upset Maria.

Fortunately, Ned stirred and whimpered a bit, then nestled his little head back into the crook of her chin.

"Did you come to calm me down?" Maria asked as she led Eleanor to the bed so she could gently lay Ned down. Again, he stirred and whimpered, then settled back into a deep sleep.

As they walked out on the porch, Eleanor had to laugh at Maria's question. "You know us too well. Jared asked me to come check on you and see if I could be of any help."

Maria gazed off into the distance to the north for a moment. In her mind's eye, she could see every detail of the mountains through which Raton Pass cut a path. Her husband was up there somewhere, most likely feeling miserable because of the way they had parted. Turning back, she said, "I do not need help with the chores. I could use a friend though." She looked away, then burst into tears.

Eleanor went to her friend and embraced her. For a time, Maria sobbed in Eleanor's arms. Finally, the sobs subsided and Eleanor stepped back to look her friend in the eyes. "What's got you so upset?" Eleanor felt a stab of fear at Maria's reaction which seemed unusually intense.

Maria choked back another sob. It was a moment before she was able to collect herself. "I have a bad feeling, Eleanor," she said as she wiped her eyes with her dress. "I don't know why, I just do. I was so mean to Juan. He's only doing his job to put food on our table. I said terrible things to him. What's worse, I wouldn't even speak to him after that." Maria turned and pounded her fist on the wall of their adobe dwelling. "What if he doesn't come back? I didn't even tell him I love him."

Eleanor searched for words to comfort her friend. She resisted the urge to tell her that Juan would return; she knew there were no guarantees of that. From her own experiences in life, she knew that loved ones are sometimes lost. Harsh words can't be taken back once they're said. If the person you care about doesn't come back, you have no chance to repair the damage. "You and Juan have had fights before, Maria," she finally said. "Juan knows once you calm down, things go back to the way they were . . . and more importantly, he knows you always love him, even when you're angry."

"I hope so," Maria said in an anguished voice, "but I have a bad feeling."

Walking back to her home, Eleanor felt a

sense of dread settle in the pit of her stomach like a piece of bad meat. There was no good reason to believe that Juan would not return home from this particular cattle drive, yet Maria's premonition seemed to have been contagious. Perhaps he sensed her mood. Perhaps it was just that she stumbled slightly and awakened him. Ned began fussing in her arms and demanding to "get down, Mama." She put him down and took his little hand as they walked along the pathway that had been worn by their footsteps over a number of years. They hadn't gone far when Ned demanded to be picked up again.

Please, Lord, give me patience, Eleanor spoke in the voice inside her head. In the voice outside of her head, she said, "Ned, I will carry you or you can walk. You have to choose which one and stick with it."

The youngster squinted hard, apparently giving serious thought to the problem his mother had presented to him. He said, "Walk." They hadn't gone a hundred yards before he began whining and demanding to be picked up again. Eleanor was at her wit's end as she tried to decide how to respond to Ned. If she picked him up again, she would be going against what she had just told him. If she didn't, he was in for a long and, for a three year old, grueling walk. She was most likely in for a temper tantrum. It was at times like this that she wished Jared could be there to see what she had to deal with. *Why does he struggle so much with me and then just do whatever his papa wants him to do with no fuss?*

Setting aside in her mind the possible future option of snatching a switch off of a tree and tanning his little hide, she presented an alternative for both of them. "Ned, you decided you would walk, so that's what you're going to do." Before he could get his face screwed up to begin squirting tears, she said, "Listen to me. When you get tired, tell me and we'll sit down on a rock until you say you're ready to go again. We can sing a song together while we rest." Squatting down so that she was eye-level with him, she said, "You already decided that you're going to walk. Now you get to decide if you want to rest now or walk a little further before we stop."

Ned was delighted with this state of affairs, which seemed to give him a burst of energy. "Let's walk some more, Mama."

As she walked hand in hand with her son, Eleanor contemplated the irony of her circumstances. Even as a young girl, her parents had included her in family discussion and she was given the right to make her own decisions. The upshot was that she developed a sense that she was in control of her own destiny. What had prevented her from becoming a spoiled brat was that they also held her accountable for whatever path she chose. Losing her parents when she was still a child had reinforced her strong need to be in control of circumstances in her life. If someone was not conforming to her expectations, she either found ways to change that person or she cast them out of her life. Before she married Jared, they'd both recognized the necessity of his making changes in order for them to make a successful go of it.

This is different, she thought ruefully. *I could never cast my child out, no matter how frustrated I become. I suppose we'll have to adjust together.* The trip home took twice as long as it might have. It was worth it as they arrived home a happier mother and son because of the adjustment.

CHAPTER 17

June 19, 1884

The sun was coming up when Nathan rode out to the east to take a look for any signs of troubles from the rustlers. The glare was in his eyes as he searched for signs of foul play. He had no specific reason to think they were up to something out this way, he just figured the more his presence was felt, the less likely those egg-sucking dogs would be to try to pull something shady in range of town.

While a part of his mind focused on the job at hand, another part roamed back over the landscape of his youth. He grew up in the sandhills of Nebraska on his father's ranch. He was sometimes mystified as to how he wound up being a law man in northern New Mexico. Unlike Jared and his other compadres, there were no sad tales of family being killed by outlaws or Indians. His father taught him the meaning of hard work. *He sure enough taught me the difference between right and wrong. I can still feel the sting of those switches sometimes when I wake up in the middle of the night,* he thought. His father taught him about the consequences when young Nathan chose to do wrong, which happened less and less often as he grew into a young man. On the other hand, his father was always generous in his praise when Nathan did what he knew to be right. He could be hard when he needed to be. Though he never said the words, Nathan never doubted that his father loved him.

His mother was the one who had no problem saying the words "I love you." Maybe it was because he was her only child to survive. Intuitively, he knew that she lavished on him all the love she could not share with her lost children before him. He grew up feeling special thanks to his mother. Included in that feeling, though, was the need to be as responsible and accountable as he could be. The few times he let his mother down, the pain on her face was far worse for him than any whipping his father ever inflicted on him. He learned to walk the straight and narrow from his father. He learned compassion from his mother.

Reckon I was in trainin' to be a law man

long before I ever knew it, he thought. *I remember that last year I was in school before I took to cowboyin' full time. That boy who was two years older than me, what was his name? Oh, yeah, Billy Hauser. Big kid from a German family. He'd been pickin' on the younger boys. He'd messed with my friend, Johnny . . . danged if I can recall Johnny's last name. I remember gettin' fed up, steppin' up to him out back of the school house. I was scared to death. Even then, though, I knew not to let it show. Maybe that came from workin' with horses all those years from the time I could barely walk. You got to let'em know you're in charge. Anyhow, he took a swing at me. I ducked it and came back at him with a right hand. I got lucky. I popped that big old German boy right smack in the nose. It was layin' to the side, Lord, he was bleedin' like a stuck pig. He started cryin' and ran all the way home to his daddy's store.*

I got in some trouble with my teacher but my daddy surprised me. He sat me down, told me to tell him my side of the story. Before I did, he told me I needed to give him my word I was tellin' the truth. I did that. I told him what happened and I'll never forget what he told me. He said he trusted me. He said it sounded like this boy needed someone to stop him from hurtin' people who couldn't defend themselves. He told me he was proud of me. He said it real quiet like, then he patted me on the shoulder and went on about his business. Nothin' else was ever said yet I'll never forget that moment, baskin' in the light of my daddy's pride. Sticks with a man.

A sound from the present intruded on Nathan's reverie. Off to his right, he heard a commotion. He scanned the trees and underbrush until he caught sight of a color that stood out. He slowly slipped his Winchester out of the scabbard. He loosened his feet in the stirrups, ready to spring out of the saddle if he needed to. He saw movement and through the brush, the form of a cow gradually materialized. He relaxed a bit and continued to observe as she moved forward a few feet. Then he saw the dead calf she was nudging. He figured she was a mama cow who'd broken loose from the herd to come back to her calf. For some reason, that made him think about his own mother. A stab of pain shot through his chest. At first, he thought his heart might be giving out. It took him a moment to realize it was a wave of sadness. Sadness for the losses his mother experienced. Sadness for the loss of the brothers and sisters he never knew. Sadness for his parents, gone these many years. Maybe most of all, sadness for the loss of his youth.

You're gettin' soft, Averill, he thought. *Better leave all that rememberin' for another time and pay attention to the job in front of you. We got some bad men in these parts again. Looks like they're on the prowl.*

"This gettin' old business ain't much fun, Miguel." Nathan sat at a table in the Marés café. Stretching out his right leg to try to ease the pain in his hip, he reached for his coffee. "I used to ride all day long, go out dancin' all night. These days, I get sore after a mornin' ride."

Miguel Marés chuckled. "I know what you mean, amigo. The other day, I was leaving the house. I turned around to say good-bye to Anita, the light of my life. You know what happened?"

"This ain't some love story you're about to tell me, is it?"

"No, I wish it was. If that was the story, I would not be telling you about it." Miguel grinned at his old friend. "What happened is that I stretched a muscle in my neck when I turned my head around. I hurt for a week. I had to look straight ahead every minute because if I turned my head, the pain shot down my neck and shoulder like someone was poking me with a hot iron."

"I know what you mean. Things that use to be easy, things that you'd take for granted, now they're a real pain in the behind. I rode out this mornin' to see if anything was goin' on to the east of us. Nowadays, just gettin' a foot in the stirrup is a chore." Nathan shifted again, trying to get comfortable. "That old saddle of mine used to be softer, too. Danged if it don't hurt to stand up or sit down, both."

"It's hard to get used to. More and more, I'm thinking we have to face it," Miguel said softly. "It's time for younger men to take over these things that we do. You and me, amigo, we have slowed down. It's the way it goes."

"I expect you're right, Miguel, but I don't reckon I can see who'll take over what I do." Nathan frowned. "I mean no disrespect to your boy Tomás; I just wouldn't want to throw him in head first with that bunch of Santa Fe Ring poltroons right now. He just don't have the experience to handle it."

"I understand, amigo," Miguel said. "Tomás is strong and steady yet I fear he may be too kind. He always looks for the good in people. With these hombrés of the Ring, there is no good. I worry that if a showdown came, he would hesitate before doing what needs to be done."

133

Nathan nodded vigorously, risking a pulled muscle in his neck. "That's just what I was talkin' about. Your son is a good man. A piece of that is he's willin' to extend mercy to folks. Problem is, some of those folks will take his mercy and pay him back with lead." His eyes narrowed. "Some of those outlaws don't deserve mercy. Knowin' when to be merciless takes some practice. It's tricky stayin' alive while you're learnin'. That ain't an easy trick to pull off."

"Funny, is it not?" Miguel paused, got up and went to the kitchen for the coffee pot. After many years, he knew without asking that his friend wanted his afternoon coffee. Sitting back down, he said, "It takes many years and much experience to learn about life and all its troubles. About the time you think you understand, you are too old to do much about it."

"Reckon that's what they call wisdom," Nathan said pensively. "Much as we can, we got to pass that along to these younger fellas . . . Jared, Tommy Stallings, your other boy Estévan."

"Ah, Estévan," Miguel said with a sigh. "I don't know what to do with that boy. He is smart as a whip yet so many times, he does not think before he acts. I'm afraid he will get into trouble that he can not get out of one of these days."

"The boy's got a good heart, Miguel," Nathan said. "His biggest trouble is that he cares too much sometimes. It clouds his thinkin'." Nathan sat back and chuckled. "You know, he and Tomás could learn a lot from each other."

Miguel nodded. "Es verdad, amigo. But they won't learn it unless they talk to each other."

"Is there bad blood between'em?" Nathan asked curiously.

Miguel shrugged. "Not so much bad blood, just that they do not spend time together anymore. Estévan used to follow his older brother around like a puppy. Now he wants to make his own way. Besides, Tomás is spending much of his time working to learn his job as deputy. Estévan hires on whenever he can to handle the wagon on the drives up to Trinidad. They go down separate paths."

"I heard he was doin' that," Nathan replied. "I know he's done some work for Bill Merritt in the past. He just got back from the last drive that Jared's outfit made, didn't he?"

"Sí," Miguel said. "Now he's off again right away."

Nathan sat up quickly. He groaned at the

response from his hip. "You say he just took off again? Who'd he go with?"

"Jared received a request to send some steers up to Morely," Miguel said. "They needed them quickly because someone ran off with their herd. Jared sent Juan, Tommy and Joe Hargrove. Estévan is handling the wagon."

Nathan stood up quickly, ignoring the pain that shot down his leg from his hip. "Sorry, Miguel, I got to run. I got to round up Tomás and see if we can catch up with those boys."

Nathan hurried over to his office as quick as his sore hip would allow. He needed to arm himself and he hoped to find Tomás as well. Unfortunately, his deputy was not there. Assuming that he must be making rounds of the town, Nathan set out to locate him. His frustration grew as every place he went, he was told that Tomás had just been there. Finally, he caught up with him at the bank and told him they needed to saddle up immediately. When Tomás asked him what was going on, he told him he would answer all of this questions once they were on the trail.

They pushed their horses hard and made Raton Pass by dusk. Caution would dictate that they find a place to camp and head out at first light. Nathan had a bad feeling. He said to hell with caution and decided to push on. With very little help from the moon, their going was slow . . . the pass could be treacherous if not treated with respect. The sun was just coming up as they cleared the pass and headed out on the meadowlands north of it. Within the hour, they found the Kilpatrick outfit and what was left of the herd. They were too late. Nathan swore.

CHAPTER 18

June 20, 1884

Estévan and Joe had tended to Tommy's leg. They stopped the bleeding and got him into the wagon. This took some doing as he was in a blind rage and initially resisted their efforts to get him off his wounded leg. After the dust and smoke had settled from the attack, they'd found two bodies . . . one of the rustler's, the other, Juan Suazo. Estévan and Joe were stunned beyond words. Tommy was wild with grief and anger. He wanted to mount up to go after the rustlers and it took some convincing to dissuade him. This was the scene Nathan and Tomás rode into at daybreak.

"What on God's green earth happened here?" Nathan asked of no one in particular.

Joe Hargrove took off his hat and slapped the dust off his pants leg. "Rustlers, sir," he said in a toneless voice. "They came in the middle of the night. We was sleepin'. Juan was ridin' night herd." He shook his head as if he were in a daze. "They killed Juan." He said it almost as if he were asking a question.

Estévan walked over to his brother. Joe's bald statement regarding the death of Juan Suazo seemed to have snapped him out of his fog. "This is Jared Delaney's fault, Tomás," he said angrily. "He knew there could be trouble. In his greed to make money from our sweat, he sent us out anyway without enough hands to get the job done."

Tomás was stunned. For a moment, all he could do was stare at his younger brother. "You are talking out of your head, Estévan. This is the work of outlaws. We most likely know who they are." He reached out and grabbed his brother by the shoulders to steady him. "Jared Delaney did not do this."

"Bah," Estévan spit out with venom in his voice. "He may not have pulled the trigger but he killed Juan Suazo all the same. That is the truth. Es verdad!"

Nathan stepped over to where the brothers were standing. "We don't have time for this, Tomás. We've got to gather the cattle they didn't make off with and get Tommy to Raton to a doctor."

"Sí, sheriff," Tomás said. Turning to Estévan, he said, "Brother, we need to do as the sheriff says. Your compadré is wounded. We need to get him help. We have a job to do. There is no time for this talk."

Estévan eyed his brother with contempt. "The master speaks, the dog obeys. This is what you have become?"

Tomás clenched and unclenched his fists, then took a deep breath. It took all of his patience to ignore his brother's insult and stay focused on his job. He said, "You need to saddle your horse and help Hargrove gather what is left of the herd. We will speak of this later when our work is done." He turned on his bootheel before his brother could say anything else and went over to where the sheriff was looking at the body of the outlaw.

"Do you recognize him, sheriff?" Tomás asked.

Nathan leaned over and squinted at the body. Straightening up, he said, "I ain't sure. He kinda looks familiar. I think I've seen him hangin' around the tavern with Chapman's bunch."

"That's not a surprise," Tomás said quietly. Turning to his left, he saw something lying in the dust. He went over and picked it up. "Look, sheriff. This must have come from one of the rustlers." In his hand, he held a brown derby hat.

Nathan's eyes narrowed. He had a very clear image in his mind of the last person he'd seen wearing such a hat. *Hell, no,* he thought with a stab of anger in his gut. *Wearing that very same hat.*

It was noon before they were able to get the herd moving south. Estévan and Joe made a circle looking for the scattered steers, hoping to recover the strays. In their haste to get Tommy into Raton to see a doctor, though, they hadn't been able to take as much time as they would have liked. Once they had them gathered, they counted sixty-five head. How many had been taken by the rustlers and how many had wandered farther than they could look was anyone's guess.

They made it through the pass without incident and arrived in Raton by late afternoon. They left the cattle spread out to graze in a meadow northwest of town. Nathan sent Joe Hargrove to fetch the doctor while he and Tomás stopped in to pay a courtesy visit to the Raton sheriff, Hugh Jackson. Jackson had been sheriff for two terms now. Nathan had to say he was not much impressed with how he was running the town. Raton had the reputation of being wide open and wild. It appeared to Nathan that Jackson had done little to change that during his time in office. The rumors he'd heard, in fact, suggested that the man had found ways to profit from the shady dealings, accepting financial favors in return for looking the other way. Nathan didn't expect much help from the man. Still, he felt he owed him the respect of reporting in on what had happened.

They found the sheriff's office. Nathan walked up and knocked on the door. A voice from inside told them to come in, which they did. Inside, they found the sheriff sitting at his desk with his feet up, puffing on a big cigar. His three deputies were seated around a table, deeply involved in a card game. They barely looked up.

"Sheriff Jackson, I'm Nathan Averill, sheriff down in Cimarrón. This is my deputy, Tomás Marés. We'd like a word with you if it's not too much trouble."

Jackson took his feet off his desk and set all four chair legs on the floor. He rose, set the cigar on the edge of the desk and walked toward them with his hand extended. In a booming voice, he said, "Well, if it's not the legendary Nathan Averill right here in my office. Now that's something." He hollered over his shoulder to his deputies. "Boys, put those cards away and come over here. You don't have the chance to shake the hand of a legend all too often."

Nathan took a deep breath. He prayed for patience as he reached out to shake the sheriff's hand. "No legend, Sheriff Jackson, just a flesh, bone and blood man. I need to tell you about a situation that occurred last night, north of here, up near Morley. Rustlers attacked a herd. One of the cowboys was murdered. They were trailin' a herd from one of the ranches down my way. Since it happened close to your territory, I figured you'd want to know."

"Well, now, technically, that's outside my jurisdiction, Sheriff Averill," Jackson replied, averting his eyes. "I sure do appreciate you letting me know though." Waving a hand as if to brush away all this unpleasant talk about rustlers and murder, he turned and hollered across the office. "Come on boys, you need to get on over here and shake this man's hand." The deputies seemed much less impressed with the legendary Sheriff Averill. They reluctantly laid down their cards and came over, offering perfunctory handshakes. Nathan tolerated this for as long as he was able. As soon as he had shaken the third hand, he turned back to Jackson.

"I know it didn't happen in your jurisdiction, sheriff," he said testily. "I just thought you might want to be aware that these outlaws were in the area in case they decide to attack someone who *is* in your jurisdiction."

Jackson picked up on Nathan's irritation and said deferentially, "Of course, sheriff, I understand. I didn't mean to imply that I was discounting the information." Glancing over his shoulder at his deputies, he said, "We'll be on the lookout, won't we boys?" The deputies ignored him as if he didn't exist and returned to their card game.

Nathan sized up the situation and decided any more time spent with the local authorities would be wasted. In disgust, he took his leave . . . although not before having his hand pumped several more times by the sheriff. As the door closed behind them and they headed up the street, Nathan heard Tomás chuckle softly. He turned to his deputy and said, "What?"

Tomás grinned at his boss. "I was thinking now might be a good time to ask for a raise, sheriff. It looks to me like I do the work of three deputies for you."

Nathan had to grin back at Tomás. "I reckon you're right about that. I don't think the citizens of Colfax County really appreciate what a bargain they got with the two of us." They walked on a ways. Nathan said out of the corner of his mouth, "Don't hold your breath waitin' on that raise."

They'd agreed to meet up at the Wild Mustang where they knew they could count on the aid of Big Jim Rogers. When Nathan and Tomás arrived, they found Tommy Stallings stretched out on a table with the doctor examining his wound. Big Jim paced the floor. He saw them walk in and immediately came over.

"Sheriff, this is awful," he said. "I can't believe Juan is dead. I just saw him a few weeks ago." He shook his head as he tried to digest the tragic news. "You've got to catch the sheepherdin' trash that did this terrible deed."

Nathan had never met Big Jim Rogers but he'd heard a great deal about him from Jared Delaney and Juan Suazo. He knew he was a true friend and a formidable foe. "Mr. Rogers, I'll do my dead-level best to find and catch these outlaws, you have my word on that. We have a pretty fair idea of who did this. We'll get to work trackin' em down as soon as we make sure young Stallings here is taken care of."

That seemed to focus Rogers. They walked over to the table where the doctor was treating Tommy. "What's the verdict, doc?"

Nathan inquired of the physician.

The doctor looked up at Nathan and peering over his spectacles, said, "And you are?"

"I'm Sheriff Averill from Colfax County," Nathan said peremptorily. "I'm in the midst of investigating a case of murder and cattle rustling. I'd appreciate it if you'd let me know if this cowboy is gonna make it or not. I've got business to attend to."

Somewhat taken aback by Nathan's tone, the doctor said, "Sorry sheriff, no offense intended. I just didn't know who you were." He finished bandaging Tommy's wound and straightened up. "He is a lucky young man, sheriff. The bullet passed clean through the meat of his leg without striking bone or major arteries. If it had done either or both of those things, he might have bled to death or been crippled for life. As it is, if he doesn't develop an infection and lose his leg, he should be able to recover fully in time." Turning back to his patient, he said, "That means you have to stay off the leg for now, young man. It also means you have to keep that wound clean and change the dressing every day."

Nathan turned to Big Jim. "Can Stallings stay with you for a spell until he's healed up enough to travel?"

Before Big Jim could reply, Tommy raised

146

himself up to a sitting position on the table. "Hold on just a dang minute, Sheriff. I ain't plannin' on stayin' here. Juan was my friend. I'm goin' with you after the no-good cull that shot him."

Putting both hands on the table and leaning over so he was eye to eye with Tommy, Nathan said in a low but very clear voice, "No, son, you're not. I don't have the time nor the inclination to argue with you so let me just say this straight. I'll be movin' fast. I don't need a crippled up cowboy slowin' me down. For all we know, the men that did this deed could be in Colorado or even Texas by now. I've got to see if I can pick up their trail and track'em down. You'd just be in the way." Seeing the crestfallen look on the young cowboy's face, Nathan softened his tone just a tad. "I know Juan was your friend. Hell, son, he was a friend to all of us. The important thing is to bring these outlaws to justice. If that means you have to stay here and heal up, then that's your part in the deal. Savvy?"

Tommy stared at Nathan for a long moment, then exhaled slowly. "Yes, sir, I reckon I savvy . . . I don't like it much but I savvy."

"Good," Nathan said, all business again. Turning back to Big Jim, he said, "Can you tolerate this boy for a week or two, Mr.

Rogers?"

Big Jim grinned at the sheriff. "Sheriff, that'll work out just fine. It'll give me a body to play cards with. The best part is, he can't run away even if he wants to." Turning serious, he said, "Just funnin' sheriff. Me and my daughter Ellie, we'll take care of the boy, keep that wound cleaned and bandaged fresh every day. I can ride out and check on what's left of the herd tomorrow. I'll make sure they don't stray too far."

"Much obliged, Mr. Rogers," Nathan said. He turned to Joe and Estévan. "You boys got a tough job ahead of you. You need to get down to Cimarrón as fast as you can and let Jared Delaney know what happened to his herd. He'll have the unpleasant task of lettin' Maria know about her husband."

Joe Hargrove nodded but Estévan Marés shook his head violently. "You don't want me to talk to the man responsible for Juan Suazo's death, sheriff. I don't trust myself not to shoot him."

Nathan looked at the young man he had known since he was a small boy. Estévan had always been hot-headed and impulsive. Nathan figured this was just one more incident in a long string. "Estévan, that's loco. I don't know how you got it into your head that Jared is responsible for Juan's

148

death. You need to listen to me. It's plum loco."

"It's the truth, sheriff. You can talk all day and all night. I know the truth."

"I don't have time to talk all day and all night, Estévan." Nathan shrugged wearily. "I reckon maybe it'd be better if you just take the wagon on into town, then. Let your pa know what happened." He turned to Joe Hargrove. "It looks like it's on your shoulders, cowboy. I'd appreciate it if you'd ride on ahead of the wagon. Get there as quick as you can. You may need to stop and make camp tonight. As soon as the sun is up, though, you light a shuck for the Kilpatrick place."

"Yes sir, sheriff," Hargrove said. He looked around and asked uncertainly. "Now?"

"Yes, now!" Nathan fairly shouted. Hargrove nearly fell over backwards. Taking yet another deep breath, Nathan said, "I'm sorry son, I'm on edge. Tomás and I need to get started back up through the pass so we can try to pick up the trail of those rustlers first thing in the mornin'. Now get goin'."

June 23, 1884
Nathan sat at his desk staring out the window at nothing in particular. Tomás was

149

just finishing sweeping the office for the second time that morning. They had arrived back in Cimarrón the day before empty-handed.

They'd followed the outlaws' trail south for miles. About halfway between Raton and Cimarrón, the riders had split up and lit out in two different directions. Some of the outlaws had taken the steers west but a couple of the riders had clearly gone east. Since the tracks were at least a day old, Nathan figured it didn't make much sense trying to follow them. He decided to head back to town. When they arrived, they discovered that Bill Chapman had made himself quite visible in town during the time the attack on the herd took place. Clearly, he had not been one of the night riders who'd stolen the cattle and shot Juan Suazo. Daughtry and his gang, however, were nowhere to be found.

"We know the whole story. Provin' it's another thing," Nathan said, shaking his head in frustration. "Even though I know Chapman ordered this deed, until I get those letters from Taos, I can't prove it. The mere fact that Daughtry ain't here makes him look guilty as sin. Without one of the boys bein' able to identify him, though, we got no proof."

"We have the derby hat, sheriff," Tomás said quietly. "Can we prove that it is the one Daughtry wore?"

Nathan shook his head wearily. "I don't know, Tomás, maybe we can. That's pretty thin, though. If we don't come up with some more evidence, those varmints may get out of this."

"When do you plan to ride to Taos to get the letters from your deputy friend?" Tomás asked.

Nathan stood up creakily from his desk chair. "Reckon I ought to send him a telegram to make sure he'll be there when I ride in. From the sound of his last communication, he was mighty skittish about them Ring boys tryin' to shut him up permanently. For all we know, he might've lit out for the hills." Nathan walked toward the door. Looking back over his shoulder as he went out the door, he said, "I expect that floor's clean enough, Tomás. Why don't you go down to the tavern. Ask around to see if anybody's heard anything that could help us."

A week went by, then two weeks with no word from Ronald Markstrom. By the end of the third week, Nathan decided to ride over to Taos to check on his friend. What he

151

found there was not encouraging. The folks he talked to hadn't seen Markstrom in over a month. He had given no clue that he would be leaving or where he might go . . . one day he was there, the next he was gone. There were no signs of foul play, he just vanished.

While he was there, Nathan talked with an attorney he knew about how he might proceed if and when he got sufficient evidence to make an arrest. His friend advised him that the district court would send a judge and a prosecutor over from Taos for a preliminary hearing to see if they had a strong enough case to go to trial. If they did, it would go on the docket. His friend advised him, though, that he might be looking at a long wait as there was quite a backlog of trials scheduled.

"Lots of rustlin' and murderin' goin' on, Nathan," his friend had said. "It's like an epidemic is what it is. Folks say it's those fellas with the Santa Fe Ring but nobody can live long enough to make any of the charges stick." Nathan returned to Cimarrón feeling pretty dispirited.

Through July and into August, Chapman stayed around Cimarrón and made the Colfax Tavern his headquarters. Daughtry and his crowd, on the other hand, seemed to have vanished into thin air. First Tomás, and later Nathan, talked with customers at the tavern. No one would admit to knowing anything. From the frightened expressions and the way they tended to look over their shoulder while he questioned them, it was evident to Nathan that if anyone did know something, they were deathly afraid to reveal it. Whenever he brought up the subject of the rustling and the murder of Juan Suazo, folks looked around nervously. They suddenly remembered an errand they had to take care of immediately. The investigation was dead in the water.

In late August, Nathan stopped in the tavern as he made his rounds and discovered that Chapman was gone. Tom Lacey reported that he'd left earlier that day. Said he'd mentioned to him that he'd probably be away "on business" for several weeks.

"He told me not to worry, he'd be back. Said he likes it here in Cimarrón," Lacey said. "Said he was even thinking about going into the cattle business. Winked at me. Said he knew where he might get a ranch on the cheap." Lacey's face was a mask of concern as he said, "These men are getting downright brazen. I don't know what it will take to stop them, sheriff. Whatever it takes, I hope you figure it out pretty quick."

Pretty quick has come and gone, Nathan thought to himself. *Tom's right, though, I got to do somethin'.*

Things were quiet in town during the month of September. There was no sign of Chapman or Daughtry and no new leads for Nathan and Tomás to follow in the case. Tommy Stallings had returned to town from Raton. He was able to walk with a cane but he wouldn't be riding a horse anytime soon. Nathan spoke with him on several occasions about the events of the night in June. While Tommy was convinced that it was Daughtry and his men who had attacked them, he couldn't say with any certainty that he had recognized Daughtry that night. Joe Hargrove and Estévan Marés had not gotten a good look at the rustlers either. He had Daughtry's derby but he was skeptical that they could convince a judge that it belonged to him. Nathan had no witnesses and no solid evidence. *Other than that, things are just, dandy.*

October 4, 1884
Nathan and Tomás were sitting in the office after their noon meal when the door burst open. One of the girls from the tavern rushed in. She was trying to say something

154

but she was out of breath from running and they couldn't understand her.

"Slow down, miss," Nathan said in a firm tone. "Looks like you got somethin' important to tell us. We can't make head nor tails of it until you catch your breath." He pulled up a chair. "Here, have a seat. Take a minute."

The girl sat down gratefully and took some deep breaths. "Mr. Lacey told me to come get you and your deputy. He said to remind you of your last conversation when he said you needed to do something quick." She shook her head and gave Nathan a baffled look. "I don't know what he meant, sheriff, I'm just telling you like he told me to. He said the time to do something is now."

Nathan had a pretty fair idea of what Lacey was communicating to him. He knew what he had to do. Even though he knew it wouldn't stick, he would do it. He hoped it would send a message. "Why don't you walk on back to the tavern? Take it easy so you don't get all out of breath. Tell Tom I understand. I'll be there in good time. Tell him I don't want him to say or do anything until I get there." He patted her on the hand and said, "You can do that, can't you?"

The girl nodded. Nathan helped her up

and escorted her to the door. With a gentle and fatherly pat on the shoulder, he ushered her out. Turning to Tomás, he said urgently, "Get your pistol rig, your ammunition belt and your shotgun. We're goin' to a get-together down at the Colfax Tavern."

Although Tomás hadn't been a party to the conversation between Nathan and Lacey, he was a quick study. He figured out who'd made a triumphant return to town. "Do we have a plan, Sheriff?"

"We do," Nathan said. "You walk in behind me. As soon as you get through the door, you spread out to the right side over by the bar. Try your best to get a line of fire so no innocent bystanders are between you and our boys. Once you're in position, don't do anything except keep your shotgun ready."

"Sí Sheriff Averill." They walked out the door and down the street.

Bill Chapman sat at a table with Daughtry and the man with the top hat. At the moment, he couldn't recall his name which didn't really bother Chapman. He wasn't important; he was just a tool to use when he was needed. In fact, the same was true of Daughtry although Chapman would never say that out loud. If Daughtry was a tool, he was a mighty sharp and dangerous tool. He required careful handling.

The three had ridden in mid-day. They came straight to the Colfax Tavern. Chapman had a soft spot in what passed for his heart when it came to the tavern. The owner . . . he thought Lacey was his name . . . gave them the best whiskey, the best girls and he left them alone. Chapman thought the man might be suspicious about what had happened to his bartender. To tell the truth, though, he didn't think he was going to raise too big of a stink about it. In the meantime, as long as the whiskey and women kept coming their way, he had no complaints. All in all, things were going well.

While he was away, he'd spent quite a bit of time with Tom Catron and they had come up with a plan that would put the final nail in the coffin for Delaney. The Kilpatrick Ranch was a nice spread. With some money invested in it, it could become quite a profitable venture. Chapman suspected that he could easily get used to being a gentleman rancher with plenty of hired hands to take up the business of supplying beef to the miners to the north.

Chapman was so caught up in his daydreaming about acquiring the ranch he was slow to notice that Daughtry had visibly tensed. In fact, he looked like he was about to leap out of his chair. He followed the gunman's line of sight to the door. That old sheriff and his young deputy had quietly entered the tavern. The deputy moved over toward the bar. His shotgun was pointed directly at Chapman. The sheriff had his shotgun pointed at Daughtry, which accounted for the fact that the gunman hadn't already made a play. Once again, the old sheriff had the drop on them.

"So we meet again, Sheriff Averill," Chapman said jovially. "It's always a pleasure to see you although I have to say, it's a bit tiresome the way you're always pointing a shotgun in my direction. Some folks might interpret that as downright unfriendly."

"Those folks would be right," Nathan said evenly. "We're not friends." Turning his head slightly, he kept his eyes glued to Daughtry and said in a louder voice, "All you folks need to clear out of here pronto. Anybody that sticks around here is in peril if lead starts flyin'."

Most people wasted no time at all, clearing out before Nathan's last words had echoed off the back wall of the tavern. Tom Lacey came out from behind the bar and began ushering his girls into the back room. A few folks lingered in their chairs, whether out of curiosity or paralyzed with fear, it was unclear.

Nathan said a little louder this time, "I don't know if you have a hearin' problem. I'm only gonna tell you this one more time. Get out of here . . . *now*!"

That seemed to do the trick. The rest of the customers got up and beat a hasty retreat out the door. Nathan turned his full attention back on Chapman and Daughtry. "You and Daughtry are under arrest, Chapman. You got a choice about how you go . . . alive or dead . . . but go you will. You got about five seconds to decide your play."

Tomás had gradually edged closer to the table. While Chapman was making up his mind about what to do and Daughtry was twitching as he searched for an opening, the nameless man in the top hat suddenly sprang out of his chair towards Tomás. He was holding a large knife in his hand.

With a lifetime's worth of experience in these perilous situations, everything seemed to slow down for Nathan. He saw the man jump. His initial impulse was to take his shotgun off of Daughtry, but he knew that would give him the chance to draw. Before he had to make that choice, Tomás took a quick step forward and rammed the barrel of his shotgun sharply into the gut of the man in the top hat. He made a "whoosh-ing" sound as the air rushed out his lungs. His knees buckled and he fell to the floor. Before Chapman could do anything, Tomás had his shotgun back up and trained on him.

Chapman carelessly glanced down at his fallen minion. He looked back at Nathan. "Sheriff, exactly what is it you're arresting us for anyway? You failed to mention that."

"Daughtry is under arrest for cattle rus-tling and the murder of Juan Suazo," Na-than said in a clear and firm voice. "You, Mr. Chapman, are under arrest for conspir-acy to rustle cattle and conspiracy to com-mit murder."

"That's ridiculous," Chapman chortled. "Where's your warrant, sheriff?"

Nathan smiled. "You're lookin' down the barrel of my warrant, Chapman. It's signed by Judge Remington."

Top hat was beginning to stir uncomfort-ably on the floor. Tomás eyed him warily as he rose slowly and painfully to a sitting posi-tion. Without taking his eyes off of Nathan, Chapman said out of the side of his mouth, "As soon as you can ride, you get yourself to Santa Fe. You go to the office of Robert Elkins. He's my attorney. You tell him to get his no-good lawyer carcass to Cimarrón right away and get us out of this elderly sheriff's pathetic jail." The man shook his head to clear it. Chapman said more adamantly, "Do you understand what I'm telling you?"

"Uh, yes sir, Mr. Chapman, I reckon I do," the man mumbled in a hoarse voice. "Get your lawyer, Elkins, from Santa Fe. I understand."

Chapman turned back to Nathan. He glared at him through eyes that seemed to shoot sparks. "You're going to be sorry you did this, sheriff. That's a guarantee." He turned to Daughtry and said, "We'll go peacefully, do you understand?"

Daughtry looked at him in disbelief and cocked his head in an unspoken question. Chapman gave Daughtry a hard look. He said, "Now is not the time . . . but don't you worry. The time will come." He moved forward unhurriedly and said, "Would you like to lead the way, sheriff?"

"No thanks," Nathan said. "I believe I'll let you two poltroons go first." He stepped to the side, careful not to position himself directly across from Tomás. "Let's head on out. If you value your lives, you'll move mighty slow."

Nathan and Tomás were sitting in the front

161

office. Things were quiet in the back where Chapman and Daughtry each sat on identical narrow benches in identical narrow cells. The walk from the Colfax Tavern had been an edgy one. In the end, the men had gone peacefully into their cells. Chapman had told Nathan in a voice dripping with venom that his lawyer would have him out by tomorrow night. Nathan had laughed at that and told him it was unlikely.

"What I didn't tell him," Nathan said dryly, "was that he'd surely have him out by the next day."

Tomás looked at Nathan quizzically. "He can do that? They're under arrest for cattle rustling and murder. That's some serious charges. This lawyer can just walk in and take them out?"

Nathan chuckled. "He sure can. For starters, Chapman was right about the arrest warrant. We didn't have one." Tomás stared at him. "What I told him about Judge Remington signin' the warrant was accurate as far as it goes. It sure won't hold up in a court of law, though. On top of that, we don't have much in the way of evidence." With a wry grin, he said, "Other than that, we got an open and shut case."

Tomás shook his head dubiously. "What was the point then, sheriff?"

Nathan leaned back in his chair. He contemplated the question for a moment. "Couple of things, Tomás. First off, it shook'em up a bit. They were thinkin' they could just ride in here, be cock of the walk. Now they know I won't tolerate that. Second, it'll at least make'em wonder what cards we got up our sleeves. Maybe we got somethin' in the way of evidence after all. If they're unsure, they might just make a mistake." Nathan pushed his hat back on his head and grinned like a possum eating persimmons. "And lastly, seein' the looks on their faces just made me feel a hell of a lot better about things, even if it is only a passin' fancy."

"It made me feel better, too, sheriff," Tomás said with just a hint of a grin. The grin was swiftly replaced by a sober look. "I'm sorry I got too close to that polecat with the top hat. For just a moment, I thought he might stick me with that big knife of his."

"I was meanin' to ask you about that," Nathan said evenly. "What were you thinkin' that made you decide to move up within strikin' distance?"

Tomás looked down at the floor. "When I moved up closer, there were still innocent people in the tavern. I was afraid if I was too far away from the outlaws, I might accidentally shoot one of those people." He raised his head. Nathan saw a distressed look on his face. Tomás said, "I don't know. Maybe it wasn't the right thing to do, sheriff. Those people are my friends, though. I didn't want to take the chance of hurting any of them."

Nathan thought about what his young deputy had said. After a moment, he said, "You were right. We're supposed to protect the people of Cimarrón, not shoot'em while we're arrestin' the outlaws. It's always better to do what you got to do to keep the citizens safe, even if it sometimes means you put yourself in danger." Nathan leaned over from where he sat and patted Tomás on the back. "Son, you did just fine."

Two days later, Nathan was sitting in a chair behind his roll top desk when the door burst open. A man strode in decisively. He was wearing woolen trousers and an embroidered vest over which he wore a dark frock coat. He sported a silk cravat and his moustache was neatly oiled in the handlebar style. He had a short-brimmed Stetson in one hand and a set of official-looking papers in the other. He started to speak. Abruptly, his words trailed off as he stared in mute terror at the short-barrel .45 peacemaker pointed at his mid-section. He quickly raised his hands, dropping the hat and papers in the process.

"Mornin', sir," Nathan said politely. "Around here, folks generally knock first before bustin' in." He looked the man up and down. "Course, I reckon you ain't from around here, are you?"

The man, struck dumb, managed to shake his head in a weak approximation of "no."

"I'm guessin' that you're most likely a lawyer. I bet you plan on springin' those two thievin' curs I got locked up back in my jail cells. Am I right?"

The man was regaining some of his color . . . he had initially turned ashen when the pistol was pointed at him . . . and with it, some of his confidence. "Why yes sir, I am indeed Robert Elkins, attorney at law from Santa Fe and I've come to . . ." he paused as he considered using the word "demand" and apparently thought better of it . . . "request the release of Mr. William Chapman and his colleague, a man named Daughtry."

Nathan sighed wearily. "I reckon those papers you just dropped on the floor are the documents you need to make that request. Am I right again, Mr. Elkins?"

"Yes sir, that is indeed the case." Elkins started to lower his hands, then noticed that the sheriff had not lowered his pistol even an inch. Clearing his throat, he asked, "With your permission, Sheriff, might I take my hands down and retrieve the papers?"

Nathan nodded, slowly moving his gun to rest, and said, "You can even pick up your hat while you're down there, Mr. Elkins. Just don't make any sudden moves. I ain't completely made my mind up about you yet."

As he knelt down gradually to get his hat and the court papers, the attorney said, "I assure you, sheriff, I am unarmed save for the power of the law."

And a rattlesnake ain't poisonous until he bites you, Nathan thought. *Leastwise, that's what he'd have you think.* He didn't say this. Instead, he said, "You got me curious now, Mr. Elkins. Since you claim to be on the side of the law, what are you doin' here about to spring two of the most notorious lawbreakers in the territory?"

Elkins rose slowly, carefully straightening his cravat and smoothing the wrinkles out of his frock coat. "Sheriff, surely you are familiar with the phrase 'innocent until proven guilty.' That phrase accurately describes my clients."

Nathan smiled. "I have heard that one, counselor. Have you heard the saying that a man is judged by the company he keeps?"

Elkins blinked uncomfortably and looked around. "I suppose we could go on like this all day, sheriff. However, I would really like to have you review these papers and begin the process of freeing my clients."

Nathan took a deep breath and shrugged. "I can do that, Mr. Elkins. And there ain't really much 'process' to it. I just go back, unlock the cells and watch those two mankillers like a hawk until they walk out of my office." Nathan took the papers that Elkins held out to him. As he retrieved his spectacles from his desk, he said, "And you really ought to give some thought to that saying I threw out at you. A man can't be too careful about his reputation."

The door opened again and Tomás walked in from making his rounds. As had been his custom since the murders of the previous summer, he carried his sawed-off shotgun nestled in the crook of his elbow. He looked closely at Elkins. He glanced over in Nathan's direction. Accurately discerning that the sheriff was not threatened by the man's presence, he calmly walked over to the other side of the office and placed his shotgun on a rack mounted on the wall.

Without looking up, Nathan said evenly, "You might want to hang on to that hogleg, Tomás. We're releasing our prisoners to this lawyer. They may not be too happy about havin' shared in our hospitality here."

Tomás retrieved the gun and leaned back against the wall. Had Elkins been observing carefully, he would have noticed that Tomás had one foot slightly behind the other, his elbow against the wall, so that if necessary, he could push off quickly and train his shotgun on anyone bent on causing trouble.

Elkins wasn't observing that carefully but Nathan was. He looked up from reviewing the paperwork, took off his reading glasses and smiled in his deputy's direction. "Well, Mr. Elkins, I'm afraid these papers look to be in order. Let's head on back and gather'em up." Nathan got up from his chair and with his left hand, waved the attorney back toward the cells. He hung on to his Peacemaker with his right hand. "After you, sir." As he followed Elkins, he said, "Tomás, come along after me." He chuckled. "And don't get too close."

Daughtry was reclining on the rickety cot in his cell, his hat covering his eyes. Chapman was pacing his cell. When he saw Elkins approaching, he stepped quickly to the door of the cell and grabbed the bars in his hands. The look on his face suggested he would rather his hands be around Nathan's neck, or perhaps that of his lawyer.

"Elkins," he trumpeted, "what in the hell took you so long to get here? We had to spend two nights in this flea-infested jail because you couldn't be bothered to come yesterday."

"Your assistant didn't reach me in Santa Fe until after sundown day before yesterday," Elkins sputtered. "I couldn't start the journey in the night."

"For the money I pay you, you could damn sure afford a lantern." Chapman made another frenzied circuit around his cell. He returned to the door. "Never mind, we'll deal with that later. Right now, I want this old geezer to let me and Daughtry out. I'll not spend another second in this rancid place."

Elkins turned to Nathan who reluctantly took the keys to the cell off his belt. Tomás stood about ten feet down the hall in the direction of the door. As Nathan began to unlock Chapman's cell, the man leaned over toward him. In a low voice that was almost a hiss, he said, "This is not over, Averill."

Nathan looked up from unlocking the cell. He returned his stare. "You're right about that, Chapman."

169

Nathan swung the cell door open. He stepped back so that Tomás had a clear line of fire just in case he should need it. Turning to unlock Daughtry's cell, he said, "Wake up, sunshine, it's time to take your leave."

Daughtry slowly lifted his hat from his face. He gave Nathan a flinty glare. He swung his feet off the cot and stood up. Nathan opened his cell and followed the same procedure, stepping back to give Tomás a clear shot if he needed it. Daughtry didn't say a word. As he stepped out of the cell, he bumped into Elkins, knocking him into the wall. The lawyer gave an indignant gasp which was stifled almost immediately as Daughtry turned his glare on him.

"After you, gentlemen," Nathan said as he encouraged the men to file out of the cell area. Tomás carefully backed out into the office, his eyes never leaving the two outlaws. He took a position off to the side of the door. As the men walked out to the center of the room, Nathan took a couple of steps over toward his desk. He carefully arranged his position so that if gunplay broke out, he would not be firing directly at Tomás.

"We'll take our guns now, sheriff," Chapman said arrogantly.

"No, I reckon that ain't gonna happen, Chapman," Nathan responded evenly. "You'll be leavin'em with me."

"I'll be damned if I will," Chapman said hoarsely.

He took a menacing step in Nathan's direction. The unmistakable sound of a shotgun's hammers drawing back stopped him in his tracks. It was fortunate that it did because it was only then that he noticed Nathan's .45 pointed directly at the center of his chest. He looked at Elkins, whose mouth was hanging open. He shook his head and sneered.

"If it makes you feel better, sheriff, you can keep the guns." He grinned over at Daughtry. "We've got a lot more where those came from."

Nathan didn't say a word. His pistol never wavered. Tomás had quietly and efficiently shifted his shotgun so that it was pointed in Daughtry's direction.

"As I said, sheriff, this is not over. The time will come when we meet again. I promise you, we'll be armed then." Turning on his bootheel, he strode out of the office without a backward glance. Daughtry followed close behind him. Elkins looked around in confusion, perhaps wondering if there wasn't more paperwork. Apparently, he decided whatever there was would have to wait and he scampered off behind his master.

CHAPTER 19

October 21, 1884

As he waited to be called as a witness for the prosecution early in the afternoon on this second day of the proceedings, Tommy Stallings' mind wandered. He thought about justice. He wondered if such a thing really existed. Certainly, there was no justice in the fact that his parents and sister had been murdered by marauding Indians when he was a child. He had thought there might be some justice in the world when Jared Delaney took him under his wing and showed him the way to becoming a man. He thought about how Juan Suazo taught him secrets about being a cowboy that he'd never dreamed of and how hard he'd worked to earn his respect. *Is justice somethin' you earn,* he wondered? *Is it what you deserve? Or is it some high-falutin' notion that really has nothin' to do with real life?* The vigorous banging of the judge's gavel jerked him out of his musing with a start and back into the stark reality of the courtroom.

"Mr. Stallings," Judge Cardenas said sternly. "Would you care to join us?"

Tommy shook his head. "Sorry, judge. My mind wandered a bit. What did you say?"

"You were called as a witness for the prosecution, young man. That means you need to wake up, come up here to the chair next to the bench, be seated and get sworn in. Is that too complicated for you?"

Tommy felt his hackles go up. He told himself to calm down. He figured it wouldn't help the case any if he got into a dust up with the judge. "No sir, I reckon I can handle that." Leaning on his cane, he gingerly approached the chair designated for witnesses and allowed himself to be sworn in by the bailiff.

John Budagher, the young prosecutor, approached the bench and cleared his throat. In his head, he repeated the mantra he had been saying all morning . . . *speak up!* In as clear and firm a voice as he could muster, he began. "Mr. Stallings, is it true that you were one of four hands employed by the Kilpatrick Ranch to take a herd of one hundred head of steers up the trail to Morley back in June of this year?"

"Yes sir," Tom responded in a clear voice.

"I was one of the hands that was supposed to run that herd up there. Juan Suazo was in charge."

"In your own words, Mr. Stallings, would you please tell the court what happened on the night of June nineteenth?"

"Well, sir, we'd made it through the pass with no trouble, thank goodness. We decided to bed the herd down in a meadow just north of there." Tom squinted as he looked at the image in his mind's eye. "The land flattens out there pretty well. There's some good grass and a nice little stream. We camp there pretty often when we . . ."

"Objection." Robert Elkins rose and walked toward the bench. "Do we really need a description of the scenery, your honor? We're wasting time here with this cowboy's ramblings. These men have better things to do than listen to him prattle on about the sights."

"Sustained," Judge Cardenas said emphatically. "Mr. Budagher, please instruct your witness to stick to the facts and get on with his testimony." He glanced sideways over at Bill Chapman before continuing. "I'd venture to say that we all have more important matters to attend to and would like to get this business settled as soon as possible."

It occurred to Tommy that they had just

175

wasted more time complaining about his rambling than the time he'd taken to ramble. He wisely kept his thought to himself. "Sorry, your honor."

"Continue your questions, Mr. Budagher," Judge Cardenas said.

Budagher again cleared his throat and spoke up. "You were telling us about what happened on June nineteenth, Mr. Stallings."

"Yes sir. We got the herd settled down. Estévan cooked us up a mess of frijoles. I took the first watch once it got dark. Things was pretty quiet. There wasn't much light due to it bein' a wanin' moon. The night was clear and still and you could just about count. . . ." Tom started to say more about what it was like to be out there on the prairie under a million stars, then caught himself. "Around midnight, I heard Juan ridin' up to relieve me." Tommy stopped at that point. He choked up a bit as he thought about his mentor and friend. He looked down at his boots as he fought to control his emotions. "We joked around for a spell, then I rode on back to the wagon and crawled into my bedroll. That was the last time I ever saw my pard."

"What happened next?" Budagher coaxed him along.

"I woke up to a hailstorm of bullets," Tommy said. "I could hear Juan blazin' away from over on the east side of the herd. I rolled out of my blankets quick as I could. I'd just got ahold of my pistol when some varmints come ridin' into camp firin' off one shot after another. I believe there was four of'em. Tell you the truth, it was hard to know for sure cause there wasn't much light. I squeezed off all the rounds I had in my pistol. One of'em went down. I'd kept my rifle handy right by my bedroll like I do every night. I was tryin' to pull it out when I caught a round in the leg."

"You were wounded?"

"Yes sir, I was shot in the right leg." Stallings winced as he remembered what that had felt like. "It went clean through the meat on my upper leg. Reckon I was mighty lucky it didn't hit the bone or I might've been crippled for life. As it is, I ain't been able to get horseback since that night. That's how I make my livin', so it's been a tough row to hoe."

Sensing that the young cowboy was about to start rambling once more and hoping to avoid another objection that might further irritate the judge, Budagher once again nudged his witness back on course. "Mr. Stallings, could you tell the court what happened next, please."

"Yes sir, I can. I finally got ahold of my rifle. I squeezed off a couple of shots before the whole crew of lowlife rustlin' curs took off. They stampeded the herd. They was able to get away with quite a few head."

"Who else was there with you that night, Mr. Stallings?"

"It was me and Joe Hargrove ridin' herd with Juan. Estévan Marés was on the wagon."

"What were they doing during this incident?"

"Well, just like me, they was sleepin' when it first started. Estévan and Joe was both able to get their guns and pull off a few rounds. At the time, it was hard to tell who was shootin' at who." Tommy sat back in the hard chair as the chaos of that summer night flashed through his mind. "When we talked afterwards, they told me they'd fired some shots. In the middle of somethin' like that, you can't really tell who's doin' what. We never figured out who it was that hit that one scruffy outlaw. I reckon it don't much matter, long as one of us got him."

"You wounded one of your attackers?" Budagher asked quietly.

"No sir, he was shot dead. And good riddance, I say," Tommy said heatedly.

Judge Cardenas slammed his gavel down with a retort like a pistol shot. "I will not tolerate disrespect for the dead, sir! Confine your observations to what happened or I will fine you for contempt of court."

Tommy looked back at the judge with all the contempt of his own he could muster. "What about the disrespect for my dead pard, Juan Suazo, Judge? Who gets punished for that?"

The judge banged his gavel once again. "Not another word, young man, or in addition to the ten dollars I'm fining you for contempt, I'll throw in ten days in jail as well."

Jared Delaney gripped the rail in front of him with both hands until his knuckles turned white. He did everything in his power to catch Tommy Stallings' eye without making too much of a ruckus. The last thing they needed was for Tommy to antagonize the judge even further. His testimony was already somewhat shaky. To have a prayer of a favorable ruling, they had to establish every bit of credibility they could muster. Finally, Stallings looked his way and he was able to catch his eye. Prying his fingers off the rail, Jared gave him a motion to slow down by pantomiming pushing down with his hands.

John Budagher quickly walked over to where Tommy was sitting and placed a hand on his arm. He just as quickly stepped away when the judge sent a warning glance.

"Would you continue with your account, Mr. Stallings?"

Tommy took a deep breath and closed his eyes briefly. He struggled to get himself calmed down. After a tense moment, he resumed his testimony. "After the shootin' stopped and they rode off, Joe and Estévan came over to check on me. I was bleedin' pretty good. They bandaged up the wound with a piece of cloth. After a couple of minutes, that stopped the blood from flowin'. I couldn't walk just then. They was the ones that went out and found Juan."

"What did they find when they went looking for your companion, Mr. Stallings?"

Tommy felt himself getting angry all over again. He knew he had already pushed the judge to the limit. He reckoned he'd better slow himself down to a trot. As evenly as he could, he said, "They found Juan Suazo shot dead out where he'd been guardin' the herd."

"What else did they find, Mr. Stallings?"

"As they was comin' back into camp, they found a brown derby hat."

Budagher spoke as clearly as he could.

"What is the significance of the derby hat, Mr. Stallings?"

Tommy sat up straight in his chair. "It fell off one of the rustlers, sir. And it looked just like the hat that lowdown cull over there is wearin'." Tommy pointed directly at Daughtry, sitting next to Bill Chapman at the defense table. Daughtry's eyes narrowed. He looked as if he wanted to jump over the defense table and thrash the young cowboy.

"Objection!" Elkins shouted. "They have no proof whatsoever that the hat in question belongs to my client."

"Overruled," the judge said somewhat reluctantly. "You'll have your chance to question the witness when you cross-examine him, counselor." He smiled almost apologetically. "You can clarify whether or not there is any proof that the hat belongs to your client at that time." Turning back to the prosecutor, Judge Cardenas said brusquely, "I'd really like to get this wrapped up as soon as possible, Mr. Budagher. Do you have further questions for your witness or can we give Mr. Elkins the opportunity to cross-examine?"

Budagher looked around the courtroom as if searching for inspiration. Although he had a couple more questions he could ask

Stallings, he wasn't sure they would strengthen his case significantly. He knew the longer the young cowboy remained on the witness stand, the greater the chance that he would blow. "No, your honor, not at this time. I would like to reserve the right to re-call the witness at a later time, however."

The judge looked over his glasses at the prosecutor. "No, you may not reserve that 'right,' counselor," he said in an imperious voice. "It is not your 'right' unless I grant it. I'm not inclined to lengthen this proceeding any more than absolutely necessary. If you have further questions, ask them now or don't ask them at all. Am I making myself clear?"

Budagher looked crestfallen. "Yes sir, perfectly clear." He paused for a brief moment, then he shrugged. "No further questions, your honor."

As the defense attorney gathered his papers and prepared to cross-examine Stallings, Jared's mind was racing. He was angry and anxious at the same time as he watched this judge hurry through this sham of a legal proceeding. He wondered if Budagher was making a mistake by not taking a more aggressive tack in asserting his case and yet whenever he made any effort to do so, the judge slapped him down. *Nathan's just got to get here with those letters that show Chapman planned this whole shindig,* he thought. *Otherwise, we've got nothin'.*

Elkins walked over until he was about halfway between the witness and the judge, a bit off to the side so Bill Chapman had a clear view of everyone. "So, Mr. Stallings, you say you were sound asleep when this alleged attack took place?"

"Alleged attack?" Tommy looked at the defense attorney sideways. "I'm not sure exactly what that means, sir."

"What it means, young man, is that although you say an attack took place, it has not been proven in court that it occurred."

Tommy clenched his jaw. He closed his eyes for a moment in an effort to retain control of his temper. Then he spoke. "A man is dead. I got a bullet through the leg. You got the word of three good cowboys that we was attacked by rustlers. What more kind of proof do you need, sir?"

The judge banged his gavel down. "Mr. Stallings, it's not your job to bandy words with the defense attorney, it's your job to answer the questions. Do you understand me?"

Tommy took another deep breath and said, "Yes, your honor, I do."

"Please proceed, then."

"I repeat," Elkins said. "Were you sound asleep on the night in question?"

"I already said I was, sir. If you want me to say it again, I will. I'll say it as many times as you ask it. I was asleep and was woke up by the sound of gunfire."

"That must have been quite confusing," Elkins said in a sympathetic voice, "being awakened by gunshots in the dark. Would it be fair to say you were disoriented?"

Through gritted teeth, Tommy answered, "I ain't sure what that word means, sir."

"It means confused, baffled, not sure of what is happening." Elkins smiled. "Does that describe your state of mind on the night in question?"

"No sir, it does not. When a cowboy's been up the trail a few times, he gets used to bein' woke up in the middle of the night by things like thunderstorms, stampedes and such. You learn to come to pretty quick when there's danger . . . not that you'd know about any of that." Tommy looked at the lawyer with scorn. "Besides, once I got the bullet through my leg, I pretty well figured out what was goin' on."

Elkins ignored Stallings sarcasm. He partially turned so that his gaze included the courtroom. "Mr. Stallings, do you recognize anyone in this courtroom as having been present the night you say you were attacked?"

Jared winced as he waited for Tommy to answer. This was the weakest part of their case. It had been too dark to really make out faces that night. None of the cowboys got a good look at the rustlers.

"Well, sir, I can't rightly say for sure," Tommy said hesitantly. "I already said there wasn't much light. We had a wanin' moon at the time, if you know what that is."

"I'm glad you mentioned that, young man. I do indeed know what a waning moon is." Elkins' smile broadened. "It's the time in the cycle after the full moon when the light decreases, coming up on a new moon. It would be very difficult to see at this time, I would think." Elkins turned and looked directly at Stallings. "Am I correct, Mr. Stallings? Is it difficult to see during a waning moon?"

Tommy hesitated before answering. He knew what was coming next. "Yes sir, it can be pretty hard to make out faces."

"So perhaps you're ready to answer my question? Do you recognize anyone in this courtroom as having been present the night in question?"

"I reckon Mr. Daughtry over there looks a whole lot like the fella I saw with the derby hat," Tommy said heatedly. "He's about the same size. If I could only see him horseback with that hat on, I could tell you pretty quick."

Elkins smiled patiently. "Mr. Stallings, I am asking you if you can positively identify anyone in this courtroom as having been present on the night of the alleged attack."

Tommy sat back in his chair with a look of resignation on his face. "No sir, I can't say for dead certain that I can."

"That wasn't so difficult now, was it Mr. Stallings?" Elkins wore a smug look. "Let's move on to the next part of your testimony if we might. The part about the derby hat." He walked over to the bailiff's small desk. He picked up a brown object. "Does this look like the hat that was found at the scene?"

Tommy looked carefully at the misshapen object Elkins was holding. "From here, it's hard to tell. If you bring it closer, I can take a better look at it and answer your question."

Elkins shared a cooperative smile. "Certainly, Mr. Stallings, my pleasure." He walked over to the witness stand and handed the hat to Tommy. "Is this close enough?"

Ignoring the question, Tommy took the hat. He looked closely at it. "That looks like the hat we found that night, yes sir."

Retrieving the hat, Elkins set it on the defense table. He turned back to Stallings. "Do you see anyone in the courtroom who is wearing a derby hat, Mr. Stallings?"

Tommy pointed an accusing finger at Daughtry. "That lowdown bushwhacker right over there is wearin' a derby."

The judge's gavel came down like a shot. "I'm warning you, Stallings. Control your outbursts or spend the night in jail."

Tommy put his arm down. He continued to stare at Daughtry with hate in his eyes. Daughtry stared back with just as much intensity. It began to look as if violence might break out. Elkins moved closer to the witness. In the process, he broke the line of sight between the two men, temporarily defusing the situation. "Mr. Stallings, have you ever known anyone else to wear a derby hat?"

Stallings looked around as if searching for a different answer. Finding none, he replied through gritted teeth, "Yes, sir, I have at one time or another."

Elkins half turned and smiled in the direction of Bill Chapman. "Mr. Stallings, have you heard of a man named Bat Masterson?"

"I believe I have, sir," Tommy said. "Just about everyone out west has heard of Bat

Masterson."

"Did you know that Bat Masterson is known to wear a derby hat, Mr. Stallings?"

Tommy shook his head in disgust. "You ain't tryin' to say that Bat Masterson rustled our cattle and killed my pard, are you? That's plum ridiculous."

"No sir," Elkins stated emphatically. "I'm just establishing the fact that there are many westerners who wear derby hats. The hat in question might belong to anyone." He smiled a triumphant smile in Chapman's direction. "There is no proof to indicate this hat belongs to my client, Mr. Daughtry."

"Well, try it on him, dang it." Tommy was rapidly running out of patience for this farce.

Elkins shook his head and said dismissively, "It's a common size, Mr. Stallings. It wouldn't prove anything even if it did fit."

"That ain't necessarily so, Mr. Elkins," Tommy insisted. "A man's hat takes on the shape of his head. It don't fit right on nobody else's."

Elkins walked back towards the defendants' table. Over his shoulder, he said, "Judge, I believe we've wasted enough of these men's valuable time. Can we please move on?"

"Ain't you even gonna give it a try?"

Stallings stood awkwardly.

Judge Cardenas banged his gavel down sharply. "Sit down right now, young man! We will conduct this court in an orderly fashion or I will have you arrested if you don't follow protocol."

Tommy had heard enough. He put his weight on his wounded leg and almost fell before he could grab his cane for support. He glared at Elkins. "Go ahead, play all your lawyer tricks, you gutless wonder. You know the truth as well as I do . . . that lily-livered backshooter sittin' over there killed my friend. He rustled Mr. Delaney's steers." Judge Cardenas banged his gavel repeatedly and demanded that Stallings be seated. Tommy was having none of it. He was his own personal stampede at this point. There was no stopping him. "I won't shut up. You can damn well throw me in the jail for all I care. What kind of justice is it that a man who's been wronged . . . hell, I got shot . . . goes to jail? The man who done it gets to walk out of here?"

"That's enough," Judge Cardenas roared. "You are going to jail for contempt of court, Mr. Stallings. Bailiff, please escort him right over to the sheriff's office and lock him up. We're taking a recess until tomorrow." He looked around angrily. "Where is that old sheriff?"

He rested against the boulder, its sharp edges cutting into his back. The upper right side of his chest was on fire. His head throbbed like someone slammed a sledge hammer inside his skull. Where the bullet showered rock fragments on his face, it felt like a nest of wasps had attacked him, the cuts angry and inflamed. Mercifully, his gelding hadn't run all the way home to Cimarrón. It had returned and nudged him into consciousness where he lay behind the rocks. *Nothin' like a good horse,* he thought. *Prob'ly just needed me to loosen his cinch. Still, I ain't complainin'.*

It took him almost an hour of superhuman effort to retrieve his canteen and some beef jerky from his saddle bags. It was worth it, though, for that was what had kept him alive for . . . how many days had he been laying here? Thankfully, his weathered, sheepskin coat had been rolled up behind his saddle. That trusted old friend had kept away most of the chill at night. He hadn't frozen to death and he hadn't bled to death yet, which he took to be good signs. *I ain't gettin' any stronger though. I don't know if I can make it on my own. They got to be lookin' for me by now.*

The nights had been the roughest. The first two, he'd had a fever. He was seeing and hearing all sorts of things that weren't there. At one point, he thought he heard his mama calling to him. Another time, he could swear Christy had knelt beside him and wiped his brow. He was pretty sure he'd heard a mountain lion's eerie cry as it stalked its prey. Somehow that had changed into a vision of the gunman, Daughtry, smirking at him as he pointed his .45 at his head. *Reckon it don't matter whether it's a cat or that low-life cur, Daughtry. It's a good thing I got them two bullets left.*

CHAPTER 20

June 11, 1884

Where is that old sheriff? Christy thought he would probably bristle like a porcupine if she asked that question out loud. She knew that was more due to his own insecurities than anything she thought or felt about him though. As she thought about this man she had fallen in love with, she couldn't help but smile. In her mind and heart, she saw him as having the wisdom and dignity that come with age and experience. It only made him more attractive to her. *He'd better not get himself caught up in some lawman's shenanigans and miss this picnic.*

Rustlers had been on the move a month or so back and Christy knew Nathan was worried about that. More recently, though, things seemed to have calmed down a bit. They had talked for more than a week about getting away for a picnic and had finally settled on this Saturday to get it done. There were only a few high, thin clouds in the sky. The sun had warmed things up nicely to just take the chill out of the air without making it unpleasantly hot. It was a fine spring day that held out the promise of an array of wildflowers and the smell of piñon.

A sharp rap on the school house door jarred Christy from her reverie. "Who is it?"

Nathan cracked the door open just enough to peek his head around. "Did you give up on me?"

"I was just about to," she said with a frown on her face but a twinkle in her eye. "You're lucky you got here when you did. I was just about to take one of my other suitors up on the offer of a picnic." She couldn't maintain the severe look, however. She burst out laughing.

"Well, then," Nathan said merrily. "Looks like I got here in the nick of time. Let's hop in the buckboard and clear outta here 'fore them other fellers show up."

They followed a trail southwest of town, climbing gradually but steadily. Though the sun was out, it was cooler as they got in among the fir trees. Christy heard the harness creak like a rusty gate hinge. She felt the horse strain just a bit pulling the buckboard up over the gentle rise. As they crested the hill, she saw a sight that took her breath away. In front of her was a large meadow that appeared to contain all the colors of the rainbow. Wildflowers in varying hues of red, blue, yellow, orange and pink spread out before her eyes over a canvas of green grass. In the background, Bear Mountain, Black Mountain and Cimarróncito Peak provided a stunning backdrop with a delicate forest green shade blending into the white snow-capped peaks.

"Oh, Nathan, it's beautiful."

Nathan pulled back gently on the lines. The horse responded and the buckboard rolled to a stop. He sat back in the seat, looked at the vastness of nature's artwork surrounding them and smiled. "I thought you'd like it. I didn't know if you'd ever been out this way. It seemed like the perfect spot for a picnic."

Christy glanced sideways at him. She leaned over, threw her arms around his neck and whispered in his ear. "This is perfect. Thank you." The moment could have been awkward. Somehow, it wasn't. Christy gave him a final squeeze, a peck on the cheek and then sat back in the buckboard seat.

"Well, thank you, m'am." Nathan looked at her with a twinkle in his eye. He appeared more at ease than Christy had ever seen him. "I figured you'd like it just fine." He shook the lines and they moved forward again. "Now let's find a nice spot to settle down. I'm ready to dig in to that fried chicken you cooked up for us."

In the middle of the meadow stood a solitary cottonwood tree that had grown to massive proportions. Under its shade, the grass had thinned out. Nathan pulled the buckboard to a stop there beneath its massive bows. Christy unpacked the picnic basket and laid out the comforter that she had brought for them to sit on while Nathan unhitched and hobbled the horse to allow him to graze. When he was done, he walked back over and looked at the meal she'd laid out. In addition to the chicken, she had biscuits that she'd baked, an apple cobbler and sweet tea in a mason jar.

"A feast fit for a king," Nathan said expansively as he looked up at the mountains in the background. "Now, if only we had a king."

"Oh, I don't know, you make a pretty good king." Christy said mischievously. "Or at least a knight."

"I don't know much about knights," Nathan said with a smile. "You'll have to educate me."

"I can do that, you know," Christy said proudly as she handed him a piece of chicken. "I've been teaching the students about King Arthur and the Knights of the Round Table in England. I've had to read up everything I could find. Lucky for me Eleanor has a good library that she inherited from Hattie O'Hanlon."

Eleanor Delaney had been taken under the wing of Hattie O'Hanlon, the school teacher, when she was a girl. She'd taken over as school marm when Hattie passed away. In turn, she had trained Christy for the job, passing it on to her when she was ready to handle it. Eleanor had chosen to get married instead of "passing on" like her predecessor had done, however.

"That sounds mighty interestin', Miss Johnson. I believe I could sit quiet and listen to you tell me about them fellers."

Christy looked carefully at Nathan to determine if he was patronizing her. As best she could discern, he genuinely seemed to want to know. "Well, there's a whole lot to the story. I'll just tell you a bit about the part that reminds me of you." She leaned back on her elbows and continued. "A long time ago in England, there was this man named Arthur. He'd had a pretty rough go as a boy. Some good folks helped him out, though, and before you know it, he got to be king. He was different than a lot of the kings back then . . ." Christy shook her head and grinned ruefully, ". . . or a lot of the folks in charge now, for that matter. He wanted to do good things for the people. He gathered a bunch of men around him who were good fighters and good men, too. They'd take a vow to follow his lead and he'd tap them on the shoulder with his sword. They were called knights."

"I hope he used the flat side of the blade," Nathan said with a chuckle.

"Hush up, silly," Christy said with mock irritation. "Let me tell the story." Nathan gave her a look of contrition. She continued. "They had meetings at this big table where King Arthur would come up with the jobs he wanted them to do to help folks. He called them 'quests.' King Arthur decided the table should be round. That way, no one was sitting at the head of the table. It made them all equal."

"That's a nice idea," Nathan said thoughtfully. "In my experience, though, every man doesn't have the same abilities."

"I know that," Christy said. "I just think he wanted them to feel like they all had an equal chance to succeed at the quests that he laid out for them."

"I reckon that's fair enough," Nathan said. "What sorta jobs did old King Arthur come up with for'em back in ancient England?"

Christy looked thoughtful. "You know, I hadn't quite thought about it this way until I started to talk to you about it." She sat up and brushed a strand of hair out of her eyes. "There were some greedy and wicked folks who tried to take things away from the decent people who lived in King Arthur's kingdom. It was the job of King Arthur and the Knights of the Round Table to stop them. I guess things haven't changed much in all these years." She looked up at the mountains and then back at Nathan. "That's the part that reminds me of you."

For a moment, Nathan held Christy's gaze. Then he chuckled. "Good. I was afraid I reminded you of the part about King Arthur bein' around for such a long time."

Christy gave Nathan a gentle shove on the shoulder and laughed. "Here I'm trying to be serious and you're just being silly."

"I know," Nathan said. "It's real interestin' stuff, I just like to have a little fun." He took his hat off and scratched his head. "I tell you what else I'd like. I'd like to have a whole table full of deputies, the way he had all those knights. It's not easy tryin' to watch over this whole county with no more than one or two deputies at a time."

Christy sat up straight. "I understand why

you'd think that. Do you know what, though? His knights got jealous of each other. They did all kinds of underhanded tomfoolery to try to out-do each other and win King Arthur's favor. That's why they weren't able to defeat the villains in the story."

Nathan said, "Reckon I should be less crabby about what I got to work with, don't you know. Tomás does his job as deputy and he sure doesn't pull any monkeyshines." Nathan chuckled. "Don't know who he'd pull'em on, for that matter."

"You have other knights helping you, though," Christy said earnestly. "Miguel and Estévan, Juan and Tommy Stallings. They all help you out when the chips are down." She smiled wistfully. "Jared is sort of like your Sir Lancelot."

"Who the heck is that?"

Christy sat back and looked at Nathan. "Are you sure you want to hear about this dreary history?"

Nathan smiled. "Well, first off, if you like it, it can't be all that dreary. I kind of like hearin' about how these old timey fellas handled their business, too. Maybe I can learn somethin' from'em."

"All right," Christy said, a bit hesitantly. "If you really want to hear."

"You should know by now, Miss Johnson, that when I say somethin', I generally mean it," Nathan said with another smile. "Go on, tell me all about these knight fellas. They sound a tad bit like cowboys to me."

Christy sat forward and continued eagerly. Nathan wasn't sure whether the glow around her golden hair was from the reflected sunlight or if it came from within. "Oh, Lancelot was a young knight, brave and loyal and a great fighter. He'd come up kind of hard compared to some of the other knights. They were jealous of him because he was King Arthur's favorite."

"I've seen that happen," Nathan remarked. "Cowboys gettin' their noses out of joint when they think the boss favors one of'em. They oughta be takin' care of their own business. Instead, they want to find fault with someone else."

"That's the way it happened," Christy said, nodding her head excitedly. "Pretty soon, it seemed like everyone was plotting against everyone else. As you could imagine, that got in the way of their doing the deeds they were supposed to be doing . . . and these were the good men!" Christy shifted around, straightening her dress so that she was more comfortable. "I haven't even told you about the evil people . . . men, and women, too . . . who were plotting against King Arthur."

"Sounds like that old boy had his hands full," Nathan said, chuckling. "I reckon I don't feel quite so bad now. I got some bad folks to deal with but as far as I can tell, none of my friends are plottin' against me."

"You're right about that." Christy laughed along with Nathan. "You've got some of the most loyal and steadfast friends of anyone I know." She paused, a pensive look on her face. "Before I got to know you, Jared and Eleanor, I really didn't believe that a person could trust anyone. I'm glad I found out that's not true."

Nathan leaned over, took her hand and looked into her eyes. "Whatever happens in the days to come, Christy, I'm glad you found that out. In my job, I've had to handle a lot of mean, ornery folks. Knowin' there's good upstandin' people in this world is what keeps me goin'."

The rest of their day was a private affair, one that would remain fixed in their memories as one of the finest days of their lives. The tales of King Arthur and the Knights of the Round Table had never been told with such flair, fried chicken never tasted better, and love had never been sweeter. There are very few times in life that seem perfect . . . this was one of those times. Perfection never lasts. When you have the opportunity, you'd better grab on and enjoy it to the fullest. They did.

Nathan put away the buckboard at the livery and brushed down the horse. He found himself whistling a tune as he did it and laughed at himself. He was in such good spirits he decided he would continue to live the high life and enjoy a nice big beefsteak at the St. James Hotel. Before doing that, however, he thought he should probably go by the jail house and check in. As he walked up, he saw someone pacing up and down the boardwalk in front of his office. He proceeded cautiously. As he got closer, he recognized Bill Merritt, a rancher from south of town.

Merritt saw the sheriff coming. He strode resolutely over to meet him. He was not a tall man; in fact, looked a bit like a bookkeeper. Nathan knew him to be a good hand and he ran a good outfit. "Sheriff," he said urgently, "we got big problems. I sent a couple of hundred head of steers up the trail with five of my best hands about two weeks ago. When they didn't come back, I rode out to find'em." Merritt's face was pale. His hands were shaking. He tried to speak but choked up.

"Take it easy, Bill," Nathan said. He put a hand on the rancher's shoulder. "Maybe we ought to step inside, set a spell."

They walked into Nathan's office and Merritt sat in the rawhide chair next to Nathan's roll top desk. "You got any whiskey?"

Nathan looked at the expression on Merritt's face. He nodded slowly. "Matter of fact, Bill, I believe I do have a bottle somewhere here in the back of this desk." He pulled out his private stock of good whiskey and handed Merritt the bottle. "I don't have any clean glasses. Reckon you'll have to do it the old fashioned way."

The rancher snatched the bottle from Nathan. He took a big swallow. He sat back in the chair and closed his eyes for a moment. Then he straightened up and continued in a raw voice. "Sheriff, I seen a lot of things since I come out west . . . seen what Apaches do to settlers, seen cowboys run over in stampedes. I'll tell you straight up, what they did to my boys is worse than all I ever seen." He still had the bottle in his trembling grasp. He took another stiff belt which led to a fit of coughing. When he finally caught his breath, he said, "Sheriff, they cut the throats of two of my hands.

They shot the other three right there in their bedrolls." He took one more swallow. "Then they ran the herd through the camp. If any of those cowboys wasn't dead from the bullet wounds, they died a horrible death from the stampede."

Nathan didn't know quite what to say. He knew Merritt looked after his cowboys and thought of them like family. "I'm sorry for your loss, Bill." He took off his hat and put it on his desk. "Any idea who might have done this?"

"Oh, you know who done it, Sheriff," Merritt said heatedly. "That lowdown Santa Fe Ring political hack, Bill Chapman, ordered his mankiller, Daughtry, to do it. You know it and I know it."

Nathan scratched his head. "I reckon you're probably right, Bill. Now I just got to figure out a way to prove it."

"Well, you just do what you got to do, Sheriff," Merritt said firmly. "In the meantime, if I see anyone sneakin' around my place, I'm gonna give'em a couple of barrels worth of buckshot. We'll sort out provin' who did what after the smoke clears and the dust settles." With that, he stalked out of Nathan's office.

Nathan leaned back in his chair. He stared

morosely at the ceiling. *There goes my perfect day.*

CHAPTER 21

October 21, 1884
Lord, this is a mess, Jared thought. *The one thing that crooked judge got right today was wonderin' where that old sheriff was.* When Tommy Stallings finally lost his temper with the farce of a trial and started telling the judge what he really thought of him, it was all Jared and Tomás Marés could do to get him under control and out of the courtroom. Currently, he was cooling his heels in one of the jail cells in Nathan's office. Belatedly, he was worried that he might have damaged their flimsy case with his outburst. He showed not the least bit of remorse for having explained to Judge Cardenas what a low-down, dirty snake he was. The judge was not pleased.

"Tomás," Jared said, "we've got no chance at all if Nathan doesn't get here pretty quick with those letters."

"Si, es verdad," Tomás said. "He should

be here by now. I'm worried that something has happened to him."

"I been thinkin' that, too," Jared said musingly. "You reckon one of us ought to ride out into the canyon, see what we can find?"

"I think someone should do that," Tomás said. "It seems to me that you are needed here, though. I don't know if I should leave either, since I'm the only lawman in town. I'm thinking my brother should go."

Jared considered Tomás's suggestion. "You're likely right about both of us bein' needed here. Do you think Estévan would be of a mind to go?" Since the ambush, Estévan had been angry almost all the time. He focused much of the anger on Jared. He had idolized Juan and still held Jared accountable for his death. "It might be a good idea for you to be the one to talk to him about it. I don't think he'd take kindly to me suggestin' it."

Tomás nodded. "I apologize for my brother's actions, señor Jared. He's always been the wild one. He is most upset at the death of Juan. He looked up to him like he was some kind of hero. I don't understand why he blames you and not those cabrónes who killed him but that is the way it is. I'll go talk to him now about going to look for the sheriff. I'll ask him to leave right away."

"Thanks, Tomás," Jared said. "Maybe if we can find some justice for Juan, he'll come to see things different. If Nathan doesn't get here with those letters, though, there ain't gonna be any justice."

Tomás walked away from Jared and headed towards the Colfax Tavern. Even though it was only the middle of the afternoon, he was fairly certain he would find Estévan leaning on the bar with a beer and a shot of rotgut whiskey in front of him. Since Juan Suazo had been murdered, his brother had taken to drowning his grief in a river of alcohol. Tomás was not proud of his brother's behavior. Even so, he was still family.

As he'd expected, he found his brother standing at the bar, deep in conversation with one of the flash girls who worked there. He walked over to where they were standing and tipped his hat to the lady. "Por favór, señorita. I need a moment with my brother in private."

The girl, who couldn't have been more than seventeen years old, nodded meekly and hurried away to the other end of the bar with a swish of skirt and petticoat. She knew Tomás was the deputy sheriff and although he had never been anything but polite to her, she didn't want to take any chances.

"And why did you do that, big brother?" Estévan Marés' voice was slurred from the whiskey. "I just about had Rosa convinced that I was going to inherit a ranch now that Juan is . . ." Estévan's voice cracked. He turned away from his brother until he regained his composure. Turning back, he looked his brother in the eye and asked, "What is it that you want?"

Tomás looked at his brother with a heavy heart. Estévan had always been the light-hearted, adventurous spirit while Tomás was steady and serious. Now when he looked in his brother's eyes, all he saw was pain and desperation. "I have a favor to ask of you."

"Are you asking as my brother or as the deputy sheriff?" Estévan continued to look his brother in the eye, his blistering gaze radiating contempt. "The one who works for the gringos."

Tomás felt his anger begin to rise like flood waters through an arroyo during the monsoon season. He struggled to maintain control. He did not speak for almost a minute. Unwaveringly, he held his brother's gaze. Finally, Estévan looked away.

"I'm sorry, brother," Estévan said sullenly. "I had no right to say that."

"I don't even know why you think it,"

Tomás said with a tinge of sadness in his voice.

Estévan sighed deeply. "As a man, I don't understand how you can work for people who treat us like dirt under their boot-heels."

"That is all you see?" Tomás frowned. "The ones who are blind and ignorant? What of the ones who stand with us against the outlaws? What of Sheriff Averill or Eleanor Delaney or even the man you seem to blame for all your misfortunes . . . Jared Delaney? What about them?"

Estévan turned and spit on the floor of the bar. "Jared Delaney sent Juan Suazo to his death. For this, I should be thankful?"

Tomás shook his head. "If that's how you see it, then maybe *you* are the one who is blind and ignorant. If Juan Suazo was here right now, he would be the first to tell you that Jared Delaney gave him a chance to be his partner, not just some hired hand. Juan knew the risks when he became a cowboy." Tomás closed his eyes. He prayed for patience. "Are you not my brother? Have things changed that much between us since we were boys?"

"Many things have changed. We are still brothers . . . we are no longer boys."

Tomás nodded slowly. "No, we are not. It

is time to act like men." He slowly looked around the room, then he turned back to his brother. "To answer your first question, I'm asking both as your brother and as the deputy sheriff." He clinched his jaw for a moment, biting off the bitter words he might have said. "I serve all the people in this place, gringo and Spanish alike, as long as they follow the law."

Estévan looked at his brother. He slowly smiled. "All right, then, mister deputy sheriff. What did you want to ask of me?"

Tomás exhaled. Finally, he returned his brother's smile. "One day, you will succeed in making me loco." He reached out and playfully shoved his brother. Then he turned and leaned against the bar. "I'm worried about the sheriff. He should have been back by today. Without the papers he carries, we have no chance to find justice for your friend, Juan Suazo."

Estévan's eyes narrowed. "If I get the chance, I will settle for revenge. I don't see that it's possible for a man named Suazo to get justice in a gringo's courtroom."

Once again, Tomás shook his head. He sighed. "Maybe you are blind after all. Have you not noticed, brother, that the judge is named Cardenas? You think just because someone's skin is brown, he's your friend?

Open your eyes."

Estévan shrugged. "You may be right, quien sabé? My head is beginning to hurt from all this talk. Ask me your favor, get on with it."

"For once, we agree," Tomás said with just a hint of a grin. "I can't leave town because I'm the deputy sheriff. Jared can't leave because he may be called as a witness. I want you to ride into Cimarrón Canyon. See if you can find any sign of the sheriff. If he's hurt or has been ambushed, we must have the papers that he carries." Tomás reached out with both hands. He took his brother by the shoulders. "I can't tell you how important this is, brother. We are counting on you. Maria Suazo is counting on you."

At the mention of the widow of Juan Suazo, Estévan's eyes became misty. He looked down. He swallowed hard. When he looked back up, his eyes were clear. "I will do this for Juan Suazo." He paused, then he spoke again softly. "And I will do it for you, brother."

Tomás clasped his brother's hand in both of his. He could find no words. Finally, he nodded, released his brother's hand and walked out of the Colfax Tavern. Estévan looked over at the bar where his whiskey sat, unfinished. He started to reach for it, then stopped. Turning, he walked out of the tavern as well. Neither brother noticed Jim, the bartender, standing close by during their conversation. He'd paid a great deal more attention to their words than good manners should have allowed.

Bill Chapman leaned back in the chair with his feet propped up on the battered old desk. He had a glass of whiskey in one hand, a big cigar in the other. A wreath of smoke surrounded his head. He was feeling first-rate. "Well, Mr. Elkins, I'd say we had a fine day in court." He took a sip of whiskey followed by a puff on his cigar. "Yes sir, mighty fine."

Daughtry sat in another chair, leaning back against the wall facing the door. He raised his glass of whiskey in salute. The ghost of what might have been a smile played on his lips. Elkins noticed that his eyes still resembled those of a rattlesnake as it circles a field mouse . . . no hint of pity or compassion. A chill went up his spine. *Good to know I've still got one.* He suppressed a shiver.

"Yes, Mr. Chapman, I believe it went rather well," Elkins said with an enthusiasm that he didn't really feel. "The judge seemed sympathetic to our cause. He certainly recognized that they don't have much of a case." Elkins considered his words and hastened to add, "Well, of course, that's because you're innocent. That should go without saying."

Chapman arched an eyebrow as he gazed at Elkins, which made the lawyer squirm in his chair. After a long moment, Chapman smiled again and said, "No, counselor, it shouldn't go without saying. In fact, it's your job to keep saying it over and over until the judge believes it beyond the shadow of a doubt. Wouldn't you agree?"

Elkins began to sweat and hated himself for it. "Well, certainly I agree. I mean, I will continue to present the overwhelming evidence that you could not possibly have been involved in this incident. It goes without saying . . ." Elkins stammered and caught himself. "What I mean is that it is, of course, *understood* that you are both innocent. That doesn't mean I won't keep saying it over and over . . ." Elkins realized he was babbling. His voice trailed off. He didn't know what to say that would not draw the ire and ridicule of William Chapman and yet he felt compelled to say more. He was about to begin babbling again when a knock at the door gave him a temporary reprieve.

Daughtry immediately put all four of his chair legs on the floor. His hand was poised by his pistol. Chapman set his glass of whiskey on the table, turned to Elkins and said quietly, "Counselor, why don't you see who's at the door."

Elkins sat there for a moment, terrified to move. It was hard for him to fathom that a simple knock at the door could create such a crackle of tension in the air . . . he felt it nevertheless. The danger-ladened air was hard to breath. He reached for his collar to loosen it. Chapman cleared his throat. Momentarily confused, Elkins finally picked up his cue. He rose and rather unsteadily walked to the door. He didn't know whether to ask who was there or just open the door. He was afraid if he tried to speak, nothing but a squeak would come out. He opted just to open the door . . . slowly and carefully. What he found when he opened the door was a surly young man whom he recognized as the bartender at the Colfax Tavern. John, it was. No . . . Jack? No, that wasn't right. Jim, that was it. "You're Jim from the Tavern, aren't you?" Elkins was embarrassed at the high, reedy quality he heard in his voice.

"Yes, sir, that's right. I have some informa-

215

tion for Mr. Chapman."

"Mr. Chapman is rather busy at this moment, young man." Trying to regain some modicum of self-respect, Elkins stated in as haughty a manner as he could muster up under the circumstances, "We have some very important legal matters we are discussing. I don't think he has time for any gossip from the tavern."

Chapman slammed his fist down on the table, causing Elkins to nearly jump through the roof. "Dammit, Elkins, let the boy in. Have you not got a brain in your head?" Chapman shook his own head in disgust. He stood up. "Come in, Jim. Have a seat, make yourself comfortable. Fill us in on what you've heard."

Jim came in, hat in hand. He found an empty straight-back chair on which he perched uncomfortably. "That's it, Mr. Chapman, I did hear something. I was pretty sure you'd want to know about it."

"Call me Bill, son." Jim started to speak but Chapman cut him off. "On second thought, call me Mr. Chapman," he said with a wicked grin. "No need of us getting confused about who's the boss here, now is there, boy?"

Jim looked down at his dusty brogans. He looked up again. "No sir, Mr. Chapman,

I'm not confused at all about who's in charge." He grinned back at Chapman. "That's exactly why I'm here."

Chapman laughed out loud. "Splendid, son," he boomed heartily. "Carry on."

"Well, sir, while I was tending bar, I couldn't help but overhear that deputy . . . Marés is his name, I guess . . . talking to his brother. Something about riding out into Cimarrón Canyon to look for the old sheriff. I thought you'd want to know that."

Chapman looked reflexively in Daughtry's direction. Daughtry's eyes narrowed as he looked back at him. Casually, he said, "That's interesting. Any idea when the other Marés boy was going to head out?"

Jim nodded. "I got the idea that the deputy wanted him to leave pretty soon. I doubt he'll go until the morning, though. It'd be dark by the time he made it to the canyon if he left today." He smiled thinly. "Besides, he was drunk as an old coot. He's not in any kind of shape to ride anywhere right now."

Chapman pondered this information. Finally, he looked the young bartender square in the eyes. "You strike me as a man of high aspirations, son. Am I right?"

The young man nodded emphatically. "Yes, sir, I am that. Whatever I can do to help, you just let me know and I'll do it."

"You're looking me in the eyes, boy, saying you'll do anything I ask you to do? Is that what you're saying?" Chapman stared into the young man's eyes with even greater intensity.

Jim didn't flinch. "Yes, sir, I'll do whatever you ask me to do."

Chapman nodded and smiled encouragingly. "Where did you grow up, boy?"

Jim looked puzzled. "Well, sir, I grew up in Georgia, leastwise until I was about twelve. That's when my daddy hauled us out here to the New Mexico Territory." He nervously crushed his hat in his hands. "Why do you ask?"

Chapman's smile broadened. "If you grew up in Georgia, I'll bet you did some squirrel hunting. Am I right?"

The young bartender cocked his head curiously. "Yes, sir, I did that . . . squirrel, then deer when I was older."

"Were you any good?"

A grin slowly spread across the young man's face. "I was a pretty fair shot if I do say so myself. I once shot a ten point buck right at two hundred yards."

Chapman returned Jim's grin. "Well, then, son, I've got a job for you."

Jared felt he should head back out to the ranch so he could be with Eleanor and Ned. He also was beside himself with worry about Nathan, though. Torn between his family and his friend, he agonized over who was most in need of his attention. He finally decided he would go to the sheriff's office and wait for Tomás to return so he could hear the result of his talk with Estévan.

When Jared got to the sheriff's office, he went in the front door. He looked over at Nathan Averill's rolltop desk. As he would have expected, it was neatly arranged with a stack of a few papers on it and little else. Nathan was organized and orderly in everything he did, so much so that you could set your pocket watch by him. When he said he would be someplace, he would be there or die trying.

As this painful thought floated to the top of his consciousness, Jared felt a wave of sorrow come over him. It sapped his energy and left him feeling hopeless. The absence of Nathan Averill and all that it implied was devastating. He went over and stretched out on the old cot where he had lain as he recuperated from the gunshot wound Morgan O'Bannon had inflicted on him several years ago. Memories flashed through his mind . . . Nathan's kind and patient counsel and most especially, of how when Jared needed his aid most desperately, he was there. *I would return the favor a thousand times over: I'd be there for him right now,* he thought, *if I just knew where in the Sam Hill he was.*

Jared almost jumped out of his skin when Tomás shook him awake. He rubbed his eyes and looked around. The world was gray and totally devoid of color or life. He shook his head to clear it. As he looked up at Tomás's face, he realized he had slept for over an hour. Dusk was upon them. He needed to head back to the ranch soon before Eleanor went out of her head with worry.

"Did you speak with Estévan?"

Tomás sighed as he thought about his conversation with his brother. "Sí, we spoke." Tomás shrugged "He agreed to do what I asked. He is in no shape to go today, I'm afraid. No matter, it would've been dark before he got in to the canyon. He would not have been able to look for the sheriff anyway. He promised to leave right before first light tomorrow." Another shrug. "We will see."

Jared read between the lines of what his friend was reporting. He realized that the conversation had been difficult and painful. Tomas, not being one to share family business and Jared, not being one to pry, they spoke of it no more.

"Reckon there ain't much more for me to do here tonight then." Jared slowly sat up, feeling much older than his twenty-seven years. "If it's all right with you, I'll mount up and ride for home."

"Sí," Tomás replied. "Go home to your family."

He stuck out his hand. Jared grabbed it firmly. Without words, they said as much as they could in a handshake. Jared walked out of the sheriff's office.

CHAPTER 22

October 22, 1884

It was still pitch-dark when Jim tip-toed furtively from his room underneath the stairs in the Colfax Tavern. *Room, hell, it ain't much more than a closet.* He had his boots in one hand, his old Henry rifle in the other. *About the only damn thing my daddy ever gave me that was worth anything.* As he walked softly past the old grandfather clock, he could see by the light of the moon that it was three in the morning. He smiled to himself. He was right on time.

Creeping stealthily out the back door of the tavern, he made his way over to the old hitching post. He put a saddle on the beat-down old brown nag that passed for his horse, then bent over to tighten the cinch. Completing the task to his satisfaction and the horse's discomfort, he stepped into the saddle. Without a backward glance, he headed west out of town toward Cimarrón

Canyon. He had done some deer hunting in the canyon since he came to town and he knew a place about a mile in where a makeshift stand was. If it worked for deer, he reasoned, it would most likely work just fine for human prey.

In his dream, Estévan looked down at the knife protruding from his body, bare inches above his manhood. Fiery pain radiated from the knife wound down his legs and across the lower part of his body. He looked up at the man who had inflicted this dreadful insult on his person. His head was turned away. Estévan could not recognize him. He tried to speak . . . the words just wouldn't come out of his mouth. Who was this stranger who would so callously render such a grievous personal injury on his body, then turn away as if nothing had happened?

"Who . . . who . . . who?"

Estévan sat up with a start. He had no idea where he was. He was lying in a pile of straw; some had found its way into his mouth. He spit it out, then shook his head to clear away the cobwebs. He immediately regretted it. He felt as if someone had driven a spike right between his eyes and in to his brain. Very carefully, he lay back down in his straw bed. With all the energy he could muster, he tried to figure out where he was.

He was dimly aware of a noise . . . "who, who, who? After careful and painful consideration on his part, he discovered the source of the repetitive question to be a barn owl. With this new bit of information, he retrieved a memory from the previous night in which he stumbled to the livery stable where his horse was kept and staggered into the barn. There was something about needing to be close to his horse so that he could get an early start in the morning. *What was it?* Wondering hurt his head. *I can't remember.* The pain got worse. *Ah, yes,* he recalled, *my brother's favor. Aaaaahhhh. Relief . . .* but only fleetingly.

Feeling an intense pain in his lower abdomen, he briefly flashed on the frightening image of a knife protruding from his body. As the fog in his mind continued to dissipate, he realized the source of the pain was his need to relieve himself rather than a mortal wound from a blade. *More relief.* Recalling the precarious state of his head, he very carefully pulled himself to his knees. After resting in that position for a moment, he managed to slowly and painfully drag himself to a standing position. His head throbbed. Unfortunately, it was not enough to distract him from the fact that his stomach seemed to be rolling over and over.

I will NOT be sick, Estévan thought as he gritted his teeth. If there was one thing in the world he absolutely abhorred, it was vomiting. Along with the unpleasantness of the taste and the obligatory retching invoked, he found it to be so . . . undignified. After a moment during which he swayed dangerously in his tracks, the queasiness passed.

Estévan had no idea what time it was. He knew that he'd wanted to get an early start and he was afraid he had failed in that endeavor. He stumbled out of the barn. To the east, he saw a narrow crimson band of light just above the foothills. He cursed, but gently so as not to agitate his head and stomach. He was already later than he would have preferred. This left him no time to clean himself up and find a bite to eat. A promise was a promise, even when it was an ambivalent one. He had told his brother he would do this thing and do it, he would, however reluctantly. But first, he would answer nature's call. *Even more relief.*

Once nature was satisfied, he had his horse was saddled within minutes. He rode out of town with the first rays of the sun on his back. He urged his horse into a lope, both because he'd wasted enough time already and also because it was slightly less painful to his head than a trot would have been. Although he continued to feel as if his head had been kicked by a mule, his thought processes gradually became more lucid. He remembered his conversation with his brother the previous afternoon in the Colfax Tavern. He felt a pang of regret as he recalled his provocative comments about Tomás working as a lackey for the gringos. He actually loved and respected his brother a great deal. Unfortunately, their temperaments could not possibly have been more different. Where Estévan was quick to speak his mind and lash out when he perceived an injustice, Tomás was ever careful in considering the many facets of a thing. In his heart, Estévan understood that this allowed his brother to move ahead with certainty and conviction once he was sure of himself. Estévan's pride would not allow him to acknowledge this, at least not out loud.

The sun had cleared the foothills by the time he entered Cimarrón Canyon. He could feel its warmth on his back. After a few twists of the trail, however, the temperature dropped and he was riding in shadows. He was aware that he should be feeling a chill and yet he found himself sweating profusely. He felt as if a blacksmith was pounding on his head with a hammer. His stomach resumed its rolling and flopping. Throughout his self-inflicted and hard-earned suffering, he vowed to remain focused on his task and ignore the ravages of the alcohol from the night before. Moving along slowly now on his horse, he squinted to make the most of the limited light in the canyon and searched from side to side looking for signs of the sheriff.

His perception of time was skewed by his physical discomfort . . . it seemed as if he had been in the canyon for half of his young life. However, the gradually increasing light on the trail told him that he had only been riding long enough for the sun's rays to begin to peek into the canyon. This would mean he'd probably only been searching for about an hour. It occurred to Estévan that if he didn't start feeling better soon, he might need to dismount and take a rest. As reluctant as he was to do this, he was concerned that if he didn't, he would become violently ill. *I'll just keep going a little longer,* he thought, *then I'll find a shady place to lie down for a few minutes.*

Much of the trail was made up of a mixture of grass and dirt compressed from the plodding of many riders over the course of time. Other parts of the trail over which the creek had once run were rocky. The footing was a bit tricky. In the middle of one of these sections covered with round stones, his horse stepped wrong on a rock and almost lost his footing. Estévan was roughly slung sideways in the saddle. The lurching of his body caused his stomach to finally rebel completely. Try as he might to repress the urge, it became evident to him that he was, indeed, going to be violently ill in a matter of seconds. All he could think of was that he had to get off the trail before he was sick. It would be undignified to despoil this thoroughfare over which people he might know would travel.

Estévan made it to the edge of the trail where the trees started before his body betrayed him. Just as he bent over to purge himself, he thought he heard a shot. His horse bucked. He found himself flying through the air. His progress was stopped quite abruptly when his head encountered a low but sturdy branch. His world went dark.

Startled by the sound of a hoof hitting a rock, Jim came out of his reverie. He looked around wildly. It had been dark when his eyelids began to get heavy. Now it was broad daylight. The smell of piñon was strong in his nostrils. He was aware of a cacophony of birds signaling to one another that an intruder was in their midst. It took a moment for his mind to sort out and discern the nature of the sound that had awakened him. As he looked up the trail to the west, he realized that his prey had almost eluded him. Estévan Marés was at least a hundred yards beyond his makeshift hunting stand. He'd nearly reached a bend in the trail that would have made it impossible for Jim to take the shot. This would have necessitated his trying to track him on horseback and running the risk of the rocks giving away his location as they had Estévan's.

Got to hurry, he thought, *but don't hurry the shot.* He rested his elbow on the branch that lay across the group of rocks he was nestled in. He had to twist his body around at an uncomfortable angle to sight in on his prey. He scraped his knuckles bloody on the bark as he swung around to line up his shot. *Damn, I should have stayed awake. Chapman will give me hell if I miss.* This thought made him jittery. He told himself he needed to clear his mind like his daddy had taught him. *Don't get that buck fever. Take a deep breath, hold it, then let it out slow. That's it, stay calm. There he is . . . I got him now.*

In his mind's eye, Jim was a bit unclear as to the progression of the next series of events. He squeezed the trigger. The horse bucked, then bolted. Estévan fell from the saddle. *Got you, you tortilla-eatin' varmint!* He wiped away the sweat that had somehow appeared as if by magic, dripping from his forehead and down into his eyes, clouding his vision. *Leastwise, I'm pretty sure I got you.*

Jim sat as still as he possibly could for several minutes although it seemed longer to him. He saw no movement from where Estévan had fallen. He considered walking up the trail to double check to make sure that his prey was dead. After some thought, he decided against it. *That pepper-belly could be playing dead, trying to lure me into a trap so he can shoot me.* Jim wiped more sweat from his brow. *Besides, I know I got him. Yes sir, that's it.*

Having made his choice, Jim gathered up his rifle. He walked back further into the brush where he'd tied his old nag. He figured Mr. Chapman would be mighty pleased with him. He pondered the reward he had in store. *Wonder how much it'll be worth to the boss. Reckon I deserved a pretty fair bundle of silver.* He mounted up and headed back to town.

CHAPTER 23

October 21, 1884

Jared made it back to the ranch just as the sun was setting in its colorful splendor over the hills to the west. There was a venison stew simmering in the pot . . . Jared had killed that fat doe himself . . . and he could smell the aroma all the way from the corral. It went up his nose, then straight down to his stomach, making him painfully aware of the fact that he hadn't eaten all day. He looked at the house and could see that Eleanor was playing a game of hide and seek with Ned. She would pretend not to see him as he hid in plain sight behind the rocking chair. Finally, she would make a big to-do about discovering him. Then she would chase him all around the room. When he stopped to allow her to catch him, she would snatch him up and tickle him until he was screaming with laughter.

After unsaddling and brushing down his

horse, Jared watched this interaction from the door for several minutes. The sight of his beautiful wife and his whirling dervish of a son playing together with such joy and abandon lifted his spirits in a manner that he couldn't have imagined just an hour previously. If he could just stay here with his family, the two people in the whole wide world who loved him unconditionally, he thought he would be a contented man. *Reckon a man can't live in a cocoon, though. You got to come out to make a livin'.*

"I think she caught you, pard." Jared spoke up from the door, unwilling to remain just an observer any longer. "You can't outrun your mama. I know that for a fact!"

Eleanor looked at him with a flash of mischief in her eyes. "The way I remember it, I didn't have to run after you, cowboy. I just let you chase me until I caught you."

Jared laughed out loud as his mind skipped over a mental montage of memories. "I think you're right, Eleanor my love. That just about describes the situation. You had me from the get-go, from that first day Nathan introduced us." He chuckled as he reminisced. "It just took me a little while to figure it out."

Ned had demonstrated far more patience than was typical of him. Finally, he grew tired of this "talkin' thing" his parents were doing. "Papa, you chase me!"

Jared squatted down. He started stalking Ned, growling as he went. Ned screamed with laughter and took off out the front door. For the next half hour, father and son played chase, hide and seek, and a number of other games they invented on the spot. Finally, the darkness and their rumbling stomachs chased them inside where the venison stew was waiting for them in the little ranch house.

After supper, they got the dishes cleaned up and put Ned to bed. He insisted that his father tell him a story about being a cowboy. His eyes got droopy, however, before Jared's characters had ridden very far down the trail. He went to sleep dreaming about galloping his horse across the prairie in pursuit of a runaway steer.

Eleanor made a pot of coffee. They took two steaming mugs out to the portál where they sat side by side in their rockers. The moon was just coming into view. It was in that declining stage of the cycle, after the full moon, that they called the waning moon. As Jared stared at the sliver of light, his light-hearted mood began to wane. He took a deep breath and let it out slowly in a big sigh.

"A lot on your mind?" Eleanor reached over, covering his big hand with her small, sturdy one.

Jared sighed again. "I just wish I could keep nothin' but you and Ned on my mind all the time. Seems like that's the only real contentment I got in life."

Eleanor squeezed his hand. "It warms my heart to hear you say how much joy Ned and I give you. You and I both know, though, that if you just hung around with us all day long, you'd get restless. Pretty soon, you'd arrange a cattle drive and off you'd go." She smiled sweetly at him and said, "Besides, if you were here all the time, you'd drive me completely to distraction."

Jared grinned in spite of himself. "Reckon you're right. I'm just feelin' sorry for myself." His smile faded. "Eleanor, the days of the cattle drives are just about done. The trains are comin' in, takin' over. I'm afraid it won't be long before there won't be any work for a cowboy." He ran his fingers through his hair. "Pretty soon, the life I've always known will be a thing of the past."

Eleanor was silent for a few minutes. They sat there side by side in their rockers, not needing words to make them feel close. Finally, she spoke. "You're right. That's what happens . . . things change. People change. You grow up, live your life, get old and then die." She looked at him with a quizzical expression. "This isn't brand new information you just discovered, Mr. Delaney. Why is it bothering you so much now?"

Jared had to smile again. "You have a way of cuttin' right to the heart of the matter, don't you, Mrs. Delaney." He shook his head. "It's botherin' me because I think Nathan is in some kind of trouble and I can't help him. I owe the man my life yet I don't know what to do to help him."

Eleanor considered his words. "So you really are worried that something bad has happened to Nathan?" She hesitated, then plunged ahead. "That's part of what's causing you to have nightmares again, isn't it?"

Jared shook his head in surprise. "What makes you think I'm havin' nightmares again?"

Eleanor sighed. "Jared, you toss and turn all night long. You mumble in your sleep. Sometimes you even yell out. I'd have to be deaf and blind to not know what's happening." She reached out and tenderly took his hand. "I'm worried about you, sweetheart. This thing is eating you up."

"It's bringin' back some awful bad memories, that's for sure," Jared said quietly.

"But maybe that makes you worry even

more than the situation calls for," Eleanor said evenly. "Maybe Nathan is all right. Maybe this trip is just taking longer than he expected."

"I don't think so," Jared said wearily. "If he'd gotten held up in Taos, he'd have sent me a telegram. He knows better than anyone how important those letters are to the outcome of this trial. No, I'm afraid he's come to no good on the road. I don't know what happened or if it had anything to do with this trial business." Jared shook his head in consternation. "Heck, it might not have anything at all to do with the trial. Eleanor, he's gettin' along in years. If his horse shied from a rattler or some such hub-bub, he could be laid up with a broken leg."

"That's part of what got you to thinking about life changing, isn't it," Eleanor said softly. "The man you've looked up to isn't the man he used to be anymore."

Jared rocked a bit in silence. "No, he ain't. I reckon he's been tryin' to tell us that for a while now. I've sure enough had a hard time hearin' it. Ever since I've known him, he's been larger than life. Now, all of a sudden, I guess I realize he's human like the rest of us."

"Jared, he's always been human. He gets scared, he gets tired, he even gets old."

Jared chuckled. "He's done a fine job of hidin' it until here lately. He plum had me fooled."

"Don't get me wrong," Eleanor said. "He's always been braver, stronger and smarter than anyone I've ever known. It's just that it doesn't make him immune to fear, fatigue or age."

"I know what you're sayin'," Jared said. "It's just hard for me to square it with the man Nathan is . . . or at least the man he was."

"It does fit, though," Eleanor said. "That's why you're worried."

"That's it in a nutshell," Jared said. "I think Nathan needs my help now more than he ever did in the past."

"So what are you going to do?"

Jared sighed. "Tomás and I figured we were both needed in town right now. He has to keep the peace. I'll most likely have to take the stand tomorrow. He's asking Estévan to take a ride up into the canyon to look for him. I don't know if he left this evenin'. I'm guessin' he's more likely to head out early tomorrow."

At the mention of Estévan's name, Eleanor got quiet. Finally, she said, "Estévan blames you for Juan's death. Lord knows why," she added.

"I know he does. He says 'the gringo always takes advantage of his people.' You know, a lot of the time, I think he's probably got the truth of it. I don't know what I can do about it, though, other than to do what's right myself. Tomás was gonna talk to him man to man and ask him to lay his personal feelin's aside for now. You know," Jared said with a touch of sadness in his voice, "this reminds me of when we had to deal with the O'Bannons. I'd made such a mess of things with you and Lizbeth and Ned, as I'm sure you recall. In spite of that, you all did what needed to be done. You set your hard feelin's aside until it was over. I reckon that's what Tomás is gonna ask Estévan to do."

"Estévan comes from a fine family," Eleanor said. "I don't know if he'll ever get over his hurt feelings. Do you really think that will stop him from doing what is right though? The Marés family may have brown skin while we've got white but we've got a whole lot more in common than we have different. They're our friends. They'll be there when we need them."

"Mrs. Delaney, how do you do it?" Jared asked with a touch of awe in his voice. "You see the best in people. You keep goin' when I'm so disheartened I don't know if I can take another step. You tell me people live, grow old and die. That sounds pretty dog-gone bleak to me, yet you just keep movin' on down the trail like nothin' was the matter. What's your secret?"

"Jared," she said, giving him the look she used to reserve for students who couldn't see the answer right in front of their faces. "Sometimes you make things more complicated than they really are. You answered your own question, you just didn't realize it."

"What on earth are you talkin' about, Eleanor my love?"

"You said it . . . listen to yourself. You said, 'people live.' That's the secret. You live every day, every moment. You don't stop until you're dead. You treasure your time with your loved ones. Look at you. You have a beautiful wife . . ." she reached over and playfully gave his shoulder a gentle nudge. "You have a strong young son who wants nothing more than to be a cowboy like his daddy." She paused again. Then she smiled. "And you have a daughter on the way."

Jared was thunderstruck.

"I've lost them," Jared mumbled to himself as he stumbled around in the foothills outside of Cimarrón. The world was grey. Everywhere

he looked, there was ground fog. He didn't know if it was early in the morning or just after sunset, he only knew that he couldn't see more than a few feet in any direction. He felt a terrible sense of urgency as he staggered and tripped over the rocks and brush. Somehow, he'd managed to lose them all . . . his parents, Nathan, Eleanor, Ned and a small infant that he knew was his baby daughter. He was responsible for all of them and he had failed miserably in his responsibilities. Now they were gone. In his heart, he knew they were in terrible danger. He had to find them and save them, yet he had no idea where to begin. "This is not right," he cried out. All of a sudden, someone or something had him by the arm. He struggled but couldn't seem to pull free. They called out his name . . . "Jared. Jared."

"Jared," Eleanor said softly, "wake up. You're having a bad dream." She shook him gently, then ducked quickly as he came awake with a start. A round-house right barely missed her jaw. "Jared, it's me. It's Eleanor."

Jared stopped his thrashing around. He rubbed his eyes. He looked over at his wife. Slowly, recognition settled in. He was in his home, in his own bed with his wife . . . having another nightmare. He took a deep breath and untangled himself from the bedclothes. He was soaked in sweat. "I thought I'd lost you."

CHAPTER 24

October 22, 1884

The third day of the trial was called to order promptly at nine o'clock according to the old grandfather clock that stood scarred but dignified behind the judge's bench. Although the day was just beginning, Jared felt a wave of weariness wash over him. There had been no word of Nathan's whereabouts from the deputy in Taos. Jared didn't even know if Nathan had made it that far. Tomás informed him that Estévan left sometime earlier that morning so it was doubtful that he would discover any useful information and make it back to court before late afternoon. That meant that in all likelihood, the preliminary hearing would end without the incriminating letters ever being brought before the judge. Considering that the only other witness for the prosecution's side was currently residing in jail for contempt of court, the prospects for justice seemed pretty bleak.

Jared was sitting next to John Budagher. He noticed that Budagher was nervously tapping his fingers on the table as Judge Cardenas strode into the courtroom. Jared didn't know if that was a good sign or a bad one. So far, Budagher had been singularly ineffective. He'd shown little grit in the process. He seemed to be in over his head and Jared was afraid that the young attorney would not only go down in defeat but would go down with barely a whimper.

Glancing back over his shoulder at the crowd gathered to witness this pretense of justice, Jared was surprised to see Maria Suazo. She was dressed from head to toe in black and her face and hair were covered by a black veil. Since he'd broken the news of Juan's murder to her last summer, Jared had only seen Maria a handful of times and then, only briefly. He felt guilty that he hadn't been on the drive with Juan although Eleanor pointed out to him that it would've made no sense for him to have gone. She told him he had nothing to feel guilty for and that Maria understood that. Jared guessed she was right because, unlike him, she'd spent many hours with Maria, consoling her and helping her deal with her grief. Still, he felt like he'd failed his old friend in some way. Maria lifted her hand in a small wave. Jared nodded and smiled in return. He then turned his attention to the judge as the bailiff called the proceeding to order.

Judge Cardenas banged his gavel to silence the small rumble of conversation that reverberated through the courtroom. When he had everyone's undivided attention, he cleared his throat and began.

"Gentlemen, I fully intend for this preliminary hearing to be over by early afternoon. I'm telling you this so that neither of you wastes any time with pointless rambling or grandstanding of any kind." He stared deliberately at Budagher for a moment before continuing. "I also want to state unequivocally that I will not tolerate another outburst like the one we experienced yesterday afternoon from that rude young cowhand. If anything like that occurs, I will clear the courtroom immediately. Do you understand me?"

"Yes, your honor," Budagher said quietly. Then, remembering the admonishing from the previous two days, he spoke up in a louder voice. "Yes, your honor, I definitely understand you."

"Good," Cardenas said, looking slightly disappointed that he'd missed out on another occasion to bully the young attorney.

He didn't even bother to look at Robert Elkins. "Let us proceed then. Did that old sheriff ever make it back from Taos with those alleged letters?"

Budagher cleared his throat. "Not yet, your honor. We're hopeful that he will make it back today in time to allow you to look at this vital evidence."

"You're hopeful, are you?" Judge Cardenas peered over his glasses at Budagher. "Well, let us stress that your only hope is that he makes it back before the end of today's session. Tomorrow will be too late. Am I making myself clear, counselor?"

"Yes, your honor, you've been clear on this point," Budagher said. The judge began to speak. To his surprise, Budagher quickly added, "I do want to go on record as saying this is critical information that is relevant to making a fair and just ruling on whether to move ahead with further legal action against the accused. It is my opinion that it would be worth waiting longer to give the sheriff a chance to get here with the evidence."

Cardenas slammed his hand down on the bench and glared at the young attorney. "I don't recall asking for your opinion on this matter, Mr. Prosecutor. You are coming dangerously close to being in contempt of this court."

For the first time, Jared detected a sense of determination on the part of the young prosecutor . . . if not exactly moral outrage, at least a hint that he was reluctant to continue to be pushed around in such a demeaning fashion by this judge.

"No disrespect intended, your honor," Budagher said in a strong, clear voice. "I believe, however, that I am within my legal rights to state this for the official record in the event that further legal action is pursued by the state."

Cardenas stared at the prosecutor. The young man returned his gaze. Apparently, the judge's desire to get the proceeding over with promptly outweighed his need to further humiliate the young attorney. "Fine, then," he said perfunctorily. "You've made your point for the record. Is that the sum total of your case or do you have other witnesses to call?"

"Yes, your honor, we do," Budagher responded calmly. "The prosecution calls Mr. Percival Daughtry."

There was a buzz in the courtroom as everyone looked around in confusion. Finally, it dawned on Robert Elkins that his client, Daughtry, actually had a first name. He had been so intimidated by Daughtry that he'd never inquired. Daughtry, for his part, had never volunteered this information to him. In fact, he had been so frightened of his client that he had refrained from discussing with him the possibility that he might be called upon to testify . . . or discussing anything else with him, for that matter. He was in a bit of a quandary about what to do and was shuffling papers on the table in order to gain some time to think. Judge Cardenas was staring at him, awaiting his response and showing the first hint of impatience that he had directed towards the defense table in the entire three days. At that moment, Bill Chapman leaned over and whispered something in the ear of Elkins. His eyes grew wide. He turned to stare at Chapman. Chapman motioned to him to listen again and whispered a few more words to him.

Elkins rose unsteadily from his chair and in an uncertain voice, said, "Defense requests permission to approach the bench, your honor."

Budagher was immediately on his feet. "Prosecution insists on being included in this discussion, your honor."

Cardenas glared at Budagher. This time, he refused to wilt. Knowing that he would be on unsustainable legal ground if he didn't allow the prosecutor to be involved in his talk with Elkins, he relented. "Oh, all right, Mr. Budagher, you may approach the bench, too."

Jared watched as the two attorneys walked over to the judge's bench. Elkins leaned in to speak. He couldn't hear what the man was saying but from the judge's reaction, it was something totally unexpected. Judge Cardenas's eyes grew wide with astonishment. He appeared to be asking Elkins questions which the defense attorney could not answer. In the meantime, Budagher's jaw dropped. Jared could see that he was becoming increasingly agitated as the discussion went on. After several minutes, both attorneys turned to head back to their tables. The judge rose.

"This court will take a thirty minute recess. The prosecutor and the attorney for the defense will join me in my chambers in five minutes." With this statement made, Judge Cardenas turned and amid the flurry of discussion and confusion in the crowd, he walked through the door to the small closet that served as the judge's chambers.

Budagher hadn't even taken his seat at the table before Jared was on him. "What's going on? Is this some sort of trick that Chapman is pulling?"

The prosecutor looked at him for a moment. "Daughtry can't speak."

Jared shook his head in confusion. "What do you mean, he can't speak? He's been called on to testify. He can't just refuse."

"No," Budagher said quietly. "I mean he can't speak. He literally can't talk."

"What does that mean?" Jared sputtered. "How . . . why . . . I mean, what . . ." He trailed off helplessly. Finally, he collected his thoughts sufficiently to formulate the question. "So what do we do?"

"That's what we'll be discussing in the judge's chambers," Budagher said quietly.

As the two attorneys moved to join the judge in his chambers, the inquisitive on-lookers grudgingly got up from their seats. They went outside to roll smokes and gossip with one another, speculating wildly on what was transpiring in the back room. Jared waited until the courtroom was quiet and nearly empty before rising. When he turned, he saw Maria Suazo, frozen in the same spot she had occupied earlier. He felt like a fool because he didn't know what to say. One thing he knew for certain, though, is that it would be wrong to take no notice of her. He walked over to where she was sitting and took a seat beside her.

"I want to ask you how you're doin'.

Somehow, that just seems like a stupid question," Jared said quietly.

Maria lifted her black veil. Jared saw a slight and familiar smile on her face. He also noticed the tears that were brimming over and slowly trickling down her cheeks. "I know what you mean, Señor Jared. You know my life is over, yet you still care about me. I understand. There are really no words to ask about this."

Jared nodded. He wanted to tell Maria that her life wasn't really over but he realized that it was not his place to do so. Instead, he said, "I know that bringin' these men to justice won't get Juan back for you. I just hope maybe it'll provide a bit of satisfaction. Me, I can't stomach the notion that they could shoot down my best friend in cold blood and just walk away."

"I know what you are saying," Maria said quietly, "but it really doesn't matter. My life, my corazón, is gone. You can kill every bad man in the territory. Juan is still gone."

"I can't argue with you about that, Maria. I just know that I've got to try to do somethin'." Jared closed his eyes for a moment, trying to collect his thoughts. "Maria, I loved Juan like a brother. It was more than that, though. I respected him. I respected him for what he knew, for who he was.

These people treat him like he didn't matter at all, like he was just dirt under their boots. That ain't right." Jared's hands curled into fists. He had to restrain an almost overpowering urge to slam those fists on the bench where they sat. "They can't just do that and walk away," he said vehemently. "They can't. It ain't right. They need to know it, by God."

Maria reached over and took Jared's hand, smoothing out the fist. She clasped it in both of hers. "I understand what you say, Señor Jared. I appreciate it. I know Juan would appreciate it, too, because the two of you always thought alike. All I'm saying is that it doesn't change anything for me."

Jared was truly at a loss for words now so he just sat there quietly with Maria. In a while, people began to meander back into the courtroom and take their seats. Maria gently squeezed Jared's hand, then let go. She carefully placed her veil back over her face. Jared sat for a moment longer, then got up and returned to his seat at the prosecutor's table.

Sunlight streams in through the window on the east side of the courtroom. Dust motes dance in the light. As people talk quietly among themselves, Maria's mind wanders away from the courtroom, back in time. She's a young girl coming into the flower of womanhood, the oldest child of Patricio and Rosa Gonzales. With her parents and five brothers and sisters, she lives on a small plot of land that her parents hold by the grace of God and the land grant of Guadalupe Hidalgo. They don't have much . . . some goats, many chickens, a small herd of cattle . . . but they get by. They are happy.

Maria's prize possession is a black mare with a white diamond on her forehead that her father took in trade when he thinned his goat herd. She is just a young filly when she comes to live with the Gonzales family and Maria claims her straight away. The mare is high-spirited, which suits Maria just fine. She names her Diamanté. As she struggles to break the filly to ride, Patricio is worried that his oldest daughter may break her own neck instead. Over time, human and horse learn together. They forge a partnership based on mutual trust and affection, resulting in an amalgamation of spirits that is wild and abandoned. They ride like the wild wind across the wide plains north of Cimarrón.

Another memory slowly eases its way into Maria's consciousness. She and Diamanté have been exploring the foothills; they are now on the trail headed home. As they lope gracefully along, she sees a vaquero riding toward them. She slows to a trot, prepared to bolt in the other direction if there is any sign of danger. She is confident but alert. When the vaquero is within ten yards of her, he pulls up. With a flourish, he doffs his hat.

"Buenos días, señorita. Are you out for a ride on this beautiful day?"

Maria eyes the stranger carefully. There is something rakish and wild about him. This appeals to her. He has a nice smile as well. She senses no immediate danger.

"Sí," she answers haughtily. "I ride every day. I go where I please."

The vaquero chuckles at her response. "That must be nice," he says. "I work cattle for Señor Kilpatrick. I ride where it pleases him." With his hat in hand, he bows in the saddle. "I have forgotten my manners, señorita. I am Juan Suazo."

Maria is intrigued by this young cowboy. She notices that beneath the laver of dust he is wearing, he appears to be quite handsome. "Buenos días, Juan Suazo. It is nice to have met you." Spurring Diamanté, she says, "Now I must be going."

As she surges past him, he calls out, "You forgot to give me your name."

Over her shoulder, she laughs and says, "I

did not forget, señor. You will have to work harder than this to get my name."

He turns and lopes after her. She allows him to catch up. As he rides up beside her, he asks, "What would a man have to do to earn the privilege of knowing your name, señorita?"

"For you?" She gives him a long appraising look. With a wicked grin, she says, "I think you would have to win a race with me." She sinks her spurs in Diamanté's flanks. As he bolts forward, she shouts back at Juan. "This will never happen. I have the fastest horse in the territory."

Juan spurs the gelding he is riding. He shouts, "Wait, where are we racing to?" All he hears is the sound of her laughter carried back to him on the wind. He pushes his horse harder. Soon they are both flying over the land. At times, he fears for both their lives as Maria leads him through a thicket and jumps Diamanté over a stream. Finally, she rounds the bend that leads to her home. She reins in at the front gate. Seconds later, Juan pulls up beside her.

"You did not win, Juan Suazo," she says with a grin. "I guess you will have to wait to learn my name. Perhaps you should try harder the next time."

Juan pauses to catch his breath. He takes

off his hat. With one hand, he places it over his heart. He bows to her and says, "Trying harder would make no difference, señorita. You were right. There is not a horse and cowboy in this territory that could catch you and that magnificent caballo you are riding. I will have to find some other way to win the privilege of knowing your name." Putting his head down, he mumbles something softly.

"Pardon me, Señor Suazo, I'm afraid I did not hear that last thing you said."

He looks up at her ardently. She sees a fire in his eyes. "I said that I will have to find a way to win your heart as well." With a final flourish, he places his hat back on his head. "Adiós, señorita. I will see you again very soon, I promise."

He turns and rides away. This prevents him from seeing the smile that is glowing on her face and in her heart.

A door closes as someone enters the courtroom and abruptly interrupts Maria's reverie. The memories fade. Once again, she is sitting in the courtroom, alone in a crowd of people, a widow with a hole in her heart.

The thirty minute recess stretched into forty-five minutes. At times, Jared could hear muffled noises from the judge's chambers, which he interpreted as voices raised in conflict. Finally, the door opened and the parties returned to their places. Budagher's facial expression was stony. Jared could see the muscles in his jaws clench.

"What happened?" Jared asked anxiously.

The young prosecutor turned to look at Jared. "Daughtry can't speak above a whisper. Seems someone tried to hang him once." Budagher made a wry face. "Regrettably, they weren't successful in finishing the job. They did do sufficient damage to his throat that he has difficulty talking."

Jared threw up his hands. "So what do we do? You need to be able to call him as a witness."

"Oh, I can call him to testify," Budagher said. "He'll be accompanied by Mr. Chapman who will 'interpret' to us what his answers are."

"You can't be serious." Jared was incredulous. "Chapman's a lawyer. He can say anything he wants in answer to your questions."

"Yes, Mr. Delaney, that's correct. You understand the situation."

At that moment, Judge Cardenas banged his gavel down sharply. "Let us resume this proceeding. Mr. Budagher, you called Mr. Percival Daughtry as a witness. Unfortu-

257

nately, Mr. Daughtry suffered an injury that makes it both painful and nearly impossible for him to speak above a whisper. He will be accompanied to the stand by Mr. William Chapman who will speak on his behalf."

Budagher was on his feet in an instant. "Judge, as I stated in your chambers, I object to this course of action. Mr. Chapman can say anything he pleases and it will go down in the court record as Mr. Daughtry's testimony."

The judge slammed his gavel down again. "And I told you in my chambers, Mr. Budagher, that I did not want to hash this out in front of these good people. I thought we were clear on that."

"Then let *me* be clear, Judge Cardenas," Budagher said as he stared directly at the man. "I will not sit by in silence and not comment for the record on what I perceive as a miscarriage of justice."

The judge stared back. Then he smiled. "Mr. Budagher, you blatantly disregarded my instructions. I am fining you ten dollars for contempt of court."

"Be that as it may, Judge, I am stating for the record that I object to the manner in which you are conducting these proceedings." Budagher stared at the court clerk to make sure he was taking down his words. He started to sit down, then straightened up again. "And by the way, Judge Cardenas, you are absolutely correct. I have nothing but contempt for this court."

"Another ten dollars for contempt of court," Cardenas said loudly. "Would you care to try for thirty dollars and a night in jail, Mr. Budagher?"

Jared could see that Budagher's jaw was clenched again. He wasn't sure what the young attorney was going to do. Their only friendly witness was already in jail. If the prosecutor joined him, they would have absolutely no chance. Jared wasn't sure what to do. Finally, he cleared his throat. This seemed to have the desired effect of bringing Budagher back from whatever precipice he was standing on.

"No thank you, Judge," Budagher said with surprising calm, "I am ready to proceed."

"Fine, then," Cardenas said as if nothing untoward had just happened. "The prosecutor calls Mr. Percival Daughtry to the stand. He will be accompanied by Mr. William Chapman who will assist in illuminating for the court Mr. Daughtry's answers to the questions."

The bailiff quickly jumped up and put

259

another chair next to the one where the witness would sit. Daughtry and Chapman took their seats and were sworn in. As Budagher got up to begin his questioning, Daughtry looked directly at Jared and smirked. Jared felt his temper flare. It was all he could do to remain in his seat.

"Mr. Daughtry," Budagher began. "Can you tell me where you were on the night of June 19th?"

Daughtry turned to Chapman and whispered a couple of words in his ear. Chapman turned to face Budagher. "Sir, the night you mentioned was quite a ways back. Mr. Daughtry can't exactly remember where he was." He smiled ingratiatingly. "He thinks he was probably in a saloon somewhere having a drink or two, spending time with some lady."

Budagher raised an eyebrow. "Mr. Daughtry whispered all that to you just now, Mr. Chapman?"

"Every bit of it," Chapman responded with the same infuriating smile. "I passed it on to you just the way he said it."

"Very well, sir, if you say so," Budagher replied with disgust. "Do you deny being in the vicinity of a meadow just north of Raton Pass?"

Daughtry leaned over and whispered for

several moments in Chapman's ear. "Mr. Daughtry says 'yep.' "

Budagher shook his head in disgust. "Thank you for your able assistance, Mr. Chapman."

Chapman shot the young prosecutor a look. Although the smile remained on his face, his eyes emitted sparks. "Oh, you're welcome, prosecutor. I hope you remember this . . . you know, in case we meet again. I know I will."

"I will, sir. I guarantee it." Budagher turned to the table. He took the derby in his hands. "I won't need an interpreter for this, Mr. Chapman." He walked toward the bench. "This is the derby that the cowboys found in their campsite after the attack on the night of June 19th. I would like for Mr. Daughtry to try on this hat."

As Budagher approached Daughtry, Chapman glanced urgently at Elkins who was sitting at the defense table, apparently lost in thought. Once he realized that Chapman was expecting something from him, he hastily rose and tentatively said, "Objection, your honor."

Before the judge could respond, Budagher responded heatedly. "On what grounds, sir?"

Judge Cardenas angrily banged his gavel

down once more. He said, "Mr. Budagher, that is not yours to question. Do not do that again."

"Yes, your honor." He waited expectantly. Finally, he said, "Were you going to respond to Mr. Elkins' objection?"

Cardenas glared at the young man. He turned his gaze to Elkins. "On what do you base your objection, Mr. Elkins?"

Elkins seemed confused by the question. Feeling the heat of Chapman's gaze, he looked around briefly for inspiration. Finally, he said, "Well, it's just that I thought we had covered that previously and decided it was not relevant."

Cardenas shook his head in resignation. "We did cover it previously, Mr. Elkins, when you questioned that young cowboy. However, this is a different witness. The prosecutor has the legal right to raise the question again."

Elkins appeared baffled. Finally, he said, "Oh, I see." He sat down. Chapman continued to glare at him.

"May I continue, your honor?" Budagher looked at the judge as he walked toward Daughtry with the derby in his hands.

"I suppose so, Mr. Budagher."

The young prosecutor walked over to where Daughtry sat staring at him with his reptilian eyes. If Budagher was intimidated by this, he hid it well. He handed the derby hat to the witness. "Would you please try this on, Mr. Daughtry?"

Daughtry hesitated. He looked at Chapman. Chapman gave the prosecutor a withering glare, then nodded at his henchman to cooperate. Daughtry gingerly placed the hat on his head. It seemed to slide into place, cocked a bit to one side at that jaunty angle they call "acey-deucy."

"Well, judge, it appears to fit quite nicely," Budagher said in a cheerful voice.

Elkins was more alert at this point. "Objection," he said in a strong voice. "That could fit any number of people in this courtroom."

"Really," Budagher said. "Would you care to try it on, Mr. Elkins?" He neatly plucked the hat off Daughtry's head. He held it out to the defense attorney.

"That's ridiculous," Elkins said, nonetheless shrinking away from the proffered hat as if it were a snake.

"What about you, Mr. Chapman?" Budagher turned. He extended the hat to Chapman. The man said nothing and just glared at the attorney in response to his question.

"Enough," Judge Cardenas said with a

bang of his gavel. "You have proven that the hat fits Mr. Daughtry's head, Mr. Budagher. Perhaps it fits the heads of others in this courtroom, perhaps not. This does not conclusively place Mr. Daughtry at the scene of the incident north of Raton Pass last summer."

"I beg your pardon, your honor. As Mr. Stallings said in his testimony yesterday, a man's hat is a very personal thing. It fits him . . . and *only* him . . . in a way that is unique. I want the record to reflect that this derby hat fits Mr. Daughtry like a glove."

"All right, Mr. Budagher," Judge Cardenas said wearily. "You've made your point, although I do not find it compelling. Do you have any more questions for the witness?"

Budagher weighed his choices. He realized that there was little useful information he could gather from Daughtry and Chapman. Clearly, they would deny any knowledge or involvement in the affair. Other than the derby, he had no other way to link them to it at this time. "No sir, I do not."

"You gentlemen may step down," Judge Cardenas said. "Where's your old sheriff, Mr. Budagher?"

Budagher looked at Jared who shrugged and shook his head. "He has not arrived yet, your honor. We are expecting news of his whereabouts at any time."

"I'm afraid that isn't good enough, sir," Cardenas said smugly. "We will take a recess for the noon meal and return in two hours. If your sheriff is not here, I will make my determination at that point on how to conclude these proceedings." Before Budagher could say anything further, he banged his gavel and said, "This court will take a two hour recess."

Chapman and Daughtry were enjoying a fine meal that Elkins had ordered delivered from the St. James Hotel when they heard a knock on the door of the office.

"You want to get that, counselor?" Chapman said dismissively to Elkins without looking up from his repast.

Elkins set down his utensils and reluctantly walked to the door. In his mind, he obsessed about how he could have been foolish enough to get involved with these vicious, arrogant men. He opened the door and found the bartender, Jim, standing there. Having learned from his previous experience, he immediately invited him in. The young man tentatively walked over to the table. He stood there with his hat in his hand.

Chapman and Daughtry glanced up when the bartender walked up to the table. "Well, look, Mr. Daughtry. Our young deer slayer has returned," Chapman said heartily. "How was the hunting?"

Jim stood up a little straighter. "I got it done, Mr. Chapman. Just like you told me. It would have been a tough shot for some folks but I . . ."

"Enough," Chapman barked. "I don't need to hear details, I just need to know that you accomplished what you set out to do."

Jim looked crestfallen. "Sorry, Mr. Chapman. I just thought you might want to know how it happened."

"Well, you thought wrong," Chapman said brusquely. He turned back to his meal and began eating again. Confused, the young man stood there, waiting expectantly. Finally, Chapman glanced up and acknowledged his presence again. "Was there something else?"

Jim stammered for a moment. "Uh, well, I thought maybe I would get something for having done this deed for you."

Chapman stared at the bartender. Finally, he said, "You thought you'd get something? And here I thought you just wanted to do me a favor." He turned to Daughtry and asked in a beleaguered voice, "Why is it that people always have their hand out? Doesn't anyone ever just do something out of the goodness of their heart?" Daughtry shook his head and frowned.

Jim continued to stand in their presence, feeling more confused than ever. Chapman continued to eat his meal. He ignored the young man. After an uncomfortable few moments, Jim spoke up again. "Mr. Chapman, I don't mean to be impertinent . . ." For a moment, he seemed to lose his nerve. Steeling himself, he continued. "I did a job for you. It wasn't easy but I did it. I deserve something for it." He shifted uneasily from one foot to the other.

Chapman looked up thoughtfully at the young man. "You know, you have a point." He shot a meaningful look at Daughtry. "Mr. Daughtry, this young man did some work for me. Now he feels like he deserves something for it. Apparently, he feels strongly about this. I can see that if I don't cooperate, who knows what a ruckus he might make." A smile tugged at his lips. "Would you please see that he gets what he deserves?"

Daughtry looked back at Chapman for a moment, then he returned his grin. He nodded and slowly got up from the table.

As Daughtry stepped away, Chapman said to the bartender, "If you will follow Mr. Daughtry, he'll take you and give you what you deserve, sir." He turned back to his meal and said, "I swear, all this stopping and starting is giving me indigestion. Elkins, can you make sure there are no more interruptions. I would like to finish this fine steak before we go back and wrap this legal mumbo jumbo up once and for all."

As Daughtry walked to the door, Jim turned to follow him. He turned back and said, "Thanks, Mr. Chapman, I'm glad you understand. I didn't mean to be pushy, I just want what's coming to me."

Without looking up, Chapman said, "And that's exactly what you'll get."

Daughtry strode purposefully up the street toward the north end of town where the livery stable was located. Jim wanted to ask him where they were going. He had a feeling, though, that the gunman wouldn't answer him if he did. Lost in thought as he was, he didn't notice an unkempt man wearing a top hat loitering outside of the tavern as they passed it. Daughtry gave him an almost imperceptible nod. He fell in step about twenty paces behind them.

Daughtry came to a derelict old adobe hut just before the livery stable. Without a word, he walked inside. Jim hesitated for an instant, puzzled, then walked in behind him. The man in the top hat followed a few paces behind. As he stepped inside, there was a whisper of metal as he pulled a bone-handled hunting knife from its sheath.

CHAPTER 25

October 22, 1884

Christy had aged noticeably in the past four months. The lines around her eyes and on her forehead had deepened. She did not smile as readily as she had prior to that day last June when Nathan told her she could not be with him because it was too dangerous. Having this come right on the heels of their magical day in the mountain meadow magnified the pain she felt at the exile he'd imposed. She'd thought about their conversation many times in the interim. The events that played out seemed to support his conclusion. Still, she felt a stab of resentment accompanying the sadness that was a constant companion. *You damn fool,* she thought bitterly. *You wouldn't even let me make up my own mind about the chances I was willing to take. You had to protect me whether it was what I wanted or not.*

With school in session, she had classes to

teach and hadn't attended the hearings. She had, however, gotten detailed reports from Miguel Marés. Miguel had left his wife in charge of the cooking at their café while he watched over the proceedings. He didn't want his older son, Tomás, to feel that he was hovering over him or lacking in confidence in his abilities as a deputy. On the other hand, these were some bad hombrés they were dealing with. He had reported to Christy that Nathan had ridden to Taos to get some incriminating documents and had not returned yet.

Her students were taking a break out in the school yard playing games, as was their custom in the middle of the morning session. Most of the time, Christy joined them. They seemed to enjoy it when she participated. Today, however, she just didn't have it in her. She was worried sick about Nathan . . . she felt as if she had a large stone in the pit of her stomach. Even as she'd gotten to know him better and he'd gone from being "the sheriff" to being "Nathan," she still was prone to look upon him as being larger than life.

Christy thought back to their beautiful day in the magic meadow full of wildflowers with Cimarróncito Peak in the background. She had initially felt foolish when she began telling him about the magnificent story of King Arthur and the Knights of the Round-table. He'd seemed truly interested, though, and before she knew it, she was sharing her passion for the romantic tale with him. She smiled as she remembered how one thing had led to another and how they truly had shared their passion. *I guess he really is my King Arthur.*

The memory quickly turned bitter-sweet as she reflected on the events that had transpired since that wonderful time . . . the treachery, the double-dealing, the murder. She understood that Nathan was human. No matter how good he was at his job, he was not infallible. He'd worried a great deal lately that he was slowing down. His pride wouldn't let him acknowledge this and ask for help. His sense of honor wouldn't let him walk away from the evil deeds inflicted on the good people of Cimarrón by these greedy and heartless scoundrels from Santa Fe. It occurred to her that things had not ended well for King Arthur.

Jared paced the floor in the sheriff's office, too nervous to eat. Budagher sat at the desk making notes for his summation. After a few minutes, he looked up.

"He's not coming, is he?" There was an

air of resignation in the way Budagher asked his question.

Jared stopped. He took a deep breath. "It don't look like it, does it?" He resumed his pacing. "Mr. Budagher, I don't know what to say. I'm worried sick about Nathan. I'm afraid that crooked judge is gonna shut this thing down before we can get those letters. If you got any good ideas, now would be a good time to lay'em out."

Budagher pursed his lips and pondered the question. "Well, I have an idea. I don't know how good it is and it's not an easy one to swallow. I can tell you almost for certain that today is not going to end well."

"Yeah," Jared responded wearily. "I kinda had that notion. That damned judge hasn't even had the decency to pretend like he was tryin' to be fair."

"Exactly," Budagher replied. "We had the misfortune to draw one of the judges who are at the beck and call of the Santa Fe Ring. You can bet that Thomas Catron had a hand in selecting Judge Cardenas to preside at this hearing."

Jared threw up his hands in frustration. "So what do we do, Mr. Budagher? How do we fight these political hacks who can pretty much do anything they damn well please?"

Budagher smiled gently. "Well, the first

thing you can do is start calling me John. We're going to be working together on this for a while. We might as well be on a first name basis."

With a quizzical glance, Jared cocked his head. He looked at the young attorney. He considered how the man had gone from a stammering, hesitant and ineffectual greenhorn to a more assertive and confident advocate in just three days time.

"John it is then."

He walked over to the desk and extended his hand. Budagher looked at it and looked up at Jared. Uncertainly, he reached out to shake. "Good to be working with you, Jared."

"And the same to you, counselor." He looked at the lawyer inquisitively. "This can't be all that good for your career, goin' up against these thievin' poltroons. You plan on leavin' the state once you're done?"

"No, Jared, I don't." He looked down at his notepad on the desk as if searching for the proper words. "We don't know each other very well and I imagine you haven't been all that impressed with my performance during these proceedings." He looked down again. "When this hearing began, I was terribly intimidated by the whole bunch . . . Chapman, Elkins, the judge." He shivered. "That Daughtry fellow gives me nightmares. I don't know that I've ever been in the presence of anyone more frightening."

Jared grinned. "No, he ain't exactly the kind of fella you'd want to invite home for dinner, is he . . . maybe introduce to your wife?" Jared's grin faded. "Do you have a wife, John? I don't even know that about you."

"I do have a wife, Jared," Budagher replied. He smiled wistfully. "She's the light of my life. Introducing Mr. Daughtry to her is about the last thing in the world I would want to do."

Jared thought back on his previous encounters with the gunslingers the Santa Fe Ring had sent his direction and how close Eleanor had come to being killed. "You got that one right, John. You don't want any of that bunch comin' around your family." He began to pace again. "So I still got the same question. What are you gonna do once this is over?"

"In the first place, Jared," Budagher said, "this won't be over after today. This is just the first step. I intend to go back to Santa Fe and try to find a way to get this hearing overturned. Not all the judges in this territory are dishonest and in the pay of the Ring."

"Why would you do that, John?" Jared gave the attorney a curious look. "Whatever they pay you in Santa Fe, it can't be enough to make you want to take on these back-shootin' outlaws."

Budagher laughed. "You're right, it is most definitely not for the money. We barely scrape by on my salary."

"Well, what is it, then?"

The young attorney scooted his chair back from the desk. He looked around the sheriff's office. "It's so basic that it probably will sound silly to you, Jared. I believe in the law. It's as simple as that. I believe in right and wrong. I believe in justice. That's why I became a lawyer."

"I respect you for that, John," Jared said. "I have to say that justice can be mighty hard to come by seein' as how it's folks like Chapman and Catron who make the law. They seem to be able to twist it to fit their own purposes."

Budagher stood up and clapped his hands together vigorously. "Don't you see, that's the challenge of it all. They don't just twist and bend the law. In their arrogance, they often break it. When they do that, I have to find an authority who respects the law.

When I do, it's my job to present the best case I possibly can to that authority. No one should be above the law, Jared."

"I agree that's how it should be, John. Unfortunately, it sure don't seem to work out that way all too often." Jared shook his head. "Even the part about findin' someone who's in charge and willin' to listen don't add up. Most of these politician fellas I've seen seem to think they know it all. They got no interest in listenin' to what common folks like me got to say."

"That is where people like me come in, Jared. It's my job to find someone who will listen to the common folk. It's my job to try to make the laws apply evenly to everyone."

"That sounds good to me, John," Jared chuckled. "I'd have to say it was an uphill struggle though."

"To answer your question," Budagher said, "I'm convinced that it's my mission to engage in that struggle. When this is finally over, I intend to continue to fight for the common folk. I intend to see that the same rules apply to everyone."

Jared eyed the lawyer with a newfound respect. "Well, I got to admit I wasn't all that impressed with you that first day. Since then, you seem to have found a little starch somewhere."

Budagher shifted his feet nervously. "I understand why you weren't impressed with me that first day. I admit I was intimidated by the judge and unsure of myself. In my defense, I would attribute my behavior to the fact that this is the first actual case I've prosecuted on my own."

Jared's jaw dropped. "You mean you'd never even been in a trial before?"

"Oh, I've assisted other prosecutors on a number of occasions. I did legal research and provided them with information. I just hadn't been in the role of primary prosecutor before."

Jared shook his head. "Well, I reckon I shouldn't be too surprised that the weasels in Santa Fe would send someone who was still wet behind the ears to do this job." He looked over at Budagher. Seeing that he appeared crestfallen at his comment, he added, "I think they'd be surprised at how well you're doin'. I thought old Judge Cardenas was gonna slap you in a cell next to Tommy Stallings."

Budagher tugged self-consciously at the sleeve of his jacket. He straightened his collar. "I found myself not caring what the judge thought at that moment. That's probably as close as you will ever come to seeing me lose my temper."

Remembering how Tommy had needed to be restrained the day before, Jared had to laugh. "I expect folks got all different kinds of ways of losin' their tempers, John. Maybe it's the quiet ones like you that we ought to watch out for." He chuckled again. "Maybe Cardenas and Chapman don't understand who they're up against with you, mister prosecutor."

"I don't know about that, Jared. I can promise you this, though. Whatever happens, I will not give up. If there is a legal way to obtain justice for your departed friend, I will find it."

The door opened. Tomás walked in. He saw Jared and the young prosecutor sitting with their heads close together, deep in conversation. Clearing his throat, he said, "It's time to get back to the courtroom."

"Any word from Estévan?" Jared asked.

"Nada," Tomás said.

Jared picked up his hat. They walked out together.

CHAPTER 26

October 22, 1884

Tommy stewed as he sat in his cell. He didn't have any regrets about speaking his mind to that snake, Cardenas. However, he felt rotten that he wasn't in the courtroom with his friends. Tomás had filled him in on how things were going. The news wasn't good. He knew they were waiting for Sheriff Averill to return with the letters that would support their case. Without them, they had nothing to hang their hat on, literally. Daughtry's derby hat was of no value since they had no way to conclusively prove it was his. *I swear that silly lookin' derby belongs to that outlaw,* Tommy thought. *I can see him in my mind, ridin' and shootin'.* Unfortunately, what he saw in his mind did not include the outlaw's face. Therefore, it was not persuasive enough to sway the judge.

Tomás came back to his cell. "You have a visitor, amigo."

Tomás had allowed Mollie to visit Tommy a number of times since yesterday. The judge hadn't ordered there be no visitors. Tomás figured what he didn't know wouldn't hurt him.

As he turned to fetch Mollie, Tommy called for him. "Any news of Sheriff Averill?"

Tomás looked back over his shoulder. "No, not a word. I sent Estévan to look for him in the canyon. He hasn't returned."

"What do you reckon happened to him?" Tommy asked. He could sense the deputy's apprehension. "You don't think them side-winders bushwhacked him, do you?"

Tomás slowly shook his head. "I wouldn't put anything past those cabrónes, Tommy. I'm afraid something bad has happened to the sheriff. Otherwise, he would be here."

He went into the front office and returned swiftly with Mollie. She rushed to the cell and reached through the bars to embrace him as best she could. "When are they gonna let you out of this cell?"

"I don't rightly know," Tommy drawled slowly. "The judge wasn't all that happy with me yesterday when he had me thrown in here. It didn't seem like the proper time to ask him how soon I was gettin' out." Tommy tried to look serious. "I'm afraid it

281

might be next winter. He said it'd be a cold day before I got out."

Mollie's face fell until she realized he was having her on. "You are a funny man, Tommy Stallings. Sure and you don't know when to be shuttin' your mouth. Still, you're funny enough for me."

They held hands and gazed longingly in each others' eyes for several moments. When Tommy spoke again, he really was serious. "Sometimes I got to say somethin' funny. If I don't, I'm afraid I'll go plum loco and light into anybody that's in my way." He dropped Mollie's hands. He slammed his fist into his other hand. "Mollie, this just ain't fair. It ain't right. Bad folks ain't supposed to be able to do bad things to good people and get away with it. That's not justice. And judges are supposed to enforce the law, not help'em break it."

Mollie shook her head regretfully. "Things are not the way they're 'supposed to be,' Tommy me love. They're the way they are. Rich and powerful folks all over the world have been rollin' over the common people forever. It's not likely to change anytime soon."

Tommy dropped his head and looked down. When he looked back up, he asked, "Does that mean we lay down? Do we just let'em get away with it? Is that what you're tellin' me, Mollie? Because if it is, I don't think I can stand it."

Mollie's eyes flashed with fervor as she pulled herself up to her full height of just above five feet. "Sure and you'd best not be forgettin' where I come from, Mister Tommy Stallings. I come from four generations of Fenians. We been fightin' the crown of England for hundreds of years. I never said we should give up. All I said was we don't expect fairness. But we fight on. We spit in their eye and we fight on." With her chin jutting out, the wee colleen looked daunting. "And I'll fight on with you."

Tommy was taken aback by the fire and heat coming off his lovely Irish lass. He shook his head and chuckled. "Maybe bein' in this cell is the safest place for me right now. I was thinkin' I might light into somebody. Now you got me worried that you're gonna light into me."

Mollie did not share in his levity. "I'm not joshin' with you now, Mr. Tommy Stallings. I made up me mind when I came over on the boat that I wasn't gonna take it from the man lyin' down anymore. By all the saints, I meant it. Whatever happens in that courtroom, this fight isn't over. Whatever you decide to do afterwards, just know that

I'll be standin' right by your side with a pike in me hand."

Tommy shook his head with admiration. He reached out and took Mollie's hands again. "You're a wonder to behold, Mollie O'Brien. And you know what else I wonder?"

"What's that, Mr. Tommy Stallings, criminal that youse are."

Tommy hesitated a moment. Then he looked his love straight in her green eyes. "This ain't the most romantic spot in the world to be bringin' this up, I know. Still, I was wonderin' if you'd consider becomin' Mrs. Tommy Stallings."

Mollie caught her breath. "Sure and you're not standin' behind bars askin' me to wed you, now are you?"

Tommy's face fell. He stammered, "I know, it's not the best time and place, I just thought . . ." His words drifted away.

Mollie laughed out loud. "Tommy, me love, I can't think of a better time or place. This is perfect. Yes! Saints preserve us, yes."

Tomás walked in and cleared his throat uncomfortably. "I hate to interrupt, my friends. Court is about to be back in session. Señorita, you will need to leave."

CHAPTER 27

October 22, 1884

With his gavel in hand, Judge Cardenas banged the bench with a ferocity that he had not demonstrated previously. Slowly, the buzzing of the crowd died down. The air was electric, like it sometimes is in a dry lightning storm. Jared felt the hairs on his arms tingle and stand up. He looked at his new friend, John Budagher, and gave him a wink. Budagher graced him with a tiny smile, then looked straight ahead at the judge.

"Well, Mr. Budagher, I don't see your sheriff. Would you like to offer an explanation?"

Budagher was on his feet immediately. In a voice that contained more steel than it had the previous day, he responded. "The sheriff has not returned as of this time, Judge Cardenas. We suspect foul play. We've sent a rider out hoping to determine what happened to him. We have not heard back from this rider yet. Under the circumstances, I would request a delay in this hearing until we can determine if Sheriff Averill has fallen victim to violence."

Judge Cardenas threw up his hands in exasperation. "Surely you are jesting, Mr. Budagher. I've given you more than generous leeway in this matter. Now you have the temerity to ask for more? Unbelievable!"

Budagher did not flinch. "Your honor, I repeat . . . we suspect that Sheriff Nathan Averill has been ambushed and prevented from appearing in this court to provide compelling evidence of the involvement of Mr. William Chapman and Mr. Percival Daughtry in the murder of Juan Suazo. For the record . . ." Budagher paused and looked around the courtroom. His gaze lingered on Chapman and Daughtry. Turning back to face the judge, he said, "*For . . . the . . . record,* it is the court's duty to investigate this matter as thoroughly as possible. If that investigation requires a delay in these proceedings, that's what we will request."

Cardenas glared at the young prosecutor. "All right, counselor. Your request is in the record, for all the good that will do you. For that same record, I will state that we have dilly-dallied long enough. You have presented no hard evidence to link these defendants to the events you described. It is unfortunate that these events occurred. Still, with no compelling evidence to implicate them, I see no reason to further inconvenience Mr. Chapman and Mr. Daughtry by detaining them in Cimarrón." Chapman leaned back in his chair and smirked. "Unless you have any additional witnesses to call, I will adjourn this hearing."

Before the judge could slam down his gavel for the final time, Budagher almost shouted. "Wait! I do have one more witness to call, your honor."

The judge shook his head in exasperation. "And who, pray tell, is this final witness, Mr. Budagher?"

"I call Mr. Jared Delaney, the owner of the herd that was plundered."

The crowd in the courtroom erupted in a hail of noise with people talking back and forth in surprise and excitement. Judge Cardenas banged his gavel down repeatedly and called for order in the court. Loudly, he proclaimed, "I will clear this court if there is not silence immediately."

Apparently, no one wanted to miss the show because the clamor died down quickly. The judge stood up behind the bench. He glared at the citizen crowded in the courtroom. "I will say this once more and only once more. Any further disruptions or displays of rowdy behavior will result in the clearing of the courtroom. I hope I have made myself clear." His head swiveled as he swung his scorching gaze around to include every person in the building. Several individuals shifted uncomfortably in their seats as if they actually felt the heat of his glare.

Sitting back down, the judge turned his hot gaze back to John Budagher. "What kind of trick are you trying to play, Mr. Budagher? You said nothing about calling Delaney as a witness prior to this."

Picking up on the judge's cue, Elkins rose shakily to his feet. "Yes, uh, your honor, I object to this." He looked around as if seeking inspiration or direction but found neither. He cleared his throat and sat back down.

Budagher glanced at Jared. Jared winked at the young prosecutor. Budagher smiled at him and then took the offensive. "Judge, our primary witness has been detained. He is possibly the victim of foul play. The rider we sent out to search for him has not returned either and we are worried that something nefarious has happened to him as well. Mr. Delaney has knowledge of the information Sheriff Averill was sent to retrieve and bring before this court. If you are not going to give us more time to locate the sheriff, we at the very least want to get representative word of this information in the record of these proceedings."

The judge's eyes narrowed as he considered the situation unfolding before him. Finally, he said, "Counselors, approach the bench."

Elkins and Budagher made their way up to the bench and stood before the judge. He looked at both of them and shook his head. Leaning over, he said in a low voice that still managed to transmit threat, "Budagher, I don't know where you came up with all that legal mumbo jumbo you just spouted. You don't seem to understand who you're dealing with here. I know your game. You're trying to lay legal groundwork for some sort of appeal."

Elkins started to speak. "Your honor, if I may . . ."

"You may not," Judge Cardenas said curtly to the defense attorney. "You need to be quiet." Elkins's face fell.

Turning back to the prosecutor, he said quietly, "Strictly speaking from a legal standpoint, I probably need to allow you to call this witness. However, as I said before,

I understand your game. You want to create a groundswell of sympathy amongst this rabble here in the courtroom. You think if you can get their support, it will empower you to continue this hearing at another time." He took a deep breath. "Young man, I will say it again. You don't understand the power and reach of the people you are dealing with here. They have no qualms about getting rid of anyone who stands in their way. If you continue down this road, you *will* be in their way."

For a moment, Budagher was silent. Then he squared his shoulders. He said, "I stand by my request to call Jared Delaney to the witness stand, your honor."

The judge looked at the young prosecutor and shook his head. He leaned forward and said, "It's your funeral, son."

October 23, 1884

When Estévan tried to open his eyes, he found them to be stuck together as if sap from one of the tall fir trees had dripped on them while he slept. Why was he sleeping when he had a job to do? He used his fingers to pry open his left eye. When he did, he felt a crusty substance on his forehead. *Sap,* he wondered? As his mind slowly returned to the world of the living, he turned his head slightly. He saw that the sun was just coming up over the ridge on the east side of the canyon. That slight movement resulted in an immediate awareness of an overwhelming pain in his head. He felt as if someone had taken a railroad spike and driven it into his skull a few inches above his left eye. *Maybe I will just sleep a little longer,* he thought as a wave of darkness rolled over him.

Sometime later, he came to again. Repeating the same process, he carefully pried his eyes open. They were immediately assaulted by the sun's glare from directly overhead. The pain in his head was not as acute as it had been earlier. It had receded to a dull, throbbing ache. Moving very carefully, he struggled to a sitting position. He saw his horse grazing by the stream a few yards away. He tried to piece together the fragments of images stumbling through his mind into a coherent memory that he could grab hold of. The attempt was not entirely successful. His mind flashed to an image of his horse bucking, then bolting, whereupon he ran head on into a low-hanging branch and everything went dark.

Estévan could not fathom why his horse, Amigo, would bolt like that. He was steady and loyal, hence the name. He had never given him any trouble on the trail. Had he smelled a bear or mountain lion? *Perhaps,* Estévan thought. *If he had, though, he would've let me know much sooner. His ears would've told me. He would've done a crow dance to signal the danger. He wouldn't have bolted unless the creature was right on his heels. I think I would have seen it.* He pondered the question a bit longer as more images began to come together in his mind. The humiliating vision of leaning over the saddle to empty his stomach paraded through his mind. This sparked another more alarming memory. He heard a shot from a rifle. *Who would be shooting at me?*

Very gradually, he began to collect his thoughts. He remembered talking with his brother and agreeing to venture into the canyon to find Sheriff Averill. He remembered saddling up and leaving just as the sun came up. *What day is this? How long have I been laying here?* The weight of his mission slowly emerged into his consciousness. He had to find the sheriff who had in his possession information that was crucial to finding a measure of justice for his friend, Juan Suazo. *Those back-shooting curs bushwhacked me.*

Estévan realized that whoever had ambushed him must have thought he had scored a fatal shot when his horse took off and he was knocked from the saddle. Otherwise, he would have come to where he lay helpless and finished the job. *I must have dodged the bullet when I became sick.* With a sheepish grin, he thought, *maybe emptying my stomach at that moment was the luckiest thing I ever did.*

From his sitting position, Estévan rolled over to his knees. He slowly attempted to stand. The dull ache was replaced by the railroad spike again. His head swirled, which nearly caused him to fall. He reached out his hand. It found the tree that had inflicted the wound to his head. This time, the tree was his friend. He was able to steady himself until the swirling in his head receded. He took a deep breath and prepared to rise to his feet with the assistance of the tree. *I must get moving and finish this job my brother gave me,* he thought. *I only hope I'm not too late.*

Once he was standing, Estévan managed to slowly and clumsily make his way to where Amigo was grazing. The horse looked up at his master's stumbling approach. He softly whinnied. With great difficulty, Estévan was able to get his foot in the stirrup and mount up. He cautiously urged Amigo into a trot as he turned to head west through the canyon. Finding the trot too painful, even with a horse with such a smooth gait, he urged him into a slow jog. This was more tolerable. He forged ahead, sweeping his gaze from side to side looking for signs.

A painful hour later, Estévan had covered about two more miles into the canyon as best he could estimate. Although he hurt all over, nothing seemed broken. The pain in his head had returned to a dull but tolerable ache. He found that if he kept his head stationary and scanned the trail by only moving his eyes, he could ward off the return of the railroad spike.

Estévan came around a bend. His gaze was captured by the sight of something out of the ordinary off to the right of the trail. He slowed Amigo to a walk and moved over to whatever it was that had drawn his attention. As he got closer, he realized that he was looking at a body laying face-up in the dirt. Dismounting, he left Amigo to graze. He approached the figure. At a distance of about five feet, he recognized him. His eyes widened. Cautiously, he nudged the body with his boot. There was no response. His heart pounded as he backed away. Cautiously, he made a search of the area. Were there more bodies? What he found made his head swirl again. When the swirling stopped, he quickly mounted Amigo and headed back to town as fast as his aching body would tolerate. *I don't know what has happened here but Tomás will want to know about this. I think this changes everything.* Ignoring the pain, he turned and spurred his horse back toward Cimarrón.

CHAPTER 28

October 22, 1884

"Do you solemnly swear to tell the truth, the whole truth and nothing but the truth?"

The bailiff held out the bible. Jared laid his hand on it. "I do."

"Let's get on with this circus as quickly as we can, Mr. Budagher," Judge Cardenas said with more than a touch of exasperation in his voice.

"Yes, your honor," Budagher said as he approached Jared. "However, I must say that I will need to ask Mr. Delaney a number of questions about his background and history with the town of Cimarrón, particularly as that relates to the involvement of the group known as the Santa Fe Ring."

Cardenas rolled his eyes. "Do what you think you need to do, Mr. Budagher, just do it as rapidly as humanly possible. Can you do that for me?"

Budagher smiled at the judge. "I'll do my best, your honor." Turning to Jared, he said, "Mr. Delaney, is it true that you are the owner of the Kilpatrick Ranch and the owner of the herd that was under attack on the night of June 19th?"

"Yes, Mr. Budagher, I am."

"Before we talk about that attack and your ideas about who perpetrated it, Mr. Delaney, I would like for you to tell the court how you came to own the Kilpatrick Ranch. Your name is not Kilpatrick, is it?"

Jared thought about the strategy Budagher had come up with moments before they were called back to court . . . *I hope this works,* he thought. *Here we go.* "No sir, it's not. You asked me to tell about how I got here, so here it is. I came to Cimarrón six years ago, lookin' for cowboy work. Not knowin' any better, I stumbled into a war between the ranchers in Colfax County and a family named O'Bannon. Morgan was the oldest brother in the family. He was the one who called the shots."

"And what shots was Morgan O'Bannon calling, Mr. Delaney?"

"Morgan was workin' hand in hand with a bunch in Santa Fe that goes by the moniker the Santa Fe Ring. For years now, they been usin' the land grant laws to take people's ranches and homes away from'em. When that didn't work, they would have Morgan and his bunch steal rancher's cattle and sometimes murder'em." Thinking about what he had said, he clarified. "Murder the ranchers, I mean. Not the cows." There was a quiet titter from the crowd.

Chapman elbowed Elkins sharply in the ribs. Momentarily befuddled, he finally realized his client wanted him to protest. "Objection, your honor."

Cardenas appeared bored with the proceedings. "On what grounds, counselor?"

Elkins hesitated, searching for a reasonable explanation for his objection. "Uh . . . I'm just not sure how all this is relevant to what we're discussing today." Trying and failing to think of other reasons to support his objection, he looked around the courtroom lamely, then took his seat.

Budagher quickly jumped in. "Your honor, we want to establish that what happened on the night of June 19th was part of a well-established pattern in Colfax County in which the group known as the Santa Fe Ring and their cohorts have systematically tried to steal land from the citizens. In effect, they have declared war on Colfax County. The history that Mr. Delaney is presenting is crucial in establishing this pattern . . . for the record."

"Objection overruled." Cardenas turned his glare back on Budagher and said, "For the record, mister prosecutor."

Budagher seemed to be warming to his task. Turning back to Jared, he said, "Would you tell us what happened with the O'Bannons, Mr. Delaney?"

Jared felt the hair on his neck rise. Prickles ran down his spine as he remembered facing Morgan O'Bannon under the light of the rustler's moon. What could have been the end of his life turned out to be the event that transformed it for the better. "Well, with the help of Sheriff Averill and some other good folks, Morgan and his bunch were licked." He paused as he remembered the price that had been paid. "Not before a good man, my friend Ned Kilpatrick was shot down in cold blood by Morgan O'Bannon."

"What happened after that, Mr. Delaney?"

"Lizbeth Kilpatrick, Ned's widow, asked me if I would partner up with her on the ranch. I told her I would on one condition . . . that we keep Ned's name on the spread."

"So that is how you became owner of the Kilpatrick Ranch, Mr. Delaney?"

"Well, that's how I became a partner with

Lizbeth Kilpatrick, sir. How I came to be the full owner is another part of the story," Jared said quietly.

"Would you continue with your story then, Mr. Delaney?"

Jared looked out at the townspeople sitting in the courtroom. They all appeared to be listening attentively to what he was saying. He saw frowns on some of the faces. He wasn't sure what that might mean. "We did pretty well for a few years. We started drivin' beeves up the trail to the coal mines. We were makin' a decent livin' at it."

"And who is 'we,' Mr. Delaney?" Budagher asked the question very softly.

"It was Lizbeth . . . Kilpatrick, that is. There was me and my wife, Eleanor. Not too long after we got started together, me and Eleanor had a little boy, Ned." Jared paused. He savored the temporary respite of affection that he always felt when he thought of his son. "Beyond that, we had Juan Suazo and his wife, Maria."

The courtroom was very still as Budagher carefully led Jared through the past six years. So much had happened that had never been openly discussed by the folks in town. They had kept their heads in the sand most of the time, as if they would not be affected by events if they simply ignored them. Without acknowledging it, they had depended on Sheriff Nathan Averill, Jared Delaney and the Marés family to protect their interests and shelter them from the powerful forces in Santa Fe that threatened them.

Softly again, Budagher said, "Would you please tell the court about Juan Suazo, Mr. Delaney?"

Jared took a deep breath to steady himself. "Juan was the best hand I ever knew. He could ride and rope. He knew cows. He knew when to push'em, he knew when to let'em go at their own pace." Jared found Maria Suazo in the crowded courtroom. Their eyes met. He grinned. "I'd never have admitted it to his face but he was a better cowboy than I'll ever be. We used to . . ." Jared's voice broke. He stopped, trying to collect himself. He realized that his interrupted sleep over the past several nights was taking its toll. He fought off a wave of weariness and tried to rub away the sting that he felt behind his eyes. Finally, he was able to continue. "We used to kid each other about who was the better hand. I wish I could tell him to his face right now. He was the best."

Jared looked at Maria again. She mouthed two words to him. He thought she said, "He knew." Through the mist that was suddenly clouding his vision, he smiled at her again.

"You can't tell Mr. Suazo that though, can you Mr. Delaney?" Budagher continued. "He was murdered on the night of June 19th."

There was a buzzing in the courtroom as people whispered angrily amongst themselves. "Order in this courtroom immediately," Judge Cardenas shouted as he banged his gavel down repeatedly. "Order or I will clear the room." Reluctantly, the crowd quieted.

Waiting for complete silence, Budagher paused. When you could practically hear the people's anticipation of the next question, he began again. "Would you please continue with your story, Mr. Delaney?"

"Like I said, we had us a pretty good deal goin' on, what with supplyin' beeves to the miners. We were makin' money doin' what we loved."

"Did something happen to interfere with your way of life, Mr. Delaney?"

"Yes sir, somethin' did. That bunch of murderin' thieves in Santa Fe sent a gunslinger named Barwick to Cimarrón. While me and Juan were drivin' a herd up the trail to Pueblo, he and his two henchmen tried to steal the ranch." He paused for a moment to contain the rage he felt. "They tried

302

to murder my wife."

Again there was a rumble in the courtroom. The judge banged his gavel again. The crowd quieted immediately. Apparently, they took the judge at his word and didn't want to give him cause to make them miss the show. "Would you please tell us more, Mr. Delaney," Budagher said.

"When we got the herd delivered to Pueblo, I got a telegram that told me I needed to high-tail it back to Cimarrón. I didn't know what was goin' on exactly, I just knew my wife was in trouble."

"What did you do then?"

"Well, me, Juan and Tommy Stallings . . ." Jared paused and shot a look at the judge. "The one that got thrown in jail for speakin' the truth . . ."

The judge banged his gavel. He gave Jared a contemptuous look. "Any more comments like that, Mr. Delaney, and you might find yourself joining your friend. Do you understand?"

Jared held the judge's gaze. Finally, he nodded and said, "I do . . . your *honor.*" His estimation of the judge's honor was clear from his tone. Cardenas chose to ignore it. Turning his gaze on Budagher, he said sharply, "Can we please get on with this and get it over with, counselor?"

"Yes, your honor," Budagher said. Turning back to Jared, he said, "Go ahead, Mr. Delaney, you're doing just fine."

"While me, Juan and Tommy were up the trail to Pueblo, Barwick came callin' on my wife at the ranch. He told her she needed to sell him our land . . . said if she didn't, she'd be sorry." Jared could feel his blood boil as he remembered the evil gunman. "He had a contract that had been drawn up for him by that Catron fella . . . he's supposed to be the leader of that Ring bunch." Jared turned and stared straight at Bill Chapman. "The other name that got throwed around a mess of times belonged to that man right over there. Mr. Bill Chapman."

This time, Elkins needed no urging to jump up. "Objection, your honor. Objection!"

"Again, Mr. Elkins, on what grounds?" The judge seemed to have made the decision to ride this pony to the end of the trail and give Budagher enough rope to hang his career. Clearly, he was tired of the defense attorney interfering with the process.

"Why, this man is slandering my client's good name, that's what grounds." Elkins managed to work up a pretty good case of righteous indignation. "I demand to know what evidence he has to be making these slanderous charges."

"Mr. Elkins," the judge said with scorn dripping from his voice, "I assume this is not your first trial. Am I right?"

Puzzled, Elkins hesitantly replied, "Well . . . no sir, it's not."

"Then I assume you are familiar with the concept of cross-examination. Again, am I right?"

Elkins put his head down, humiliation radiating off of his entire body. "Yes, sir, I am."

"Good," the judge said. "When the time comes, you can ask the witness about the evidence he may or may not possess. Until then, could we go lightly with the objections? I really do want to get back to Santa Fe sometime before the next century begins. You are making that even more difficult than it already was. Am I making myself clear?"

Elkins's face turned beet red. He glanced to his right and saw that Chapman was fuming. He was in a quandary as to whether to please the judge or please Chapman. He feared that in fact, he was pleasing neither. Throwing up his hands, he said, "I was just trying to look out for the best interests of my clients, your honor."

"And I'm sure your clients appreciate that,

Mr. Elkins. Having established that point, can we now *get on with it?*" His last words were spoken so sharply that Elkins stumbled backwards and nearly fell over.

"Yes, your honor, of course." Trying to preserve what little dignity he had left, he took his seat.

Wearily, Cardenas turned to John Budagher and said, "Carry on, prosecutor."

Budagher nodded. "Mr. Delaney, please tell us what happened when your wife and Lizbeth Kilpatrick refused to sign the legal documents that would have given the land to Mr. Barwick . . . and others . . ." Budagher paused. He let the implication sink in.

"What happened, Mr. Budagher, was that Curt Barwick and his henchmen attacked Sheriff Averill so they could get him out of the way. They nearly killed him; prob'ly would have if it hadn't of been for some mighty tough women." Jared felt a surge of pride and admiration as he recalled how not only Eleanor and Lizbeth but also Christy, Maria and young Mollie had stood up to the outlaws, giving them much more than they bargained for.

"Could you tell us about that, Mr. Delaney?"

"I can, Mr. Budagher. Those ladies rescued Nathan. They moved him to a safe hidin' place. They were able to stay away from Barwick and those other two murdererin' polecats long enough for me, Juan and Tommy to get back to town. We had a big dust-up that came down to some shootin'. In the end, we got Barwick and the others." Jared looked down at his boots.

"You won that battle, didn't you, Mr. Delaney? Yet a terrible price was paid, was it not?" Budagher gently led Jared down the path they had decided to follow.

"Yes sir, there was a price, all right." Jared paused again to collect himself. "When I said we had a dust-up, I mean that the ladies were in the thick of it, too." Jared aimed a sad smile in Maria's direction. "Hell, Maria Suazo's prob'ly a better shot than all the rest of us put together."

"How did that 'dust-up' turn out, Mr. Delaney?"

"Well, Tommy Stallings nearly got himself killed. Without what he done, I doubt we could have taken Barwick. And Lizbeth, she got . . ." At that point, Jared stopped speaking because he was struggling to push down a sob that threatened to escape from his mouth. All the anguish from that time three years in the past came surging back. For a brief moment, he felt like that little boy who so long ago had watched his parents be gunned down before his eyes.

The crowd in the courtroom was deathly silent. They were hanging on every word. "Take your time, Mr. Delaney," Budagher said softly. He hoped the judge would continue to give him the leeway to lay the powerful details of this story before the citizens of Cimarrón. He wanted them to understand in their collective gut that ultimately, it was their story as well.

Jared took a couple of deep breaths. After a moment, he started again. "I'm sorry, sir, I thought I was over all that." He shook his head. "Reckon there's things you just don't get over."

"And you don't forget who caused those things, either, do you, Mr. Delaney?"

Jared's eyes narrowed. With that prompt from the young prosecutor, he got back in the saddle. "No sir, you don't. Curt Barwick gunned down Lizbeth Kilpatrick. Much as I don't mourn his passin', I know he was just the puppet who pulled the trigger. One of the men pullin' the strings on that puppet is sittin' right over there." He pointed straight at Bill Chapman. He held him in the powerful light of his gaze.

The crowd erupted in angry shouts. Over the din, Jared heard snippets of what the irate voices were saying, ". . . put'em in jail . . . won't take it anymore . . . they can't do that?"

Judge Cardenas shouted for order. He banged his gavel for a full minute before he got the crowd reasonably quiet. With his face red with rage, the Judge said, "This is the very last warning I'm giving you. Any more outbursts like this and the courtroom will be cleared. I mean it." Motioning vigorously to the prosecutor to come close, he said quietly but ominously, "Mr. Budagher, you are very close to the edge. I am allowing you to go through with this melodrama because unlike you, I know how it will most certainly turn out. However, I will *not* allow you to incite a riot. Do you understand?"

With an innocent countenance, the young man said, "Your honor, I'm just encouraging my client to tell the truth. Are we to be held responsible for people's reactions to the truth?"

With a withering glare, Cardenas said brusquely, "Heed my warning, counselor. You are half-way over a cliff. Don't go all the way."

Budagher turned away and walked back to the desk where his papers lay. He went through the motions of looking at them, then turned back to his witness. "And so,

Mr. Delaney, that is how you became owner of the Kilpatrick Ranch."

Christy had been worried sick the first couple of days when Nathan was overdue in returning from Taos. She imagined any number of scenarios in which his horse was spooked by a rattler or a mountain lion. She visualized him lying by the side of the trail, unconscious with no one to come to his aid. As she agonized through these various fantasies, though, there had been a rational part of her that had rejected them. *Nathan is older now. He's not an invalid or an idiot, though,* she thought. *I just don't see that being what happened.*

As the trial progressed and Christy got her reports from Miguel Marés, she gradually began to come to terms with the likelihood that Nathan had been ambushed by one of Chapman's henchmen. *My knight in shining armor,* she thought longingly. *I guess I never thought anyone could bring him down. I thought he was . . .* she searched for one of her fancy new words . . . *invincible.* Unfortunately, as she knew Nathan would have told her if he'd been there, this was not a story book. It was real life. No one is invincible.

Christy's mind wandered through her memories of this brave and noble lawman that had served and protected the citizens of Cimarrón for almost twenty years. She remembered that even when she was employed as a lady of the evening at the Colfax Tavern, doing what she had to do in order to survive, he'd never seemed to look down on her or the other girls. He had treated them with a dignity and respect that none of them felt for themselves. It seemed a small thing at the time, yet it was precious now as she recalled his quiet compassion.

As accepting and generous as he could be with the downtrodden, Christy had also seen the harsh and dangerous side of this man whose life she was now grieving. She'd seen him use the force of his eyes and his voice to bend men to his will. She had also witnessed the power of his fists and his guns when circumstance dictated the necessity of their use. She'd heard others talk boldly about doing the 'right thing.' When push came to shove, they were nowhere to be found. Not so with Nathan. He was always there, willing to put his life on the line for the citizens of Cimarrón. She'd never known anyone who was as rock-solid in his commitment to enforcing the law and protecting the weak from the predators in the world.

She shuddered. *It sounds like I think he's dead.* She hung her head as tears filled her eyes. *I guess I do. Now what?* Help was desperately needed. She didn't think it would be coming from her knight in shining armor.

CHAPTER 29

October 22, 1884

Ned was running around outside whooping and hollering at his imaginary herd, rounding up strays and brandishing his lariat. Eleanor puttered around inside the house, sweeping and dusting areas that she had swept and dusted several times already that morning. She had picked some apples earlier and started making preserves. About halfway through, she'd lost interest and put everything away. Physically, she was at the ranch. In her mind, she was with her husband in the courtroom in town.

It was almost time for Ned to have his noon meal so she began to assemble some of his favorite foods. She hoped her picky son wouldn't engage in one of his frequent tussles with her over what, when and how much he ate. She shook her head in bewilderment. How in the world could a former teacher with a very determined personality lose a battle of wills with a creature less than half her size? *That boy is stubborn, just like his father.* A brief stab of resentment accompanied this thought. It was replaced by wry amusement when she finished the thought process. *That boy is stubborn like both of his parents put together.* She chuckled. *I think we're in for a wild ride with this one.* She placed a hand on her abdomen which was only now beginning to show the slightest bump. *Maybe she'll be the calm one.*

Eleanor felt totally powerless as she waited to hear the outcome of the court proceeding. Jared had indicated it would likely be over with today, one way or the other. Their only hope for swift justice was that Nathan would return in time from Taos with the damning evidence against Chapman. As the days passed with no sign of him, their dreams of justice began to look just like that . . . a dream.

As outraged as she was about the murder of Juan and the loss of the cattle, she was even more distressed about Nathan's disappearance. When, as a young girl, she'd lost her parents . . . her mother to illness, her father to that same gang of evil men in Santa Fe that still plagued them . . . Nathan had stepped in and quietly assumed the role of her guardian. He provided her with food, shelter and the chance to learn an honest and honorable trade. More importantly, he provided her with a moral compass. From watching him, she learned to stand up for what was right, to speak up for the weak and vulnerable who had no voice.

The night before, Eleanor had tried to comfort Jared by telling him it was the way of the world . . . things change, people get old and die. Now as she thought about her words, they seemed empty. The painful thought of losing her treasured mentor and friend dredged up the agony that she felt as a girl when she lost her mother. When a few years later, her father was murdered by these very scoundrels that seemed to be above the law even today, it was only Nathan Averill's steady and comforting presence that saved her. *The law serves the ones who make it and use it as their tool to steal and plunder from the rest of us,* she thought. *What about justice?*

"Mr. Delaney," Budagher continued, "could you please tell the court about the events leading up to the murder of your friend, Juan Suazo, last summer?"

"Yes sir, I can do that," Jared said. "Juan and the boys had just got back from takin' a good sized herd up to Pueblo. We'd planned

315

on doin' a little cow work, checkin' fences to see what needed repairin' and such." Jared smiled wistfully. "Juan had also planned to spend some time with his wife." Jared's smile faded. "Reckon he didn't get a chance to do that." He paused and glared at Chapman. "Now she's his widow."

"Did something happen to change those plans, Mr. Delaney?"

"Yes sir. I got a telegraph from Pedro Flores up at Morley. He said they'd had some steers stolen. He needed a hundred head as soon as we could get'em up to him. This cattle rustlin' business has been goin' on all over the northern part of the territory for quite a while now." Jared shook his head and stared angrily at Chapman and Daughtry. "Since right around the time those two hombrés over there showed up."

The crowd began buzzing again. Elkins started to rise. A glare from the judge stopped him. He looked helplessly at his clients. Chapman eyed him as if he were a bug on the boardwalk . . . step on him or step over him? Elkins understood the unspoken message. His features sagged. He realized that even if he won the case, he would be a loser in the long run. *No more rich contracts for me,* he thought. *I'll be lucky to get any work at all when this is done.*

Budagher continued. "How did you respond to Mr. Flores' telegram, Mr. Delaney?"

"I wired him back, said we'd get right on it. Me and Juan, we was workin' hard to make the ranch a success. When those hungry coal miners want beeves, they want'em right away."

"So you sent Juan and his hands back up the trail with a herd? Did you have any misgivings about this, Mr. Delaney?"

"Juan and I talked about it, yes sir. We both knew there'd been some rustlin' goin' on. We weren't about to let that stop us from doin' business though." Again, he stared hard at Chapman. "We ain't backed down yet from that bunch of thieves in Santa Fe. We weren't about to start this time."

"But you were still worried, weren't you, Mr. Delaney?"

"Yep, I was. We were short-handed. That made it all the more risky," Jared said. "I'd have rather sent a couple more cowboys with'em so they could have extra watch at night, there just wasn't anybody around to do it. It came down to trustin' that Juan and the boys would get the job done. They were good hands. I thought they could make it there and back safe." Jared looked down and studied his hands. "Reckon I was

317

wrong."

Tommy Stallings sat in his jail cell and fumed. He mentally berated himself for losing his temper and telling the judge what he thought of him, even if every word he had said had been the honest to goodness truth. As a result of his outburst, he was now locked up and of no use to his friends. *That's what they do to you,* he thought. *They use their laws to hogtie you. All you can do is bawl like a mama cow that's lost her calf. It don't do any good at all.*

Although he was young . . . barely twenty-one . . . he had seen a lot pain in his short life. He knew trauma and loss. His parents and sister had been massacred by Indians when he was a young boy and not a day went by that he didn't think of them. He knew that if it were not for his friendship with Jared Delaney, who truly understood his loss because of his own experience as a child, he would have continued down the road he had been on when he met him. He was bitter and angry, always spoiling for a fight. Everywhere he looked, he saw that life was unfair. He felt like the whole world had it in for him. *Jared gave me hope that maybe things could go my way if I treated folks the way I wanted to be treated. He showed me how to be a man.*

Tommy hated feeling helpless. He refused to accept that there was nothing he could do about this situation. At the same time, he could think of no clear plan of action though he wracked his brain to come up with something . . . anything. *Those no-good thievin' scoundrels are gonna get away with this if we don't figure out how to stop'em. It don't seem like the law is any help at all.* He thought about taking the law in his hands and going after them on his own. Bitter experiences in his past, however, made him question the wisdom of going down that path. The most obvious one was that after having spoken his mind in court, he found himself locked up in a six by eight foot jail cell. Another obstacle was that the powerful men like Chapman surrounded themselves with gunslingers that made their living by killing people.

Daughtry, he thought. *There's somethin' about that name that makes the hair rise on the back of your neck.* Tommy had faced off against another one of the Santa Fe Ring's henchmen. Gentleman Curt Barwick had nearly ended his life. He'd gotten off a lucky shot as he went down that wounded Barwick in the leg which gave Jared and the others the edge they needed in the ensuing gun battle. If it weren't for the efforts of Mollie and later, the doctor, he most likely would have bled to death on the floor of the Colfax Tavern.

Thinking about Mollie just increased the internal conflict he felt as he struggled with what to do about this grave injustice playing out in front of him. He knew if he went down the road of taking the law in his hands, the chances of losing his life were great. *I got a chance with Mollie to spend my life with someone who knows all my faults and loves me anyway,* he thought. *I don't want to throw that away. If I just turn my head and give up, though, what kind of a man would she be gettin'? Besides, Juan deserves better than that.* He wrestled with all these thoughts and came up empty-handed. So he sat in his jail cell and fumed.

Tomás sat at the old roll top desk. He wondered if he'd sent his brother to his death. It was still a little early to conclude that something evil had befallen him. If he'd left at first light, he could have ridden well into the canyon to look for traces of the sheriff. If he rode like the wind, he could've made it back to Cimarrón by now. On the other hand, if he had proceeded cautiously, it could take longer. Tomás smiled bitterly.

Estévan does not proceed cautiously anywhere, anytime. He always rides like the wind. Tomás smiled for a brief moment. Then he worried some more.

CHAPTER 30

October 22, 1884

"Mr. Delaney, based on your experience of living in Colfax County now for over six years and being deeply involved in the ranching business, would you tell me in your own words what has transpired behind the scenes that led to the death of Juan Suazo." Budagher knew this line of questioning left him wide open to objections from the defense. Jared hadn't been sworn in as an expert witness. Everything he was about to recount was hearsay or opinion and therefore, inadmissible. He had no illusions about winning today. He was just hoping that Elkins, after being admonished so severely by Judge Cardenas, would be timid in voicing objections. This would allow him to get away with entering the story into the record. It would also allow him to inflame the spectators.

Chapman shot Elkins a hard look. The attorney started to rise. He glanced up at the bench and was halted by the intense glare from the judge. Settling back in his chair, Robert Elkins' eyes narrowed. He thought maybe he'd had his fill of being a puppet.

Jared waited until the unspoken interplay between Chapman, Elkins and the judge was completed, then he responded to his friend's question. "Well, if you want a straight answer, here's what I can tell you. There's been cattle rustlin' goin on in these parts for a lot longer than the time I've been here. It's always been a problem for ranchers. That's why you see cattleman's associations springin' up out west here and in Texas, too."

"So, Mr. Delaney, do you believe that the rustling of your cattle on the nineteenth of June was the work of random rustlers?"

"No sir, I most definitely do not," Jared answered emphatically. "In the time I've been in Colfax County, what I've seen makes me believe that this rustlin' is part of a bigger, well-organized plan to crush us ranchers and grab our land."

The crowd stirred. People glanced angrily in the direction of the defense table. Without giving Elkins or the judge time to interrupt, Budagher methodically moved Jared along in his testimony. "Mr. Delaney, do you have any idea who came up with this plan to take over land from the small ranchers and homesteaders who live in these parts?"

Jared looked defiantly in Chapman's direction. "Yes sir, I do. There's a group of crooked politicians in the capitol city that call themselves the Santa Fe Ring." He smiled grimly. "Some of us call'em some other names." A nervous titter ran through the crowd.

"Do you know the real names of any of the members of this so-called 'ring' Mr. Delaney?"

"I can tell you a couple of'em for sure, counselor," Jared said. "One is Tom Catron. We don't see him much in person here in Colfax County. We hear his name a bunch, though, when we're dealin' with the gun-slingers and cattle rustlers he hires and sends our way. If you'll check the deeds on a couple of ranches that have gone under in the past few years, I reckon you'll see his name on them."

Budagher walked over right next to the judge's bench. He continued to direct his comments to Jared. It was clear, however, from where he stood for whom his words were actually intended. "You, Mr. Delaney, that's not a bad idea. Perhaps someone *should* check the deeds. In fact, maybe there should be a full-scale investigation into this land-grabbing scheme." The level of buzzing in the crowd increased, as if nightfall was approaching and a cicada symphony had begun.

"Order in the court!" Judge Cardenas slammed his gavel down one time. "Mr. Budagher, you are out of line. Any more comments like that and I will shut down this hearing right now. Do you understand me?"

Budagher knew the seed had been planted. He saw no need to pound it into the ground. "Yes, your honor. I understand . . . completely." He looked at the judge and smiled innocently.

The judge was not amused. Once again, however, his desire to end the hearing outweighed his impulse to humiliate the young prosecutor. "All right, then. Can we please get this over with?"

The young attorney walked back over in front of his witness. "Mr. Delaney, could you tell the court the names of any other Ring members?"

"You bet I could," Jared said firmly. "One of the names is Bill Chapman. He's sittin' right here in this courtroom."

The buzzing in the crowd grew louder until it became a low-pitched hum. All eyes in the courtroom focused on Chapman.

What they saw was a shocking sight. The big man was clenching his jaw so tight it appeared his teeth might break. His hands were balled into fists, his knuckles so white they seemed to shine. He'd turned a bright red and was breathing hard like a bull preparing to charge. Suddenly, he slammed his fist down on the table and jumped to his feet. Beside him, Daughtry also jumped up. He reflexively reached for the six-gun that fortunately had been turned in to the bailiff before the hearing began.

"Damn your eyes, Delaney," Chapman shouted. "Who do you think you are to be calling me out like this? You're nothing but a small-time rancher barely scraping by. We can make something of this land, something big-time. What can you do?" The entire courtroom, including the judge, was struck dumb as Chapman continued his rant. "You don't deserve that land. You're in the way of progress. You're damn right we mean to get you the hell out of our way! You cross the Ring, you'll get crushed."

Finally, Judge Cardenas recovered his wits sufficiently to bang his gavel and call for order. "Mr. Chapman, you need to be quiet and sit down immediately. Do you understand me?"

Chapman turned his ire on the judge.

"Oh, I understand you, judge. I just hope you understand me. I've listened to about as much of this claptrap from this no-account malodorous cowboy as I am willing to tolerate. You'd better get this business over with pronto and it better go the right way." He glared at the judge. "Do you understand *me*?"

Tom Lacey was irritated. No, in fact, he was damned mad. It was past noon. The patrons of the Colfax Tavern were both hungry and thirsty. He figured about half the town was in the courtroom. The other half all seemed to be in his bar. They demanded service. That no-good, insolent bartender of his had not shown up, leaving him short-handed. He was trying, and failing, to keep up with the orders shouted his direction by the girls.

He poured three glasses of the watered-down whiskey he served to the run-of-the-mill customers and handed them to one of the serving girls. As she took them from him and tried not to slosh out the contents, he asked, "Have you seen that shiftless Jim?"

He was not sure she even heard his question above the bedlam in the bar. She appeared to be thinking hard, then she leaned over and spoke in his ear. "I haven't seen him but I think Nell said she did."

Lacey tried to remember which girl was Nell. He looked around the tavern. He spotted a short, stout dark-haired girl at a table all the way across the room. "There she is," he said to the girl in front of him. "Go fetch her. Tell her to come over here."

The girl nodded. She slowly made her way through the crowd to the other side of the bar. Lacey saw her whispering to Nell, who then began walking his direction. Several patrons grabbed at her as she sashayed through the crowd and she stopped several times to visit. By the time she found her way to the bar, Lacey had progressed from 'damned mad' to furious.

"You took your sweet time getting here," he said angrily. A look of fear crossed the face of the girl. She began sputtering to explain why she needed to stop and talk to the customers. Lacey waved his hand to silence her and said, "It's all right. Shut up and listen." The girl clamped her jaw shut. The fear remained in her eyes. "Belle said you might know where Jim is. Have you seen or heard from him?"

Nell hesitated, trying to size up the situation and figure out if talking to her boss about Jim would lead to her catching grief from the bartender. She decided she would rather incur Jim's ire than that of her boss. "Right before I came to work, I was across the street at the mercantile." It was difficult to hear because of the noise. Lacey beckoned her to lean closer. "I saw him walking down toward the livery stable. He was with another man." She paused and seemed to be concentrating hard as she tried to recall details. "No, that ain't right. There was another man that followed them. He stayed back a ways. I don't think Jim knew he was there."

Tom Lacey wasn't sure why his bartender would have been heading toward the livery stable when he should have been coming to work. If it hadn't been so loud and busy in the tavern, he might have thought to take the time to ask Nell if she recognized the men Jim was with. Instead, he said, "I need you to run down to the stable and see if he's there. If he is, I want you to tell him to drag his lazy carcass down here right now or he'll be out of a job." He grabbed Nell by the arm firmly. "I want you to say it to him just like that. Can you do that?"

Nell flinched as Lacey's grip tightened. "Yes sir, Mr. Lacey, I can sure do that." She shifted her arm just enough to let Lacey know he was hurting her without seeming to be impertinent about it. She thought sullenly that she'd probably have a bruise on her arm come morning. When she paused to consider all the various ways she had incurred bruises in her lifetime, this seemed relatively mild.

"All right, go." Lacey gave her a none-too-gentle shove that propelled her toward the door.

Nell stumbled as she made her way to the door. Recovering with a hand from a cowboy, she headed out of the tavern. She kept her head down and didn't meet the gaze of the few women she encountered on the street. Since coming to Cimarrón, she had seen enough disapproving looks to last a lifetime. Lord knows she didn't need any more, especially today. Her life was hard enough without that kind of grief. As she approached the livery stable, she glanced over at the small adobe hut that stood next to it. She noticed the door was slightly open, which seemed odd to her since it was usually closed up tight. Thinking no more about that, she went into the stable looking for Bill, the man who looked after the horses.

"Say Bill," she said flirtatiously. "How come you ain't been down to see me at the tavern lately?"

Bill shuffled his feet and looked embarrassed. He hemmed and hawed before finally saying, "I ain't had a lot of spare coins these days, Miss Nell." He belatedly took off his hat. "I promise I'll get there sometime soon." He smiled shyly at the girl, then looked at her inquisitively. "What brings you down to the stables today? You're usually workin'."

"I am workin'," she said with a smile. "I been sent on a mission to find our missin' bartender, Jim. You ain't seen him, have you?"

Bill squinted as he thought about the question. "You know, I did see him just awhile back. He and that Daughtry fella . . . he's a scary one." Bill shivered as if someone had walked over his grave. "Anyhow, I saw'em headin' this way. I thought maybe they wanted their horses again. Those fellas are always saddlin' up and headin' out for someplace." Bill scratched his head. "Funny, though. They never made it this far. I think they turned off into that little adobe shack. Lord knows why they'd do somethin' like that. There ain't nothin' in there."

"I don't know either." Nell was puzzled, too. "Oh, well. If that's where you saw'em go, I guess I'll go have a look." She started to walk away, then she turned around. "You know, I thought it was funny that the door to that old shack was open when I walked over here. It's generally closed, ain't it?"

"That is curious," Bill said. "You're right about it bein' closed. That place is usually shut up tighter'en old Dick's hatband."

Nell shrugged. She smiled coyly at Bill. "I don't know and I don't much care. I'll go have a look and let my boss know what I find. It ain't my problem anyhow." She reached out and touched Bill's hand briefly. "Don't be a stranger now, you hear?"

Bill watched her with a muddled mixture of pleasure and embarrassment as she walked back towards the shack. He saw her open the door and stick her head inside. He knew it was dark in there. He figured it took a moment for her eyes to adjust to the darkness. What happened next was totally unexpected. He heard Nell scream like a banshee and nearly had a heart attack. Without thinking, he ran over to where she was and grabbed her out of what he feared was harm's way. Once he got her outside of the shack, he dared to look inside. He was afraid she might have surprised a rattlesnake that had crawled in to find a warm place to coil up. Once his eyes adjusted to the darkness, his jaw dropped. It was no rattlesnake.

John Budagher took several deep breaths to calm himself after Chapman's outburst. It dawned on him that prior to this moment, his concept of Chapman's power had been abstract. He knew the man pulled strings and got things done in the territory. Before now, though, he didn't really have a clear understanding of the fury and strength that drove him. What he'd just witnessed up close and personal gave him pause. *Maybe I should've let sleeping dogs lie,* he thought. *Well, I'm too far down the road now, there's no turning back.* One more deep breath. *What the hell.*

"Mr. Delaney, would you now tell us what you believe happened on the night of June 19th."

Jared glanced over at the defense table. Chapman was seething. Daughtry's eyes were narrowed as he looked around. Suddenly, Jared was distracted by the sound of the courtroom door opening quietly. His eyes widened in amazement as he watched Big Jim Rogers carefully make his way to one of the few vacant chairs in the room. Jared had no idea why the big man would show up at this most opportune of times, he just knew he was mighty glad to see him. Judging from the level of agitation at the defense table, he figured if he said what he believed to be the truth, it could be the spark that ignited a tinderbox of public outrage. Having Big Jim there to back him up sure made a big difference. *This could turn into a mighty bad wreck,* he thought. *Oh, well. What the hell.*

"I believe Juan and the boys were followed by that man right over there." Jared pointed straight at Daughtry who glared back at him. "He took along some other low-life characters with him. They waited until the herd had been on the trail a couple of days. He knew we were short-handed; he knew the night hawk would likely be tired." Jared turned to the judge and said, "You ain't as alert when you only sleep a couple of hours a night."

The judge waved his hand impatiently. "I understand, Mr. Delaney. Get on with it."

"I wanted to make sure you understood the circumstances, Judge. I didn't figure you'd ever trailed a herd before." Several people in the crowd chuckled. The judge glared at them. He turned his glare on Jared.

"You need to get on with it, Delaney."

Jared leveled a cold stare back at the judge who stared back for a moment before turning away. "Yes sir . . . your *honor.*" Jared fairly spit the last word out like he'd bitten into something foul and needed to expel it from his mouth immediately. "Daughtry and his boys ambushed my men in their

334

sleep. They killed Juan Suazo and wounded Tommy Stallings . . . two good hands."

Budagher quickly jumped in. "Mr. Delaney, do you believe that Mr. Daughtry was acting on his own or on the behalf of some other party?"

"Daughtry's a hired gun, counselor," Jared said. "A dog obeys his master."

"Who do you believe Mr. Daughtry was working for when he ambushed your cowboys, Mr. Delaney?"

Jared turned in his seat. He looked directly at Chapman. "He was working for that man right over there, counselor . . . Mr. William Chapman."

Budagher decided immediately not to go any further with the testimony. He knew it was all hearsay and would carry no weight in a jury trial. His goal had been to expose and call out Bill Chapman in hopes that a public outcry might lead to a more in-depth and fair investigation into the matter.

"No further questions, your honor." He quickly returned to his seat.

Judge Cardenas banged his gavel to still the murmuring of the crowd. "Mr. Elkins, would you like to cross-examine the witness?" With a contemptuous smile, he added, "You do remember what a cross-examination is, don't you counselor?"

Robert Elkins' attention had wandered during the last part of Delaney's testimony. It was a story he knew all too well, and it was, in fact, the truth though the prosecution had no proof. He knew no matter what the other side did, Judge Cardenas would find insufficient evidence to proceed to a formal trial. These two evil men seated next to him were about to get away with cold-blooded murder. All he had to do was to get up and ask Delaney if he could present hard evidence to support his claims. It was so simple and yet he hesitated. Chapman and the rest of the Santa Fe Ring were the type of men you did not want for enemies. They were ruthless and unscrupulous. Those who crossed them tended to disappear. *But you know,* he thought, *a man can take only so many insults and slights before he bows his back. Am I to that point?* He smiled to himself. *What the hell.*

Elkins rose and approached the witness. "Mr. Delaney, I'll be as brief as I possibly can. You have made accusations against my clients stating that Mr. Daughtry committed robbery and murder. You have further stated that he was under orders to do so from Mr. Chapman." He smiled. "Does that accurately summarize your testimony?"

Jared eyed Elkins warily. He sensed something slightly off in his approach. He thought back to the first day of the hearing when he'd sensed that the prosecutor seemed anxious and uneasy. Was Elkins having second thoughts? Or was he being led into a trap of some sort. "Yeah, counselor, I reckon that pretty well says it all."

"So," Elkins continued, "the question, then, is do you have any proof to back up your statements?"

Jared took a deep breath. From what Budagher had told him, he knew this was where the case fell apart legally. Still, there was nothing to do but go forward. "There is proof of this, Mr. Elkins. Sheriff Nathan Averill went to Taos to retrieve letters sent by Mr. Chapman that authorized Daughtry's actions." The spectators began buzzing again. "Those letters provide clear proof that he's the man behind this terrible crime." The buzzing increased.

"Order," the judge demanded as he banged his gavel. "Order right now." The crowd quieted.

Elkins smiled serenely. "Do you and Mr. Budagher have those letters in your possession, Mr. Delaney?" At the defense table, Chapman leaned back in his chair and grinned.

Jared hesitated, trying to postpone the

inevitable. With an air of resignation, he continued. "No sir, we don't have the letters here."

Chapman smiled. He nudged Daughtry. The gunslinger nodded at him. This was the moment they'd waited for. They had tolerated this charade of a hearing to get to this point. This was where they stood up and walked away scot-free. Now was the time for Elkins to say "no further questions" and return to his seat. Chapman turned from Daughtry and looked at his attorney. To his amazement, Elkins continued.

"Sheriff Averill was to have brought these letters back from Taos, is that not correct, sir?"

Puzzled, Jared answered. "Yes sir, he left a couple of days ago. We ain't heard from him since then."

"What do you suppose happened to him, Mr. Delaney?"

At the defense table, it was obvious that Chapman was becoming agitated. *What in the world is this idiot doing?*

Jared was also wondering what the defense attorney was doing. It was almost like he was helping out the prosecution with his questions. "I believe he was the victim of foul play, sir. Someone prevented him from finishing his task. Otherwise, he'd be here with the evidence."

"And who do you think might have 'prevented him from finishing his task' as you so eloquently phrased it, Mr. Delaney?"

Jared glanced over at Chapman who gave every indication he was about to erupt once more. *Well, bring it on, you low-down sidewinder,* he thought. "I'm convinced it was Bill Chapman, Mr. Elkins."

"What the hell are you doing, you idiot?" Chapman sprang from his chair. In two strides, he was at Elkins' side. "Have you lost your mind?"

Elkins stood up a little taller. "No, Bill, I haven't. I'm just trying to get to the truth of this matter."

"We're not interested in the truth, you pompous ass," Chapman roared. "Your job is to get us the hell out of this town." Chapman began to shake. Without warning, he launched a powerful right cross that caught Elkins square on the jaw. Elkins dropped like a rock. The crowd exploded as people jumped up and began jostling. Some people tried to head for the door. Others surged forward toward the bench. It was bedlam.

Cardenas banged his gavel repeatedly. "Bailiff, clear the courtroom immediately." The poor old man who served as bailiff just looked at the judge like he'd taken leave of his senses.

Over half of the crowd fled the courtroom. Jared watched as a number of his fellow citizens approached the defense table and began yelling at Bill Chapman. He didn't know where this was headed. The thought occurred to him that it had the feel of a stampede. Suddenly, Daughtry lunged from his chair. He crouched between Chapman and the angry townspeople. Jared could swear he heard a low snarl coming from the man. Even without a firearm, he appeared deadly. Everyone halted in their tracks, waiting for a sign. Would it be a spark that ignited a full-fledged riot?

Without thinking, Jared jumped up from the witness chair. In as loud a voice as he could muster, he hollered, "Everybody calm down."

Gradually, the shouting stopped and the rumbling diminished. The citizens of Cimarrón stared at Jared. He looked back at them. In the past, none of these folks had had the gumption to rally around when the bullies of the Santa Fe Ring tried to impose their will on the community. Jared wondered if this might be a sign of a new order in Cimarrón.

"It ain't gonna help if we have a riot," he

said in a quieter voice. "If we're gonna stand up to these murderin' scoundrels, we got to go about it the right way. We got to have the law on our side. We can't have that if we're breakin' the law, too."

One of the townspeople took a step forward. Jared recognized him as Thomas Figgs, the owner of the mercantile. "Jared, these boys are about to get away with cold-blooded murder. What are we gonna do about that?"

Jared glanced at the judge with contempt. Turning back to the shop owner, he said, "Tom, we're gonna track down those letters Nathan went after, then we're gonna find us an honest judge. The law is the law, no matter how much these crooks try to bend it. Even if we have to wait, we'll have justice in the end. We just got to do it the right way."

The tension in the room was palpable. Figgs and the others stood like statues while Daughtry maintained his menacing stance. The mercantile owner looked at Jared. "We're with you, Jared. What do you want us to do?"

Jared looked at Tom Figgs with a new-found respect. Allies had been few and far between in the past struggles. *Maybe it'll be different now.* The eyes of the townspeople were on him. In a firm voice, he said, "I think you should do what the judge said. Clear the courtroom. You've all seen and heard the same thing here. You know the truth." He paused, letting the word hang in the air. "We'll get this hogwash here out of the way and move on to the next step." He glanced over at John Budagher and grinned. "I think we got some pretty good help this time around. I like our chances."

Figgs nodded self-consciously. "I'm a bit late comin' to the party, Jared. I know that. I'm here now, though." He looked around at the other townspeople. "I can't speak for anybody else. As for me, I'll do what you asked."

As he turned to leave the courtroom, the others nodded and murmured amongst themselves. After a moment, they also turned and began filing out of the courtroom. Soon, only the principals remained, with two exceptions. Maria Suazo had remained in her seat. Big Jim Rogers had quietly made his way to the defense table where he stood lightly balancing his great bulk on the balls of his feet.

Judge Cardenas stood up from the bench and said, "You two need to leave as well."

Still on his feet, Jared turned to the judge. "I don't think so, Judge. Maria deserves to hear what you're gonna say about what happened to her husband. And I think we'd all be a little safer if Big Jim over there stays."

Glancing nervously at the big man, the judge threw up his hands. "Oh, all right, Delaney, whatever you say. This whole proceeding is preposterous anyway. Let's just get it over with."

Jared looked at Maria who nodded back at him. "That's about the only thing you've said that I agree with, Judge."

There was a rustling sound as Elkins attempted to get to his feet. He appeared dazed. John Budagher rushed to his aide. With the prosecutor's assistance, Elkins was able to get his footing, although he was wobbly and had to lean against the judge's bench for support.

"Elkins, you're done," Chapman said through gritted teeth. "You won't work again, ever." Chapman leaned over the defense table. He jabbed an angry finger in the direction of the prosecutor. "As a matter of fact, you might want to do what they call 'getting your affairs in order.' I can see that you might be involved in a fatal accident in the near future."

Elkins blanched at Chapman's words. Helplessly, he looked around the courtroom for any sign of assistance. John Budagher turned quickly. He took a step towards Chapman.

"Mr. Chapman, that sounds a great deal like a death threat." He also looked around the courtroom. "While it might not have been obvious from the charade of a trial we've been engaged in the last several days, this *is* a court of law." He looked around again. "There are witnesses here today who have heard what you said to Mr. Elkins. Should anything happen to him, we'll have hard evidence to present at your next trial." Budagher squared his shoulders. "You can't kill all the witnesses."

Chapman started around the table toward the young prosecutor, murder in his eye. Apparently, he disagreed with the prosecutor's last statement. It looked as if his intention was to tear him limb from limb. It appeared that he had not only the will but the strength for the job. With a cat-like quickness that belied his great bulk, Big Jim Rogers appeared at Budagher's side.

"You might want to stop right where you are, fella," Big Jim said in his oddly high voice.

Chapman was not as out of control as he had appeared and he was certainly no fool. Gauging the size and apparent strength of his adversary, he reconsidered his decision to attack. He stopped in his tracks. From a safe distance, he brought his finger up again as he continued to berate the cowed defense attorney. He never got the chance to finish, however, as the door to the courtroom banged open. Tomás Marés burst in.

"We have a murder, Judge," Tomás said in an even voice. "I thought you might want to know."

Chapman looked first at Daughtry, then at Judge Cardenas. He could see his difficulties were mounting. Realizing that their best bet was to get out of town as soon as possible, he said, "Judge, can we finish off this circus first before you go getting involved in some murder investigation that doesn't concern us?"

Tomás turned to Chapman. "I'm not so sure the investigation doesn't concern you, señor. We have witnesses providing information that could link you to what's happened."

Judge Cardenas looked at Chapman. A light of understanding dawned in his eyes. Unlike Robert Elkins, the judge knew who buttered his bread. He wasn't about to cross him. "I concur, Mr. Chapman." Turning to Tomás, he said, "Deputy, why don't you carry on with your investigation. As soon as we're finished here, I'll be glad to hear your report."

Tomás stared at the judge. Finally, he said, "Yes sir, I'll do that." He turned and walked out of the courtroom.

Everyone began talking at once. The judge banged his gavel on the bench as hard as he could and roared, "Silence." Finally, things quieted down.

"I want everyone to take their seats," he said firmly. "Once you're all in place and quiet, I will give my ruling in this matter."

Daughtry had silently moved to Chapman's side during the fracas. Now he stood, staring at Big Jim. The big man stared back for a moment. He smiled.

"You're a gunslinger, mister. Right now, it appears you ain't got no gun," Jim said softly. "Maybe it ain't the best time for you to be challengin' someone. Still, if you want to get it on, bring it on."

Daughtry continued staring at Big Jim, his hands moving reflexively toward his hips where he normally kept his pistols. His indecision was evident in his eyes. Although he was a scrapper, the odds were most definitely not in his favor in this match. His decision was made for him as Chapman reached over and patted him on the shoulder.

"Let's just sit down and get this over with," Chapman said. "We can take care of any loose ends later."

With some reluctance, Daughtry turned and went to his seat. Chapman did the same. Jared and Budagher returned to their places. Big Jim and Marie took seats right behind them. That left the defense attorney standing alone next to the judge's bench.

"Mr. Elkins," the judge said, "I told you to take your seat."

Elkins looked at Chapman and back at the judge. "I will not sit by those two murderers."

"You'll sit there or you will leave my courtroom," Cardenas said indignantly. "I am in charge here. I, alone, will dictate how these proceedings go."

Elkins looked at the judge. He slowly smiled. "There's a great deal of truth in your statement, judge. However, it is a sword that cuts both ways. You're in charge here and only here. Outside of this courtroom, there are other legal authorities who are honest. Some may even have the courage to stand up to these crooks." Chapman made a growling sound and Daughtry squirmed in his seat. "I know how you're going to rule today. You need to know this. I will do everything within my power to assist

Mr. Budagher in finding a judge who will get to the bottom of this incident and hold the guilty ones responsible for their actions." The judge started to speak. Elkins cut him off. "We'll not find justice in this court today, I know that. Mark my words, though, Judge. We will find it."

Cardenas banged his well-used gavel down yet again. "I am charging you with contempt of court, Mr. Elkins."

"Guilty as charged, Judge," Elkins said. He turned and walked out of the courtroom.

Cardenas watched him walk out the door. He turned to the prosecutor's table and said, "Mr. Budagher, do you want to jump on the bandwagon with Mr. Elkins?"

Budagher sat very still and contemplated the question. Finally, he said, "No, your honor. I just want to hear how you rule today so we can get this farce over with and move on to the next step."

The judge considered the attorney's words. Apparently, he decided it wasn't worth his time to engage in yet another skirmish around the issue of contempt. He nodded. "Very well, I will now state my ruling in these proceedings." He looked around the courtroom at the participants in this melodrama. "Due to insufficient evidence, I see no reason to proceed any further. This case is dismissed. The defendants are free to go."

CHAPTER 31

October 22, 1884

Tomás left the courtroom shaking his head and walked briskly back to the Colfax Tavern. He had sequestered Tom Lacey, Bill and the young woman, Nell, in the office in the back of the tavern. Although he would have preferred sending all the patrons home to avoid all the gossiping, he figured he'd have a riot on his hands if he tried. Better to avoid the trouble and deal with the witnesses in the cramped quarters. As he walked through the doors of the tavern and headed back to the office, he noticed the crowd was considerably less boisterous than usual. Folks gathered in small groups around tables and talked quietly among themselves. From the stunned looks on the faces of the regular barflies, they were most likely discussing the topic of who might have slit the throat of the young bartender and why.

Walking into the office, Tomás saw that Nell was still visibly upset, sobbing quietly as she sat in a chair with her head down. Bill was sitting next to her, holding her hand and trying to comfort her. Tom Lacey was sitting in a chair across the small room, studiously ignoring the two. He seemed distracted. Tomás figured he was likely concerned about the prospect of losing his customers if he wasn't able to oversee their care.

Tomás pulled a chair over next to Nell. He nodded to Bill and said, "Miss, I need to ask you some more questions." The girl looked up. Tomás noticed that the paint with which she made up her face had run down her cheeks. It reminded him of a clown he'd seen when he was a child and a small circus had come to town. There was something disquieting about the sight. He did his best to ignore it and continued. "Would you please tell me again about the last time you saw Jim. . . ." Tomás hesitated. "Do you know his last name? It seems ill-mannered to talk about him like he only had one name."

Bill and Nell both shrugged. Apparently neither had taken time to discover much about the young man which was certainly not unusual. Strangers drifting into town were often vague about where they'd lived and what they'd done prior to coming to Cimarrón. If he had given a last name, chances were pretty fair it was not the one he'd been given at birth.

"What about you, Mr. Lacey?" Tomás looked over at the owner of the Colfax Tavern. "Do you know his last name?"

Lacey took a deep breath. "I can see where you'd think I would. To tell you the truth, I don't know it either. The boy played his cards close to his vest. He didn't say much and he had a rather surly attitude. It didn't make you want to ask him a lot of questions." Lacey shook his head. "The fact is, I'd been thinking about letting him go. As bad as I need a bartender, I was getting fed up with the way he would always sneer and take his own sweet time whenever I told him to do something. He didn't seem real happy with his lot in life, I can tell you that."

"I'll ask you more about that in a moment, Mr. Lacey," Tomás said politely. "Let me finish with Miss Nell here first."

"All right, deputy," Lacey said. "In the meantime, do you mind if I go out and make sure the customers are getting served promptly? I'm really short-handed here, you know. I do have a business to take care of."

Tomás nodded. "Go ahead, sir. I understand your problem. I would appreciate it if you didn't discuss this situation with anyone though."

Nell watched him walk out of the office, her eyes narrowed. "He don't even care that a boy lost his life. All he thinks about is how much money he's makin'. He's a cold-hearted one, he is."

Tomás tended to agree with the young woman's take on Lacey. As far as he could tell, though, it didn't have much to do with his investigation. He figured he'd get further right now if he stuck to asking questions of Nell. She was the one who'd seen Jim with Daughtry.

"Please tell me again, Miss, what you saw earlier."

With a hint of exasperation, Nell said, "Well, like I already told you once before, I was over at the mercantile gettin' me some hard candies before I came to work." She paused and looked away as if she were embarrassed. "I got kind of a sweet tooth. It helps me get through busy days at the tavern if I got somethin' nice to suck on."

"I understand," Tomás said in a quiet voice. "What happened then?"

"I saw that Daughtry fella walkin' up the street with Jim followin' right behind him. I don't know where they was comin' from, I

just figured they was goin' to the Tavern."
Nell shuddered. "Tell you the truth, I was
sure hopin' they were headed someplace
else. Daughtry scares me to death."

"What is it about the man that frightens
you, Miss Nell?" Tomás remembered Sheriff
Averill telling him you catch more flies with
honey than vinegar. At first, he hadn't
understood the saying. The sheriff explained
that with some witnesses, you get more
information if they see you as kind and
understanding. As a matter of fact, Tomás
thought he probably did understand the bar
maid. *Daughtry scares me too.*

"It was the way he looked at me, like I
was just some kind of bug on the ground. I
could tell he'd think no more about killin'
me than he would steppin' on that bug."
She shuddered again. "I'll tell you somethin' else, deputy. He could be pretty rough
with some of the girls when they . . ." Nell
paused, unsure how much to say. "Well, you
know, when they went upstairs."

Tomás nodded supportively. "I do know
what you mean. I'm not concerned with
what the girls do upstairs. It does concern
me how he treated them, though. What do
you mean?"

Nell looked down. "Some of the girls told
me he had a little trouble . . ." She paused,

clearly embarrassed. "What I mean is that sometimes he couldn't take care of the business he went upstairs for. When that happened, he'd get real mean. He'd beat on the girl, like it was her fault or somethin'."

Tomás thought this was a rather interesting twist to the investigation but again, he figured it didn't have much to do with solving the murder. "All right, I understand Mr. Daughtry was scary. You said you thought Daughtry and Jim were going to the Colfax Tavern. Did they go somewhere different?"

"Like I told you already, they walked on past the tavern. They headed on down toward the livery stable. When they was just a little past the tavern, that fella with the top hat . . ." Nell paused and wrinkled her nose. "He was a smelly one, he was. He wasn't around as often as Daughtry and that Chapman fella. It looked to me like he was the errand boy for the two of'em. Anyways, he came out of the tavern and started followin'em. Jim didn't act like he knew he was there."

"You said they looked like they were heading toward the livery stable, Miss Nell," Tomás continued on calmly. "Did you actually see them go there?"

"Well, no I didn't, now that you mention it," she replied. "I was just so relieved that

Daughtry wasn't goin' in the tavern, I hurried on over and got to work."

"All right, Miss Nell, thanks for telling me your story once more and thank you for being patient with me. I'm just trying to get to the bottom of this so we can find the men who murdered Jim. I hope you understand."

"Well, now, ain't you the polite one." Nell smiled sweetly at Tomás, clearly appreciating his manners. "I do understand, deputy. I do want you to catch those murderers." With a coquettish glance, she said, "When you're done with that, maybe you could come on over to the tavern. We could get to know each other a little better."

Tomás blushed. Doing his best to ignore her flirting, he said, "That's an attractive offer, Miss Nell, I'll certainly keep it in mind. In the meantime, I need you to stay in here away from the crowd. They'll want to gossip with you and I don't want folks filling your head with a lot of confusing ideas. If we have a trial, you're most likely going to be a witness."

Nell's flirtatious attitude quickly changed to a full-fledged pout. "You mean I got to stay back here?"

"Yes, m'am, you do," Tomás said firmly. "Bill can stay here with you, though. He can keep you company. I hope that'll make your stay more pleasant."

Somewhat mollified, she glanced at Bill and then back at Tomás. "I suppose if I'm stuck here, I could think of worse people to be stuck with." She grinned wickedly at Bill. "We been stuck in rooms together before a few times, ain't we Bill?"

Bill blushed furiously and stammered, "I, uh, well, uh . . ." He cleared his throat. "That is to say, yes m'am, we have." He smiled sheepishly.

Tomás rose to leave before Nell could share any more unsolicited information. "I'll be back as soon as I can. I'll let Mr. Lacey know that he should check on you to see if you need anything."

"Thanks, deputy," Nell said. Tomás could have sworn her eyelids fluttered as she said, "Don't forget what I said about comin' back and gettin' to know me better."

Making as dignified but rapid an exit as he could, Tomás went out and told Tom Lacey to bring some food and drink to his two witnesses. Lacey wasn't pleased about this. Tomás patiently but firmly explained that he needed them kept separate from the other customers and that it wasn't up for debate. Once he was sure that the tavern owner would comply, however grudgingly, he walked back toward the sheriff's office.

As he went, he contemplated his next move. *We may be able to get these murdering varmints after all,* he thought.

Jared felt like he'd been punched in the stomach. For a moment, he thought he was going to be violently ill. He felt like poison was seeping through his veins. He was glad he was sitting down; otherwise, he might have fallen. This sensation rolled over him like a wave, then gradually receded. He wasn't sure why he was reacting this way. It'd been clear from early in the proceeding that the outcome was a foregone conclusion. Still, he realized that somewhere deep inside his soul, he must have hoped that justice would prevail. *Just a pipe dream.* He shook his head. *Reckon if there's gonna be any justice, it ain't gonna come easy. We're gonna have to keep fightin' for it.*

Judge Cardenas cracked his gavel down for one final time and said, "This hearing is now adjourned." He rose to leave.

John Budagher jumped up from his seat. In a shrill voice, he said, "Judge, you have to know this is not the end of this. We can and *will* appeal. I promise you, we will find a judge who possesses honor. When the facts of this case see the light of day, these scoundrels will pay for their actions and so will you."

The judge turned and replied angrily. "I've had about enough of your insolence, sir. You are nothing but a bumbling clerk who's still wet behind the ears. You can pay an additional fine for contempt of court."

Budagher smiled. "You may be right, sir. I may be just a bumbling clerk. I do know, however, that you can't fine me for contempt of a court that has already been adjourned."

Cardenas took a step backwards. His demeanor took on the appearance of a kettle full of boiling water. He began to speak several times, yet no coherent words came out of his mouth. If no steam actually came out of his ears, it didn't take much of a stretch to imagine it. Finally, he seemed to realize there was really nothing he could say. He turned and stalked angrily to his chambers.

Jared took a deep breath and turned to Budagher. He extended his hand. "John Budagher, I'm proud to call you friend. As us cowboys would say, you 'made a hand' these last couple of days."

Budagher nodded his thanks. He shook Jared's hand. "I appreciate that. It's important to me, however, that you know this is not over . . . not by a long shot."

"I agree with you counselor. This ain't over. I'll be mighty proud to work along side you to try to right this wrong." Jared glanced over at the defense table where Chapman and Daughtry were slapping each other on the back and reveling in their victory. Jared's expression soured. "It's a bitter pill to swallow right now, though, I guarantee."

Chapman rose and casually strolled over to the prosecution's table. "Well, gentlemen, it looks like we got this all wrapped up now, don't we?" He flashed a wicked smile. "I'd like to say there's no hard feelings. That wouldn't be the truth, though, would it? And we know how much you boys value the truth." Chapman managed to make the word "truth" sound like a vile epithet. "In fact, you've really gotten under my skin. I want you to know I will expend a great deal of effort making you pay for the trouble you've caused me."

Jared stood and stared at Chapman. Budagher stepped quickly around the table. Standing on his toes, he put his nose right in Chapman's face. Daughtry sprang to his feet. Big Jim Rogers moved over behind the prosecutor. "You haven't seen anything yet, Chapman," Budagher said heatedly. "We are going to cause you a great deal of trouble before this is over. Your threats will not stop us."

Chapman stood nose to nose with the prosecutor for a moment. Then he took a step back and laughed out loud. "Sonny boy, you still don't seem to have any idea who you're dealing with here. Apparently, you don't understand that me and my friends have the power to do pretty much whatever we want to. There is nothing . . ." Chapman's smile vanished in an instant. With an intensity that was fearsome, he stabbed his finger in Budagher's chest . . . "I repeat, *nothing* you can do about it."

Jared walked around the table to Budagher's side. "That's where you're wrong, Chapman." He paused for a moment. "As a matter of fact, now that I think about it, pretty much everything you do is wrong. It's *wrong* to take what doesn't belong to you. It's *wrong* to kill innocent people who just happen to get in your way. It's *wrong* to make a mockery of the law." Jared jabbed his finger in Chapman's chest. He said, "I promise you, we'll fight you to the death."

Chapman favored Jared with a cold stare. "That's fine with me, cowboy." He smiled. The cold remained in his eyes. "I'll make sure your death comes about very soon."

"Are you threatening my client, Mr.

Chapman?" Budagher practically jumped up and down in his agitation. "If that's what you're doing, we have witnesses, all of whom will be willing to testify in court . . ." He looked around the courtroom in disgust. ". . . in a *real* court of law."

Again, Chapman laughed. "That's fine, counselor. Go ahead and gather your witnesses. I imagine they've seen what happens to someone who tries to testify against me."

Jared said, "We do see that, Chapman. Have you seen what's happened to the gunslingers your rotten bunch has hired to scare us, bend us to your will?" His eyes narrowed. "I'll say it again, you have a lot to answer for. For these foul deeds you've done here in Cimarrón. Because of your actions, too many good people are dead." Jared paused as he considered the fallen . . . Ned and Lizbeth Kilpatrick, Juan Suazo, Reverend Richardson. "It's wrong. We *will* not allow it."

"You're a lot like your lawyer friend here, Delaney," Chapman said, his voice dripping with scorn. "You really don't understand the way things operate here in the New Mexico Territory. You say I am wrong. In reality, I can do *no* wrong. In fact, everything I do is right." He flashed a cruel smile. "Do you want to know why everything I do

362

is right, Delaney? Jared sensed that the conflict was headed toward a violent showdown. Out of the corner of his eye, he saw Daughtry reach into the pocket of his pants. He shifted his weight to the balls of his feet so he could move quickly if necessary. "Go ahead, Chapman, say your piece."

Chapman spread his arms expansively. "Why, Delaney, it's because might makes right." He smiled from ear to ear. "I have the power. You don't. It's really that simple. I can do anything I want to do. It will always be right." Again, he jabbed his finger at Jared and Budagher. "There really is nothing you can do about it."

"You damn son of a bitch!" Jared took a step toward Chapman. He wasn't sure what he was going to do. He did know that he would not accept the impotent role that this evil man was arrogantly trying to assign him. As he moved, he saw that Daughtry had pulled a derringer from his pocket. He was in the process of raising it to fire. Time seemed to slow down. Funny what thoughts go through your head at a time like this. It flashed through Jared's mind that the weapon looked like an over-under model. That would allow Daughtry to shoot both him and Budagher. *That no-good snake has been carrying the whole time.* In this split second, he hesitated, not knowing what to do. Dive for cover? Attack Daughtry and take his chances? Suddenly, Daughtry stopped. He lowered his hand. The derringer pointed at the floor. All of this coincided with the sound of two hammers being cocked on a shotgun.

"If you don't want a hole the size of a dinner plate blown right through your belly," Big Jim said softly but clearly, "you'd better put that little pea-shooter on the table over there."

Jared glanced over at Big Jim. He saw that he was aiming a sawed-off shotgun right at Daughtry's mid-section. Jared knew Big Jim favored a 12 gauge. He figured it would do exactly the damage to Daughtry's belly that Jim had described so vividly. Jared rocked back on his heels. "Looks like you're outgunned here, Chapman." He grinned. "What were you sayin' about 'might makes right'?"

Chapman glared at Jared. You could almost hear the wheels turning in his head as he calculated the odds. After a long moment, he turned to Daughtry and said, "Now is not the time. Let's head on out. We'll take care of this down the trail a bit." Daughtry scowled at him. For a second, it appeared the dog might disobey his master.

Then he slowly lowered the derringer and tossed it on the table.

Turning back to Jared, Chapman said, "If you think this means anything, cowboy, you're even dumber than I thought you were. We won this round. We'll win the next one and the one after that." In as soft voice, he hissed, "Your days are numbered."

Jared could only stand mute and wonder if he was right. Chapman turned and walked toward the door of the courtroom. Daughtry stared hard at Big Jim for a moment. Then, nodding his head at the big man, he followed Chapman as he stalked out the door. The hearing was over.

CHAPTER 32

October 22, 1884

In the aftermath, John Budagher explained to Jared that he needed to return to his room at the St. James Hotel to write down a thorough summary of what had transpired. He wanted to do it immediately while all the information was fresh in his mind. "Like I told Chapman," he said in a resolute voice, "this is not over."

Jared reached out and took the prosecutor's hand, giving it a firm shake. "However this mess turns out, I want you to know you have my respect and my friendship from now on." Looking him square in the eye, he said, "You got grit, Mr. Budagher. I admit, I didn't see it for a day or so. Darned if it didn't come out here lately though. When push came to shove, you sure enough stepped up. I won't forget that."

Budagher smiled almost shyly. "I appreciate that, Mr. Jared Delaney. I wasn't sure I had it in me for awhile either." He turned and said over his shoulder as he walked away, "We'll talk later after I take care of my paper work."

Jared and Big Jim walked slowly down the dusty main street back to the sheriff's office. Along the way, they were on the receiving end of quite a few nods, grins and tips of hats. A small thing, indeed, but Jared wondered if it might signal the beginning of a larger change in the routine of the citizens of Cimarrón.

At Jared's request, Jim explained his mysterious appearance in the courtroom. He'd received a telegram out of the blue the day before from a Christine Johnson. It said his presence was desperately needed in Cimarrón. He said he didn't know this Christine Johnson from Adam but the message had said, "Jared Delaney needs your help." That was all he needed to know. He left Raton immediately.

"Well, I'm awful glad you took her serious. I'll introduce you to her in a bit so you can meet the angel that got you all shook up and bothered." Jared shook his head and chuckled. "I'll tell you what, when I saw you pull that sawed-off shotgun out from under your coat, I felt like I was seein' a miracle happen. You couldn't have come at a better time."

Big Jim just shrugged. "We're friends. Enough said."

Jared considered shaking the big man's hand but previous experiences of nearly having his own hand crushed were fresh enough in his memory to give him pause. Instead, he reached out and patted Jim on his massive shoulder. "Thanks."

Arriving at the sheriff's office, Jared decided it might be wise to knock, given the volatility of the situation. He did so, at the same time shouting out his presence like he would if he rode up to a neighbor's home unannounced. From the office, he heard Tomás respond telling him to enter. Jared walked in, followed by Big Jim, and saw Tomás seated by the desk. Tommy Stallings was pacing the floor, limping badly despite the support of his cane. He turned and seeing Big Jim, he made his way over as quickly as his wounded leg would allow. Like Jared, he was careful not to extend a hand to be captured by a massive paw, instead opting for the swat on the shoulder approach.

"Boy, you're a sight for sore eyes," he exclaimed. "What brings you to town?"

"Got a telegram," Jim replied. "It said Jared needed help, so I came."

"Well, whoever sent it to you, they sure

enough had the truth of the matter," Tommy said bitterly. Turning to Jared, he said, "Go ahead. Give us the bad news."

Jared gave him a disgruntled nod. "You want to sit down while I fill you in? Take a load off that bad leg, you're makin' me nervous stompin' around like that." Turning to Tomás, he said, "You decided on your own to let him out?"

"Sí, he was making too much noise," Tomás said with a grin. "I believe the judge will make his way out of our town as quickly as he can. I don't think he'll stop by to make sure he's still in a cell."

"Very funny." Grudgingly, Tommy went over to one of the available chairs.

Jared took one as well. Big Jim gingerly settled his big frame in the remaining chair. "You got to know the news ain't good, I reckon," Jared began.

"How could it be with that damned judge in Chapman's pocket," Tommy said indignantly. "You could tell which way the wind was blowin' him from the git-go."

"That's true," Jared said, taking his hat off and running a hand through his hair. "And you're right, the news ain't good. The judge dismissed the case for lack of evidence. We knew goin' in we had to have those letters from Taos or we'd be shootin' blanks." He turned to Tomás. "That reminds me. Any news about Nathan from Estévan?"

"Nada," Tomás said quietly. "Now I'm worried something has happened to my brother as well as to Sheriff Averill. I'm thinking I should ride out, look for them myself."

"You could be right," Jared said. "Still, we don't know for sure. We don't know how far Estévan rode into the canyon. He only left this morning. For all we know, he might have gone all the way to Taos." Jared paused, contemplating what they all feared Estévan would find. "I think we should wait until tomorrow before we go lookin' for him."

Suddenly, Tommy struggled out of his chair. He let out a string of curses that would have peeled paint off the walls if there'd been any on them. Jared looked at his young friend in astonishment. He waited patiently until the outburst wound down. When Tommy seemed to be done, Jared tried to lighten up the situation with a weak attempt at humor. "Reckon that about says it for the rest of us, too."

Tommy wasn't through. He whirled around on his good leg. He fairly screamed at Jared. "How can you make jokes, be so calm? They killed your best friend . . . hell, maybe your two best friends in the world, if we're right about what happened to Sheriff Averill. They just got away with murder and rode out of town, nice as you please. Where's the justice in that?" Tommy was breathing hard and his face was red. Again, he asked, "Where in the hell is the justice in that, Jared Delaney?"

Jared took a deep breath before he spoke. "It ain't justice, Tommy, it just is." He shrugged. "You know better than most that bad things can happen to folks . . . sometimes mighty bad things. We all get knocked down. You either get up or you give up."

Although Tommy's breathing returned to a more normal pace, his face was still alarmingly red. "I ain't even close to givin' up, I just don't know what to do. You saw how much help the law was." Tommy resisted the urge to spit on the sheriff's floor in disgust. "For a nickel, I'd get my Winchester and ride after those no-good rattlesnakes. I don't know if I'd get'em both but I could sure as hell give it a try."

Jared's calm façade crumbled. He slammed his fist down on the desk. "Don't you know I got that same urge, too?" Jared waved his arms around in frustration. He whirled around and glared at Tommy. "You think this is easy, doin' the right thing? There's a part of me that's ready to saddle up and ride hell-bent-for-leather after those two. Let the devil take who's left."

"What's stoppin' you?" Tommy stuck out his chest belligerently.

Jared continued to glare at Tommy for a long moment. Finally, he took a deep breath. He shook his head. "There's two things stoppin' me," Jared said quietly. "They're both livin' out at the Kilpatrick Ranch. They're more important to me than anything else in the world." Jared paused. He reminded himself that from what Eleanor had told him, there'd likely be a third reason coming into the world fairly soon.

"I see that, Jared. It makes sense to me. Hell, I got Mollie to think about now. She means everything to me." Tommy threw up his hands in frustration. "Even so, that just doesn't give me the satisfaction I want . . . no, the satisfaction I *need.* I know the truth of what you said about bad things happenin' in this world, Lord knows I do. There comes a time when you've just had enough, though. When you just can't . . . won't . . . take it anymore. For me, that time is now. I've had enough."

"There's a right way to go about doin' this thing though, don't you see, Tommy. Not every judge is crooked like Cardenas. Not every lawyer is as slimy as Elkins." Jared paused. "In fact, Mr. Elkins surprised me today. He's got an honest streak hidden way down underneath that fancy lawyer suit he wears. I'd have never suspected it until today." Jared shook his head as he recollected the defense attorney's strange departure from the path on which he'd been traveling. "And John Budagher is a man to ride the river with, I'll tell you that. Sometimes facin' the worst brings out the best in a man."

Tommy walked over to his chair. He sat down dejectedly. A look of despondency came over his face. "I wish I could believe the way you do, Jared, I just don't know that I can. Far as I can see, it seems like evil's winnin' out over what's right most of the time."

"But don't you see, Tommy," Jared said passionately, "that's exactly why we got to do the right thing; we got to do it the right way. If we do things the way men like Chapman do, how are we any less evil?"

"What's the point of doin' things the right way if it don't turn out right in the end?"

Jared pondered the question. "I don't know if you're gonna like my answer. Are you sure you want to hear it?"

"You might as well go ahead, give it to me anyway," Tommy said wearily. "Ain't much

I've liked about this whole damned thing. Still, we got to find a way to get through it."

"Well, the best answer I got is this. At the end of the day, after you've accounted to your family and friends . . . your God if you got one . . . there's the one person you got to answer to that counts the most."

"Who's that?" Tommy asked quietly.

Jared looked his friend in the eye. "It's yourself. It's got to matter to *you* that you did the right thing. It's got to be the most important thing in the world. Not because it pleases anyone else. Not because it makes you look like a hero. Not because you think you'll go to heaven. Because it's right." Jared took a deep breath. "Just because it's right. I don't know how else to say it. You either get it or you don't."

"I get it," he said quietly. He scratched his head as he thought about Jared's words. "It seems to me, though, that people got a lot of different ideas about right and wrong. How come Bill Chapman gets to decide what's right? How come we're supposed to just take it without a peep?"

"The Chapmans of the world don't get to decide what's right for me and you, Tommy. Whatever other power they have, they surely don't have that power. Only you can decide what's right for you," Jared said. "Just because they got the deck stacked in their favor don't mean they're right. And I'm not sayin' we're gonna take it lyin' down. I'm just sayin' we're gonna make a stand the right way." Jared turned to Tomás who had listened quietly to the discussion so far. "When someone was causin' trouble at the tavern, Tomás, did Nathan just go down there and shoot'em?"

Tomás smiled. "No, of course he didn't. He'd talk to them, try to get them to calm down. If they wouldn't, then he'd arrest them. Most of the time they would come with him peacefully."

"Come on, now. You both know there was times the sheriff knocked some heads . . . a few times, even, when he killed bad men," Tommy interjected. "How does that square with what you're sayin'?"

"I ain't sayin' you never use force to defend you and yours. I'm just sayin' there's a right way to go about it. Men like Chapman and Daughtry, they don't think twice about killin' someone. It's easy for them . . . too easy." Jared looked around at the three men in the room.

"Think about it, Tommy," Jared said. "That ain't right. I don't ever want it to be easy for me to take another man's life. That's got to be the last resort."

Tommy snorted in frustration. "All right, I'll give you that. So what do we do now?" He shook his head. "What's the 'right way' to get these low-down, no-good bushwhackers?"

Tomás stood up. "I think we have enough evidence to arrest Daughtry for the murder of that bartender. We have witnesses who saw him with the man right before his throat was slit. While you were in the courtroom, Jared . . ." he turned to Tommy and grinned, "and you were taking a siesta in the jail cell, I was investigating this murder." His grin faded as he addressed Tommy. "I was doing it the way Sheriff Averill taught me . . . the right way. Compréhde?"

The door burst open. All four men slapped leather. They were in the process of pulling their pistols as the intruder ran straight for Jared. He grinned sheepishly. He put his gun away as his wife threw herself in his arms.

"My lord, you startled us," he said with a sigh of relief. "Lucky none of us is a real gunslinger or you might have got shot." As he hugged his wife, he looked around at the others and chuckled. "No 'quick draws' in this room, is there fellas?"

The questions tumbled out of Eleanor's mouth one right after the other. "What happened in court? Have you heard from Nathan? Where are Chapman and Daughtry?"

"Slow down," Jared said, holding his wife at arm's length. "I can't answer all your questions at once."

Eleanor took a deep breath and a step back. She looked around the room. Her eyes lit on Big Jim. She smiled as recognition dawned. "You must be Big Jim Rogers. I've heard a great deal about you." A puzzled look passed over her face. "How did you know to come?"

"Christy sent a telegram to Jim in Raton," Jared said. "She told him I needed help. He rode down straight away."

Big Jim stood with his hat in his hands. "It's a pleasure to finally meet you, Mrs. Delaney. You're even lovelier than your husband said you were."

Charmed, Eleanor replied, "And you're even bigger than my husband said you were." She smiled at him. "Thank you from the bottom of my heart for coming."

"It was a good thing he was there," Jared said. "Things got a little dodgy there at the end. If he hadn't been there, somebody might've got killed."

Jared's statement had a sobering effect on the group. Eleanor asked, "Have you heard any news from Nathan?" She looked from one man to the other. She got her answer without any words being spoken. Her shoulders sagged. "You lost the case then, didn't you?"

"We just lost this fight," Jared said with determination. "We ain't givin' up, are we boys?" The others shook their heads to back him up. "Tomás was just tellin' us what his next move is gonna be."

In his high voice, Jim spoke up. "Mrs. Delaney, it looks like we all forgot our manners." He motioned toward his chair and asked, "Would you like to take my seat?"

"Thank you, Mr. Rogers, I believe it would do me some good to sit down."

All of a sudden, Jared had an alarming thought. "Where's Ned? You didn't leave him alone, did you?"

"Of course not, silly. He's with Christy at the school." Eleanor shook her head in wry amusement. "He's giving her a taste of what she's in for once he starts going to school."

Jared breathed a sigh of relief. "He is a handful, ain't he? Reckon it could be good for both of'em."

Tommy spoke up. "Well, I'm glad little Ned is in good hands. Still, I ain't sure what we're supposed to do next."

Tomás cleared his throat. "Here's what I

think you should do." Turning to Tommy, he said, "You should go find your lovely Mollie. Be with her." To Jared, he said, "Perhaps you could take your wife and Señor Rogers over to my father's café. Have some coffee and pie." Addressing Big Jim, he said, "I think you'll like the pies. My mother makes the very best." His gaze swept the group. "I'll continue my investigation. We'll gather enough evidence to put these evil men in jail where they belong."

Jared contemplated Tomás's directives. He could find no flaw in his reasoning. *With Nathan not here,* he thought, *it looks like Tomás is steppin' up and takin' charge. He's got some mighty big boots to fill. Funny, though. I got a feelin' there's a better than fair chance he can grow into'em. Maybe there's some good in all this change after all.* "That makes sense to me, mister deputy sheriff."

Tommy hesitated. Finally, the thought of spending time with Mollie overcame his ambivalence. He didn't know how to put it in words, there was just something about being with her that made him feel whole. When she wasn't there, a part of him was missing. He said none of this. Instead, he just said, "All right."

Christy was enjoying her time with Ned

Delaney. He was a bright and happy child. He quickly grasped the notion of sitting at a desk with a pen and channeling his boundless energy onto the paper. He was currently working on his latest masterpiece . . . a work of art that he proudly proclaimed was a cowboy. Truthfully, it was a bit difficult for her to tell. She found it amusing that her friend Eleanor, who was in control of most situations, was so often baffled about how to deal with her wild young son.

A cloud of melancholy passed over. The thought occurred to her that it was highly unlikely she would ever have a child of her own. She'd allowed herself the brief fantasy that perhaps it wasn't too late for her and Nathan to start a family. Now, she suspected that dream had died on the road to Taos. *I don't believe he's coming back.*

"What now?" Jared hadn't realized how bone-tired he was until he sat down at the table in the Marés Café over coffee and pie. The determination he felt as he tried to help Tommy get back in the saddle seemed to have vanished like a summer rain shower that blows through in the afternoon and then disappears before its job is done. Now he just felt empty and unsatisfied.

Big Jim gave him a long look. "I don't

know about you, but I'm gonna have another piece of that pie." He turned to Eleanor. "Would you like some more pie or coffee, m'am?"

Eleanor smiled in spite of herself. "Not right now, Mr. Rogers. Thank you, though." She turned to her dejected husband. "You know Mr. Rogers is right, don't you?"

"I don't know what in the world you're talkin' about, Eleanor Delaney." Jared looked at her with a mixture of bewilderment and annoyance. "Are you sayin' the answer to all our problems is more pie?"

"No, of course not, sweetheart," she said patiently. "I'm saying that what we do now is go ahead and live our lives." She reached out and grabbed Jared's hand. "We get back to what we were doing before all this happened. Along the way, we'll sort things out. We'll come up with a plan."

Jared contemplated his wife's words. He saw the wisdom in them. He nodded and shrugged. "Reckon you're both right." He turned to wave at Anita Marés. "Señora, por favór. Could we get some more of your magnificent pie over here?"

Anita Marés' pies apparently possessed some sort of curative ingredient. Soon, Jared and Eleanor were asking Jim about the news from Raton and inquiring about his latest artistic endeavors. Although no one would suspect it from looking at the big man, he was a wonderful painter. The walls of his restaurant in Raton were covered with paintings he had done of horses. They were deeply involved in this discussion when John Budagher walked in. He looked around for a moment, befuddled. Upon seeing them, his countenance brightened. He walked over to their table.

"Do you mind if I join you, Mr. Delaney?" he asked.

"Only if you call me Jared," he said with a grin. As Budagher pulled up a chair, Jared said to Eleanor, "This is a young man with a backbone, Eleanor my love."

Budagher turned and doffed his hat. "It's a pleasure to finally meet you, Mrs. Delaney. Your husband thinks the world of you."

Eleanor didn't know the details of all that had transpired in the courtroom. She knew Jared's initial impression of the prosecutor had not been favorable. Clearly, the young man had done some powerful things to change his opinion. If her husband thought highly of Budagher, that was good enough for her. "Pleased to meet you as well, Mr. Budagher."

With the infusion of the magical pie, Jared seemed to have found his energy again. He sat up straighter in his chair and looked at Budagher. "You said this ain't over, John. What's next?"

The young attorney became animated. "This case is full of legal flaws and inconsistencies. To state the obvious, the judge was clearly biased in favor of Chapman and Daughtry. We have transcripts that will support that. I plan to get those transcripts and take them to Santa Fe. I'll search high and low until I find a judge who will listen and rule fairly."

Jared frowned. "We still don't have a solid case if we don't have the letters that Nathan went after."

Budagher sighed. "That's true, Jared." Another deep breath. "We do need the letters."

All the uncertainty of Nathan's situation came back to Jared and pushed down on him like a boulder. The waiting and inaction were the hardest parts. "We're givin' Estévan until tomorrow to get back from his search. If he's not back by the middle of the afternoon, I reckon me and Tomás will just have to go look for him."

"You've still got me, Tommy Stallings." Mollie O'Brien had given him a fair listen as he ranted about the injustice that had

383

taken place. Now she was ready to move ahead. "They can't take me away from you. I won't let them."

Tommy shook his head to clear it. "I know, Mollie. I know. That's the only thing that keeps me goin'. Trouble is, I ain't quite sure where it is I'm goin'. I just ain't willin' to let those low-down, thievin' backshooters get away with this."

Mollie looked at Tommy. "Where I came from, this sort of thing happens all the time. Sometimes they do get away with it. Are you gonna let it sour every part of your life, Tommy Stallings?"

Tommy took a deep breath. "I don't want that to happen, Mollie. I really don't. I just don't know what to do next."

Mollie's smile lit up the room like the sun after an Irish rainstorm. She cocked her head and looked him in the eyes. "Sure and you're no eejit, Mr. Stallings. I think you know what to do."

Gradually, awareness sank in and took root. He smiled at his love. Reaching out, he took her hand. He said, "Reckon we got us a weddin' to plan."

CHAPTER 33

October 23, 1884

Jared, Tomás and John Budagher were sitting silently in the sheriff's office, the tension palpable among them. The incessant buzzing of the flies was an irritation that grated on their frayed nerves. They'd been there all morning waiting for Estévan Marés to return from his search for Nathan Averill. They had speculated endlessly about why he hadn't yet returned. They'd managed to work themselves into quite a stew about the numerous dark possibilities. Finally, they'd run out of words. Tomás's mother, Anita, had brought over some beans and tortillas for their noon meal. They were so agitated that none of them had eaten much. Now, they were quiet. Tomás stood up.

"I'm not willing to wait any longer before I go search for my brother, amigo," he said to Jared. "In my heart, I know something bad has happened. He needs my help."

Jared had spent most of the morning trying to convince Tomás to wait a little bit longer before riding out. Upon reflection, he wondered if he'd been afraid of what they would find. Now, as much as he hated to admit it, he thought Tomás was probably right. "I reckon I have to agree with you, compadré. I expect he prob'ly shoulda got here by now." Turning to Budagher, he said, "Why don't you wait here at the office in case somebody needs one of us. You can tell'em where we went."

"Are you sure?" Budagher asked. "Maybe we should take my buckboard in case someone is . . ." He stopped in mid-sentence, trying to think of the most delicate way to phrase his question, ". . . unable to ride?"

Jared started to respond to Budagher's question when suddenly, Tomás put up his hand to silence him. "I hear a horse."

He rushed to the door and ran out in the street. Jared and Budagher followed close behind him. They saw a horse trotting toward them from the south end of town but in the glare of the mid-day sun, they couldn't identify its rider immediately. As he got closer, Jared shaded his eyes with his hand. Finally, he was able to make out Estévan Marés slumped over his saddle horn. Just as the horse arrived at the hitching posts, Estévan slipped from the saddle. In slow motion, he crumpled to the dust.

"Estévan," Tomás shouted as he ran to his fallen brother. As he knelt beside him, he turned to Jared and said, "Go get Doc Adams."

Budagher ran to assist Tomás in getting his brother into the sheriff's office. Jared beat a hasty path to Doc's office. He breathed a sigh of relief to find the man both present and sober. "We need you over at Nathan's office, Doc. Estévan Marés just rode in. He looks to be in bad shape."

The good doctor grabbed his bag and followed Jared back across the street. When they got there, they found Estévan laid out on the cot, semi-conscious. He had a head wound above his left eye. Blood had crusted down the side of his face. Doc sent Budagher to the Marés café to get fresh water so he could clean the wound and assess the damage. Suddenly, Estévan struggled to sit up.

"Easy, brother," Tomás said softly. "You need to stay down and rest. You look like you caught quite a blow to that hard head of yours."

Estévan settled back down on the cot. Although his eyes were closed, he had a slight smile on his lips. When he tried to speak, his words came out as an inaudible croak.

"Do we have anything to soothe his throat?" Tomás turned to Jared.

Jared looked around. He realized they had no water in the office. He knew Budagher would return in a short while with water but he didn't want to wait that long to hear what Estévan had to say. Shaking his head in frustration, he went to the sheriff's desk. He extracted the bottle of whiskey Nathan kept on hand for emergencies. "This is all we got. It'll have to do."

"My brother will appreciate it," Tomás said with a grim smile. "He seems to have developed a preference for whiskey over water these days." Tomás poured a bit in a dirty shot glass that was in the same drawer where the bottle was kept. He held it to his brother's lips.

Estévan slurped it greedily. This led to a coughing spell, followed by a groan as a wave of agony crashed through his head in reaction to the disruption. After a moment, he took a deep breath. He spoke.

"You're not going to believe what I found in the canyon."

CHAPTER 34

October 22, 1884

Sunlight streaked through the trees in Cimarrón Canyon, creating shafts of light and shadow that obscured their vision. Had they been paying closer attention, they might have noticed the absence of the voices of the song birds, which created an eerie silence broken only by the soft rustle of the golden aspen leaves. As it was, they were flush from their victory in the courtroom. They were invincible. When you are powerful, you fear nothing. There is no need for caution.

"Did you see the look on Delaney's face?" Chapman asked. "He looked like he'd swallowed a skunk." Daughtry chuckled.

A rifle shot rang out with an earsplitting boom. It echoed off the canyon walls and reverberated three times. Chapman looked to his right. He saw Daughtry fall back and roll off the left side of his saddle. His derby hat flew off his head and landed in the dust. Daughtry's left foot hung up in the stirrup. His horse bolted, dragging his body as it went. As Chapman's mind tried to process this information, he reflexively drew his pistol. He looked around frantically to determine the source of the assault. Off to his right, he saw a glint of sunlight reflecting off metal up in the rocks. He turned and fired wildly in that direction. All of a sudden, he felt like someone had smashed him in the chest with a sledgehammer. Almost immediately, he heard the sound of a second shot . . . an explosion really, more than a shot. Then silence.

This isn't the way it's supposed to be, Chapman thought. His head felt like it was floating. The world grew darker around him. *This isn't right.*

He was wrong.

To my lovely, intelligent and extremely competent wife, Ann — every time they knock you down, you get back up. Don't worry, darlin', I still got two bullets left.

ABOUT THE AUTHOR

Jim Jones lives in Albuquerque, NM with his wife and two dogs, Jessie and Colter. In addition to being an author, he is an award-winning Western singer and songwriter. He is an avid fly fisherman, a fair to middling snow skier and he has been known to whisper at horses (they rarely whisper back). He is working on several literary projects for young people and believes the love of reading is one of the greatest gifts we can give our children.